PLAYING WITH FIRE

Georgiana had picked Lord Roger Beauchamp with care. He was handsome, devastatingly so: tall, dark, slim, self-possessed. He was older, too, undoubtedly a man who had truly earned his reputation as society's most irresistible womanizer. In short, he was a man framed by heaven for the express purpose of making other men rage with jealousy.

As Georgiana accepted Lord Roger's invitation to waltz and slipped into his arms, she was sure that the sight would drive her young husband wild —wild enough to overcome his reluctance to make her his wife in fact as well as in name.

Unfortunately, Georgiana didn't reckon with what it might do to her. . . .

A Signet Super Regency

"A tender and sensitive love story . . . an
exciting blend of romance and history"
—*Romantic Times*

The Guarded Heart

Barbara Hazard

*Passion and danger embraced her—
but one man intoxicated her flesh
with love's irresistable promise . . .*

Beautiful Erica Stone found her husband mysteriously murdered in Vienna and herself alone and helpless in this city of romance . . . until the handsome, cynical Owen Kingsley, Duke of Graves, promised her protection if she would spy for England among the licentious lords of Europe. Aside from the danger and intrigue, Erica found herself wrestling with her passion, for the tantalizingly reserved Duke, when their first achingly tender kiss sparked a desire in her more powerfully exciting than her hesitant heart had ever felt before. . . .

Gentle Conquest

Mary Balogh

A SIGNET BOOK

NEW AMERICAN LIBRARY

SIGNET TRADEMARK REG. U.S.PAT. OFF. AND FOREIGN COUNTRIES
REGISTERED TRADEMARK—MARCA REGISTRADA
HECHO EN CHICAGO, U.S.A.

SIGNET, SIGNET CLASSIC, MENTOR, ONYX, PLUME,
MERIDIAN and NAL BOOKS
are published by NAL PENGUIN INC.,
1633 Broadway, New York, New York 10019

First Printing, December, 1987

1 2 3 4 5 6 7 8 9

PRINTED IN THE UNITED STATES OF AMERICA

1

"I HAVE SAID IT a hundred times, but I shall say it again," the Countess of Chartleigh complained, picking a speck of lint from the skirt of her black dress with two plump fingers. "I shall never forgive myself for having given birth to Ralph before Stanley."

This strange utterance was received without a flicker of surprise or amusement by her two companions. Obviously they had heard the same sentiment expressed on at least one other of those one hundred occasions. Lady Beauchamp was sitting very upright on the edge of a deep chair in the Chartleigh drawing room, sipping tea from a Wedgwood china cup. Only a close observer would have seen the family resemblance of feature between her and her sister, the countess. Lady Beauchamp was slim almost to the point of thinness and impeccably elegant.

The other occupant of the room could easily have been mistaken for the daughter of Lady Beauchamp rather than the niece. But Lady Gloria Middleton, like her mother, the countess, was dressed in unrelieved black. She looked up from her embroidery, her expression cheerful.

"It is all very well to say so, Mama," she said. "But the fact is that Ralph is the elder by three years, and no amount of wishing is going to change that."

"Well, I consider it most provoking that it has to be the elder son that always succeeds to his father's title," Lady Chartleigh said, fumbling in the pocket of her dress for a handkerchief and dabbing at her moist eyes. "It is not that I dislike Ralph. He is my own son and I nursed him at my breast. And who could dislike the boy? He is sweet-natured and always did well at his lessons. But how can he possibly take poor Chartleigh's place now that he is of age?''

"The boy is well enough, Hilda," her sister said somewhat impatiently. "One must give him a chance to prove himself now that he has passed his one-and-twentieth birthday and is to take over his duties as earl. What was so great about the late Chartleigh, after all? When he was alive you were forever complaining that he was a spendthrift among other things."

"But, Elspeth," Lady Chartleigh said, her handkerchief poised halfway to her eyes, "Chartleigh was at least a man. You have to admit that. All real men drink and gamble and, well, have other weaknesses."

"And are likely to come to premature ends like my brother-in-law," her sister commented acidly. "He would probably not have broken his neck at that fence, Hilda, if he had not been in his cups at the time. None of the other hunters had any difficulty clearing it."

Lady Gloria Middleton dropped her embroidery in a heap on the table beside her and crossed the room swiftly to her mother's side. "Aunt Elspeth!" she admonished the other lady. "Do please have a care. Mama is still very sensitive on the topic of Papa's accident, even though it happened more than a year ago. Come, Mama, here is your vinaigrette. Do take it from me, and I shall ring for a fresh pot of tea. Pray do not take on so."

"Oh, what a wretched creature I am," the countess wailed. "My poor Chartleigh dead in his prime; my dear Stanley, who resembles his Papa to the very letter, with the misfortune to be a younger son; and Ralph a dear, sweet weakling about to try to step into his papa's shoes."

"Hush, Mama," Gloria said, clearly distressed. "You are being unfair to Ralph. It is true that he has always been a sweet and quiet boy and that he dislikes hunting and gambling and such. But he is certainly not stupid. Why, that professor at Oxford who likes him so much made the effort to travel all the way to Chartleigh last year to persuade Ralph to complete his studies before taking on his new duties. And we do not know for certain that he has not matured in the year since Papa's death. He came home from university only yesterday. And, Mama, do please remember that he is barely one-and-twenty now. He is very young to bear so much responsibility. As Aunt Elspeth says, we must give him a chance to prove himself.''

"Stanley is only eighteen,'' the countess pointed out with a sniff, "but he could take his father's place at a moment's notice. What good is an Oxford education when one is to be an earl?''

"The boy will do well enough,'' Lady Beauchamp said, placing her cup and saucer on the table beside her and clasping her hands in her lap. "He needs a wife, that's all. There's nothing like family responsibility to turn a boy into a man. I wish I had insisted on Roger marrying when he was as young.''

"Well, bless my soul,'' her sister replied, looking at her in some shock. "Ralph is barely more than a child, Elspeth. How would he know what to do with a wife?''

Lady Beauchamp pursed her lips. "He would soon learn,'' she said.

Gloria bent her blushing face over the embroidery that she had picked up again.

"Do you really think it would be a good idea?'' Lady Chartleigh asked doubtfully.

"It would be the making of him,'' her sister assured her. "What man likes to appear weak before his own wife? I shouldn't wonder if he doesn't take up hunting and gaming and all those other activities you seem to think so important, Hilda, just to impress her.''

"But where is he to find a suitable bride?'' the countess asked. "There are no very eligible girls around Chartleigh except the Horsley sisters, and I always felt they were appropriately named, poor dears. They are distinctly horsey in appearance.''

"Who says the girl must come from the country,'' Lady Beauchamp asked reasonably, "just because the

last two earls chose brides from their own neighborhood? Here we are in London, Hilda, the Marriage
Mart itself. It is true that you have not gone about in the
last year because of your mourning and do not know
many eligible parties, but there are any number of
suitable girls. There would be more here if it were the
Season, of course, but even so you will have a considerable choice. I tell you what I shall do. I shall call on
Eugenia tomorrow. She knows positively everyone who
is anyone. She will name us some likely prospects."

"She must be a girl of firm character," Lady Chartleigh said. "I fear that Ralph will need a strong woman
behind him if he is to perform his duties at all well."

"I shall mention that to Eugenia," her sister assured
her.

"Is that Lady Sheldon you speak of, Aunt?" Gloria
asked. She added rather timidly, "Is it quite right, do
you suppose, to entrust the finding of a bride for Ralph
to a stranger?"

"Gracious, child," her aunt replied, "who better to
find a bride for any young man than someone with
Eugenia's connections? Your brother is the Earl of
Chartleigh and the owner of Chartleigh. He owes it to
his position to marry well. Just any girl will not do, you
know."

"Oh, why did I not produce Stanley first?" Lady
Chartleigh said on a sigh.

It was not clear whether her elder son heard this
statement or not as he entered the room. Certainly he
gave no sign of having done so, and his mother quickly
erased the stricken look that his unexpected entrance
had brought to her face.

The Earl of Chartleigh smiled at the three ladies and
crossed the room to kiss each on the cheek. "Are you
comfortable enough, Aunt Elspeth?" he asked. "Shall I
fetch a cushion for your back?"

"Absolutely not," his aunt assured him, lifting her
cheek for him to kiss. "It is very bad for the posture, my
boy, to be forever propping oneself up."

Ralph grinned, picked up the teapot to refill his

mother's empty cup, and seated himself beside his sister. She smiled across at him.

"Were you out riding?" she asked. "I saw you go downstairs in your riding clothes after luncheon."

"In a sense," he said. "I went to have a talk with Parker. His firm has handled Chartleigh's business for so many years that I thought he would know best what is to be done. When I visited Chartleigh at Easter, I rode down to the laborers' cottages. Those people had a great deal to say."

"Complaining, no doubt," his mother said. "Chartleigh—your poor dear papa, that is, Ralph—always used to say it would serve them right if he cut them off and made them move into the towns to work at a factory. That would teach them when they had been well off, he used to say."

"I daresay they are far better off where they are, Mama," the earl agreed with a smile, "but there really is room for improvement in their living conditions. Some of those houses are not fit for habitation."

"They are good enough for laborers, you may depend upon it," Lady Chartleigh said firmly. "Don't let them persuade you otherwise, my son. You must never appear weak to your servants, especially at the start. You must try to imitate your poor dear papa, who always knew how to handle his workers."

The earl continued to smile. "I am sure your advice is good, Mama," he said. "Gloria, do you still spend a great deal of time at your embroidery? You are a wonder. The work is exquisite."

Gloria smiled up at him, pleased, and looked back to her work again.

An onlooker would have noticed that although the ladies resembled one another to a degree, Lord Chartleigh bore no likeness to any of them. While Gloria was dark with strong, rather severe features and firm, thin lips, and the other two ladies were older versions of her, the one equally slim, the other plump, he was fair and had a pleasing, open countenance with steady gray eyes and a sensitive mouth that seemed to curve upward at the corners. He was a tall, slender young man who moved with an easy grace. It was not yet apparent whether age would add muscularity to his physique. He looked younger than his one-and-twenty years.

"Do you not consider the color of your riding attire somewhat inappropriate, Ralph?" his mother asked as she selected a buttered muffin from the plate he had risen to offer her.

Ralph looked down at his bottle-green jacket and buff riding breeches in some surprise.

"Your poor dear papa has been gone for scarcely more than a year," his mother continued. "I have not even considered the possibility of leaving off my blacks yet, dear, and you can see that Gloria is still in deep mourning too. As the new Earl of Chartleigh I think you owe it to your family and to society generally to show all proper respect to the dead."

The earl looked at his mother, contrition in his glance. "I have been thoughtless, Mama," he said. "I left off my own mourning after the year was over, but I should have noticed when I arrived yesterday that you are still in black. If you will excuse me, I shall go upstairs now and change. I am glad I arrived home in time to see you, Aunt Elspeth. Your pardon, Mama." He lifted his mother's hand to his lips as he passed her chair on his way out of the room.

Lady Chartleigh sighed and accepted another muffin from her daughter. "Yes," she said to no one in particular, "dear Ralph needs a bride, someone who can manage him and instruct him how to go on. Had not even noticed that we were still in mourning, indeed! The boy is a dreamer and the veriest child."

The Honorable Georgiana Burton was in disgrace again. She had been sent to her room to contemplate her many sins after a severe tongue-lashing in the library from her father. She was fortunate indeed, he had told her, not to be tipped over his knee and spanked until she was too sore to sit down. She might be eighteen years old and consider herself above such childish treatment, but if she must behave like an irresponsible hoyden, then she must expect to be treated like one. Next time . . . Viscount Lansbury had left the threat unfinished, but his daughter had looked suitably chastened as she withdrew with lowered eyes and flaming cheeks.

He would, too, he told his wife ten minutes later when he had joined her in her sitting room, his breathing still labored, his face still flushed. He would paddle the girl's bottom until she had to sleep facedown for a week. Just one more provocation!

"I have never been more mortified in my life," the viscount continued. "There they were, all lined up in the green salon, all breathing fire and brimstone. At me. Viscount Lansbury! Tradesmen and servants all of them. And I was obliged to eat humble pie in front of them."

"Dear Georgie is merely a high-spirited girl," the viscountess said soothingly, pouring a cup of tea for her husband, who looked as if he were in need of a far stronger beverage. "And she has always enjoyed a prank. She will grow up."

"When!" The word emerged as more exclamation than question. The viscount regarded the top of his wife's head in exasperation. "It seems to me you have been saying that for the past five years, my lady. When is Georgiana going to grow up? She was presented this past spring among a bevy of girls as pretty-behaved and dignified as any father could wish. And some of them were younger than she."

"You must admit that Georgie has been very popular this Season, Lansbury," his wife said. "She has certainly not lacked for admirers."

"You refer to Creeley and Vaughn and young Haines, I presume?" the viscount said, his voice heavy with sarcasm. "Not one brain to spare among the lot of them. It was young Haines who caused all the trouble this morning. Not that I believe for a moment that the fault was all his. If the truth were known, I daresay the whole idea was Georgiana's.''

"I think you make altogether too much of the incident, Lansbury," the viscountess said placidly. "All they did, after all, was race their horses through the streets instead of in the park. Georgie said it added to the excitement to have obstacles to dodge instead of just a wide green to gallop along. No harm was done. One can always trust servants and tradespeople to exaggerate and look for cause to complain against their betters."

"No harm was done!" The viscount directed his eyes to the ceiling. "If you call an apple stall being upset, a fish wagon overturned, and a pedestrian's leg bitten by a frightened dog, among other incidents, *no* harm, my lady, I should like to know what you consider *some* harm."

His wife sipped her tea and wisely refrained from comment.

"Well," Lansbury said, "I had decided to stay away from the country this summer while the repairs are being made to the house, but go there we will, and soon. We shall just have to turn a blind eye to the presence of the builders."

"So uncomfortable," his wife said with a frown. "You know how sawdust and the smell of paint give me the headache and have me sneezing all day long. Perhaps it would be better to find Georgie a husband. You may depend upon it, Lansbury, she would soon settle down if she were given the responsibility of her own home. I am convinced that it is merely boredom that drives the girl into so many scrapes."

The viscount regarded his wife fixedly. "Heaven help the poor man!" he said feelingly. "Is there anyone foolish enough to take her off our hands, Livvy?"

"I am not sure, of course," his wife said with careful casualness, "but I do believe Chartleigh might be brought to the point."

The viscount frowned. "Chartleigh," he said. "He is a mere pup, is he not?"

"One-and-twenty," his wife informed him, "and in search of a wife. Or the countess is in search of a wife for him, which amounts to the same thing. She has always ruled that family, I understand. The late earl was something of a wastrel."

"I knew him," the viscount said. "Is the son like him? I can't say I have heard anything about him."

"A very quiet, bookish sort of young man, according to Eugenia" his wife replied. "Just the sort of husband for Georgie, Lansbury. He would be a steadying influence and help her to grow up."

"Hm," Lansbury said. There was a world of cynicism in the one syllable. "I think a rakehell might do better for her. He might take a horsewhip to her hide once in a while."

"Lansbury!" his wife admonished, placing her cup back in its saucer with a clatter.

The viscount clasped his hands behind his back and regarded his wife, rocking back on his heels as he did so. "Very well," he said. "You heard this from Eugenia, Livvy? She ought to know. The woman has been matchmaking for years. I shall accompany you on a visit to Lady Sheldon tomorrow afternoon. We shall see what can be learned about this youngster. I do not set my hopes too high, though. The man who will be willing to take Georgiana off our hands will have to be somewhat touched in the upper works. Now, if it were Vera . . . How can two sisters be so vastly different from each other?"

"Vera is an angel," the viscountess said briskly, rising to ring for a footman to remove the tea tray, "but she is three-and-twenty and still unmarried, Lansbury. And without prospects. One must admit that the girl is on the shelf to stay. If we can but catch Chartleigh for Georgie, I shall be well content. It will be a quite brilliant match for her."

Georgiana sat in the drawing room of her father's house on Curzon Street, all outward docility. Since

Mama and Papa had explained to her the afternoon before that a marriage between her and the Earl of Chartleigh was a definite possibility, she had been all set to rebel. No one was going to marry her off to a total stranger.

But Papa had foreseen her reaction and her ears were still tingling from the peal he had rung over her head immediately after luncheon. The earl was to visit that afternoon with his mother, the countess. Georgiana was to conduct herself as a young lady of the *ton* who was "out" was expected to behave. She was to be courteous and agreeable. If she was not, if she did one thing to show the visitors what a bad-tempered hoyden she really was—just one thing!—she would have him to reckon with afterward.

Georgiana had dared to glance inquiringly at her father at that point. The spanking threat again? He appeared to read her mind.

"It will be home to the country for you, my girl," he said, "and there you will stay until some gentleman farmer is fool enough to offer for you. Or failing that, you may spend your declining years ministering to the needs of your mother and of the parish. You will never see London again, never attend a ball or a party, and never wear a fashionable gown. Do I make myself understood?"

Georgiana dropped her eyes meekly to the toes of her blue slippers. "Yes, Papa," she said.

And that was just the sort of threat he would keep, too, she thought glumly. She could safely disregard the threats of a spanking. Papa had never ever beaten her, though he must have threatened to do so at least once a week since she was six. He had even dismissed a governess once when he caught the woman rapping her over the knuckles with a ruler for not paying attention to her lessons. But he would send her home. That was just the sort of thing Papa would do. She would take the beating any day rather than have to go home. She would positively die of boredom.

So she had quite sincerely assured her father that she would behave herself that afternoon, and gloomily allowed herself to be turned over to Price, Mama's hatchet-faced dresser. And here she was as a result, a lamb prepared for the slaughter, sitting meekly in the drawing room wearing her pale pink muslin, which she positively hated because it was so delicately feminine. And her hair! She had not counted the ringlets as Price turned them out, like so many sausages on a string, from the curling tongs. But it felt as if there must be at least two hundred of them bouncing against the back of her head and the sides of her face. And ribbons! One pink bow on each side of her head, starkly noticeable against the darkness of her hair. Georgiana scowled, remembered her promise, and schooled her features into bland emptiness again.

Why had she never met the Earl of Chartleigh? She had never even heard of him before. Was he newly arrived from the country, still smelling of the barn? And how old was he? What did he look like? What sort of man had to have a marriage arranged for him? And with a girl he had never set eyes on! She heartily despised him already. She was going to hate him, she knew she was. But how was she to put him off without making it obvious to a hawk-eyed papa that she was doing so? She would not marry him. She was not going to marry anyone. If she ever did marry, it would be to someone like Warren Haines, a thoroughly good fellow with whom she could be herself and not have to trouble about ringlets and pink dresses and all that faradiddle. But she had laughed at Warren the week before when he had suggested that perhaps they should think of becoming betrothed. She did not really want to marry even him.

Georgiana stifled a sigh. Mama and Vera were all dressed up as for a big occasion too, and both already wore on their faces that bright, sociable, artificial expression that they reserved for visitors of special significance. Why could not this earl marry Vera if he was so anxious for a bride? She was the older sister, after all. And Vera was not an antidote, though Mama was fond of saying so when Vera herself was not within hearing. She was a little too thin, perhaps, and a trifle pale, and her hair of a somewhat indeterminate color, but she had the finest gray eyes Georgiana had ever seen. "Windows to the soul" was the phrase that leapt to mind when one really looked into Vera's eyes. And, more than that, she looked beautiful when she felt deeply about something. Her cheeks would flush and her whole face come alive. Unfortunately, that did not happen often enough. Vera seemed to think that a lady should always be calm and in control of her emotions. She was an angel—even Mama admitted that much. She never lost her temper or got into scrapes.

Georgiana jumped noticeably in her chair as the butler opened the double doors into the drawing room with a flourish and announced the Earl and Countess of Chartleigh in his best theatrical manner. Her heart fluttered painfully. How could one possibly be expected to behave naturally in such very embarrassing circumstances? She schooled her features into a smile that matched exactly in artificiality those worn by her mother and sister as her father stepped forward to greet the visitors.

She curtsied deeply to the portly countess, whom she recalled seeing on occasion at church, and to the earl, who was blocked to her view at first by the large frame of his mother.

When she did see him, Georgiana was definitely shocked. This was the husband her parents had chosen for her? This . . . this boy? He was surely no older than she. There must be some mistake. She felt an alarming urge to giggle as everyone settled into chairs and began the laborious business of making polite conversation. The older people sustained the flow of talk. The three younger ones sat mute after the opening greetings—like children who must be seen but not heard, Georgiana thought hilariously.

At first she kept her eyes riveted to the face of whichever adult was talking. But several furtive glances at the Earl of Chartleigh assured her that he was not looking her way at all. He seemed to be engrossed in the conversation. She studied him openly, losing all track of what was being said.

How old was he? Far too young to be married, at any rate. Most of the men of her acquaintance held that marriage before the age of thirty was a shocking waste of a youth. She doubted if this man was even twenty. Her eyes passed over his tall frame, slender and elegant in his mourning clothes. A boyish figure. Not the sort of godlike, muscular physique that all girls dream of. His hair was very fair and looked baby-soft, but it was thick and rather unruly. Although it was fashionably rumpled, she doubted that the effect had been created deliberately. His complexion, too, was fair. He had a sweet face. His nose was high-bridged, a rather prominent feature; his eyes and his mouth looked as if they smiled, though his face was in repose.

He was beautiful, she thought, and then realized with some revulsion just what adjective her mind had chosen to describe him. What woman wanted a beautiful man for a husband? Handsome, yes. Rugged, perhaps. But beautiful?

It was while she was frowning at the thought that the earl turned his head rather jerkily and looked directly into her eyes. He looked sharply away again, his fair complexion decidedly flushed.

Good God, Georgiana thought irreverently, he is shy.

2

RALPH MIDDLETON, Earl of Chartleigh, sat on a straight-backed chair in his room, staring into space, a riding crop swinging idly from one hand. He had left off his mourning again, at his mother's bidding. He was wearing a close-fitting coat of blue superfine, biscuit-colored pantaloons, and gleaming black white-topped Hessians, the fashionable purchases of the day before. Crisp white lace was visible at his throat and wrists. His fair curly hair, newly combed, was looking somewhat less unruly than it had appeared to Georgiana two days before.

There was really no point in sitting here ruminating, he told himself, not for the first time. Wheels had been set in motion, and it was beyond his power to stop them. In exactly forty minutes' time he was expected at Curzon Street to pay his addresses to the Honorable Georgiana Burton. Her father had assured him the day before that she would receive his offer favorably and had proceeded to talk in great detail about settlements.

Since the death of his father little more than a year before, Ralph had been somewhat dreading the approach of his one-and-twentieth birthday. It would precede the end of his studies at Oxford by barely a month. He would be an adult, equipped by age to take over his responsibilities as Earl of Chartleigh and head of the Middleton family. He had not felt old enough. He had felt inadequate. He had never wanted such a life for himself. If only time could be suspended and he could have stayed at Oxford. There he had felt thoroughly at home with his books and with people like himself, people who delighted in talking about important ideas rather than about fashions or the latest scandal. There he had felt as if he had a mind of his own. He had his own ideas and opinions, and his companions, though they might argue hotly with him, respected him too.

He had never felt quite accepted at home. It was a dreadful admission to make about one's own family. He used to look at his father sometimes without recognition. How could that man possibly be his father, the man who had begotten him? There was some slight physical resemblance, he knew, but there was no similarity whatsoever in character and personality. His father had been larger than life, doing everything to excess. Ralph had been somewhat afraid of him; he had known that his father despised him. He had felt inferior.

His mother had always dominated the whole family, though she was firmly of the belief that his father had ruled single-handed. She dominated through her complaints and her hints and suggestions. As a child, Ralph, always dreamy and somewhat absentminded, small in stature until he suddenly shot up in his fifteenth year, unaggressive, had allowed himself to be dominated more than the others. He knew as he grew older that his mother did not always rule her family wisely, but it had always been easier to give in to her than to argue. Obedience to her became almost a reflex action.

He had never been very close to his brother, three years younger than he, though there was an undemonstrative affection between the two. Stanley was very much like his father: confident, aggressive, physically active, very obviously masculine. To be fair, though, he had to admit that Stanley appeared to have a warmer heart than the late earl.

Gloria was perhaps the only member of the family of whom he was really fond. Although she looked like their mother, he could see much of himself in her. She was six-and-twenty and had considered herself betrothed to the vicar at Chartleigh since she was twenty. The countess opposed the match. The vicar was merely the younger son of some obscure baronet. She constantly found excuses to force the couple to postpone their wedding. And Gloria took it all with great meekness. The only sign of firmness she showed was in remaining constant to her betrothed. She had consistently refused to be attracted to any of the brighter matrimonial prospects her mother had presented her with before their year of mourning had forced them into seclusion.

Somehow, in the year since his father's death, Ralph had reconciled himself to the fact that his life of free choices was at an end. He had hoped to stay at Oxford even after his graduation. He had not expected his father, so full of vigor, to die for many years. That life was out of the question for him now. But if he was to be the Earl of Chartleigh, he was to be so on his own terms. He had never approved of his parents' life of selfish privilege. His estates and all the people dependent upon him had meant nothing to the late earl beyond a source of seemingly endless income. Ralph had found it hard to love his father.

It was not going to be easy, the life he had chosen for himself. It would undoubtedly be lonely. His mother would never accept his need to understand the workings of his properties and his need to see all those dependent on him as people. His brief mention of Chartleigh the day after his return from university had confirmed his fear that his mother would interpret his interest as weakness. They had always thought him weak because of his hatred of inflicting pain—even on poor hunted animals. Perhaps they were right.

Ralph sighed, realizing that in five more minutes he must move if he were not to be late at Lord Lansbury's home. He certainly had one glaring weakness, one that had troubled him somewhat for a few years but which had now been drawn well to the fore. He was unnaturally shy of women.

Mama had suggested to him a week before that it was time he was married. He owed it to his position to take a wife and begin to set up his nursery, she had said. And she even had a bride all picked out for him, a girl she knew by sight only, a girl he had never met.

He had been horrified. The idea of marriage had occurred to him before, of course, but it was a thought rather like that of death. One assumed that one must come to that time eventually, but it seemed comfortably far in the future. He had never had anything to do with girls. He had had the opportunity. There were plenty of students at university who frequented taverns where the barmaids were pretty and accommodating. Some of them had persuaded Ralph to go along with them one night. Their obvious intention had been to help him lose his virginity. They had picked out for him a very petite and very pretty little barmaid, and she had been very obviously willing.

After a few drinks he had become bold enough to look at her and had felt the stirrings of desire. She had come to their table frequently, swishing her skirts against his legs each time, looking provocatively down at him out of the corner of her eyes, leaning over the table to pick up empty tankards so that he could have a clear view of an attractive mole far down on her generous breasts. Ralph had realized afterward that his companions must have paid her in advance to seduce him. He had shamed himself by lurching to his feet suddenly and rushing from the tavern, his face burning. He had been teased mercilessly for a long time after that.

And now here he was, Ralph thought, about to propose marriage to a girl. Was he mad? How could such a thing possibly have come about? He knew he was not the weakling his family thought him to be. He was quite calmly determined to live his position according to his own conscience. But he had never considered personal matters. When his mother had mentioned marriage to him and pointed out his duties to provide his family and dependents with a countess and with an heir, he had felt almost like a child again. It was very hard to withstand his mother's persuasions unless one had a moral conviction to aid one's resistance. He had no moral conviction against marriage. Indeed, he agreed with her. It was necessary for him to marry. But not yet, surely.

That had been the only argument he had put up against her. She had demolished it with an ease that matched the feebleness of his resistance. He had finally agreed to pay a visit to the girl and her family two days before. There was no possible harm in paying an afternoon call, his mother had explained reasonably. There was no commitment in such a move. If he did not like the look of the girl, there would be the end of the matter. She would say no more to him.

Why was it, then, that a mere two days later he was dressed and ready to call again at Lansbury's house to make a marriage proposal to the girl? What had happened to his freedom to say no? The countess had been greatly impressed with the viscount and his family. And she had been delighted by the demure dignity of Miss Burton. The girl had been brought out during the spring, she had explained to her son, and had been in London all Season, gaining social experience. Lady Sheldon, whoever she might be, had assured her that the girl had spirit and that she had been much admired.

"She is perfect for you, Ralph," the countess had persuaded him. "She is pretty and clearly knows how to behave. She has good parentage and doubtless a competent dowry. And any number of young gentlemen have been paying court to her. If you delay, you may find that she will betroth herself to someone else. And what a loss that would be, dear boy. You must see it is your clear duty to marry. If only your poor dear papa had lived, God rest his soul, there would be no immediate need for you to do so. But you are Chartleigh now, my dear, and you must learn to put behind you any selfish considerations.''

It was that argument again that had finally crumbled his defenses. If it was his duty to take a wife, he would do so. Besides, he had to admit to himself that he liked the look of Miss Burton. In the brief glance he had of her, he had seen a very youthful, pretty, and shy girl. He hated his own terror of women. Perhaps if he did something really decisive like offering for this girl before he had time to consider what was ahead of him, he would overcome this one weakness in himself that even he despised. So he was going. Must be on his way, in fact, he thought, jumping to his feet.

Ralph paused on his way out of his room, his hand on the doorknob. How could he face Miss Burton? What would he say to her? How would he force himself to look at her? He had hardly done so two days before and had heartily despised himself ever since. He had been tinglingly aware of her presence the whole time, but he had found himself totally unable to turn to her, as he should have done, and engage her in conversation. He could not even look at her. He had glanced at her once, having steeled himself for five whole minutes to do so. But she had been looking at him, and—fool that he was —he had not smiled easily at her and made some polite remark. He had looked hastily away, his face burning, and sat paralyzed with embarrassment for the rest of the visit.

She really was very pretty. He had seen that much. She was gracefully slim and had looked very feminine in her delicate pink dress and with her masses of beribboned ringlets. Her eyes were very dark. At least that was the impression he had gained from that one hasty glance. She was eighteen, Mama had said. Three years younger than he. Little more than a child. It was an arranged marriage for her too. She had looked like a timid little thing. She was probably even more frightened of the afternoon before her than he was. The thought gave him courage. He must reassure her, convince her that he would not be a demandng or overbearing husband. He must tell her that he would be gentle and patient with her. Really, he had no reason whatsoever to be nervous.

With such thoughts Ralph finally turned the doorknob, left the sanctuary of his own room, and ran nimbly down the marble stairway of his London home. He even managed to grin confidently at his mother, who stood at the foot of the stairs waiting to bid him a tearful farewell, and at Gloria, who hovered in the doorway of the drawing room, smiling encouragement.

He left the house, concentrating his mind on the fluttering fright that Miss Burton must be experiencing at this very moment, a mere fifteen minutes before his expected call.

Georgiana Burton was indeed awaiting the arrival of her suitor. She was standing at the window of the green salon, glaring out at the street beyond the small front garden. Her teeth were tightly clamped together so that her jaw was set in a stubborn line. There was the small crease of a frown between her brows. One blue-slippered foot was tapping impatiently on the Turkish rug.

Mama had left the room for a moment, giving her the opportunity to display the wrath she was feeling. How had she got herself into this coil, anyway? A mere few days ago she had been as free as the wind, her only problem the difficulty of finding sufficient amusement in this off-Season period in London. With Ben Creeley and Warren Haines not yet departed for Brighton, she had been succeeding quite nicely.

Yet here she was about to receive a proposal from a beautiful boy whom she had met for the first time two days before and to whom she had never spoken. And a shy boy at that! Mama said that he was one-and-twenty, but that was a bouncer if she had ever heard one. If the truth were known, he was probably younger than she was. Well, she would just not do it, and that was that. It was cradle robbery. Why, Chartleigh was just the sort of character that she and her friends would laugh at if they saw him at any assembly. Shy. Awkward, Boyish. Et cetera, et cetera. How could she marry him? She would be a laughingstock.

"Dammit, anyway," she whispered rebelliously against the window, and then looked guiltily over her shoulder to make sure that no one had come into the room and overheard her. Of course, she could not refuse him. Why fool herself into thinking that she could? Papa had made his sentiments quite clear, and even Mama on this occasion was not taking her part. Mama thought it an excellent match. She was very impressed with the beautiful boy, could see only the advantages of such a marriage, and none of the humiliating impossibility of it all.

They would definitely take her home if she refused the earl. Mama had said so. And Mama had made it clear that she would blame Georgie for such an undesirable removal. Mama dreaded having to live all summer under the feet of the buildiers and painters. And what about her? There was no one—no one!—even remotely interesting at home. And there was nothing to do there except ride in the occasional hunt. She would die!

But what an alternative she faced! She was to marry this shy, blushing stripling. What a bore. Worse. How could one live the rest of one's life with someone one heartily despised? And she did despise him. She could not stand spiritless people, especially men.

Well, she thought grimly, turning from the window as the door opened and her mother entered again, accept him she would. She would just have to make the best of her life afterward. She would persuade this earl to live in London for most of each year, and she would carry on with her own life just as she did now. If he did not like it, it was just too bad. She would punish him for forcing her into such a dreadful situation by leading him a merry dance. She was not going to change her way of life for a blushing boy.

He was probably shaking in his boots right now. He must be due to arrive at any minute. She would have some fun with him, she decided suddenly. She was not free to be herself anyway. If she were, she would send him packing in no time at all. If she must act a part, she would do the thing thoroughly. She would pretend to be as shy and demure as he. Would he not be shocked after their wedding! Georgiana smiled brightly at her mother.

"Oh, Georgie," the viscountess said, "you do look pretty. I am sure you will quite take his lordship's breath away."

The smile stayed in place. "Price insisted on the blue," Georgiana said. "It brings out the color of my eyes better than the yellow, she said."

"And quite right, too," her mother agreed. "She has certainly done wonders with your hair. I do wish Vera's had such body."

Georgiana seated herself demurely on a sofa. She was glad there was no mirror in the salon. She had no wish to be reminded of her coiffure. If there had been two hundred ringlets on the occasion of the earl's first visit, she was quite sure there must be two hundred and fifty this time. And the blue bows were larger than the pink had been. She was very thankful that Warren Haines was not there to see her. He would hoot with laughter as he always did at elaborate hairstyles or ornate bonnets.

"Remember, Georgie, to make an effort to be agreeable and set the earl at his ease," her mother was saying. "It is always something of an ordeal for a gentleman to pay his addresses to a young lady. Papa, I swear, stuttered over every second word when he proposed to me, though I have never heard him stutter since. Papa and I will leave you alone for ten minutes."

"Yes, Mama," Georgiana replied so meekly that her mother gave her a suspicious look, "I shall do my very best."

"Remember that he is doing our family a great honor," the viscountess added.

"Yes, Mama."

The conversation was interrupted by the sound of a knocking at the street door, and mother and daughter glanced at each other self-consciously while waiting for the viscount to bring in their visitor.

Georgiana rose to her feet and curtsied, but she did not look up. The earl spoke quietly about common-places to her parents for a few minutes until they rose and withdrew. Then she was alone with him. The moment had come.

"Miss Burton," the Earl of Chartleigh said after a short but loud silence. He had jumped to his feet as soon as the viscount and viscountess rose. "I am sensible of the honor you have done me in granting me some of your time."

Georgiana peeped up at him through her lashes and looked down again at her hands, which were twisting in her lap. She said nothing.

"I believe you have been informed of the purpose of my visit?" he said.

Georgiana swallowed. "Yes, my lord," she almost whispered.

"Your father has kindly permitted me to pay my addresses to you," he said. "You would be doing me a great honor, ma'am, if you will consent to be my wife."

Georgiana's hands were tightly clenched together. "You are very kind, my lord," she said.

He stood a little way in front of her. There was silence for a little while. "Will you marry me?" he asked.

She permitted herself another swift peep up at him. "I—if you wish it, my lord," she said. "That is, y-yes, I should . . . Yes, my lord."

The blue fabric of her dress was now caught up between her hands and was being mangled into a knot.

Chartleigh stood looking down at her for a few moments. "Is it what you wish?" he asked. "I realize that this is an arranged match. We have not had the opportunity to get to know each other. I would not force you into an unwanted marriage."

Georgiana looked up at him with wide unguarded

eyes. His voice had been unexpectedly gentle. She looked down again. "Mama and Papa think it is time I married," she said. "I am sure that they have selected a suitable husband for me."

He came a few steps closer and held out one hand. She was obviously expected to place one of hers in it and did so. He held her hand in a tight clasp and drew her to her feet. She stood before him, her eyes on a level with the snowy lace at his neck. She looked downward at the silver buttons on his waistcoat.

"But what of you?" he asked, his voice still gentle. "Do you think it is time you were married? And would you prefer to select a husband for yourself?"

Georgiana could no longer resist the urge to look fully at him and see this boy who was to be her husband. She looked up into the beautiful face. His mouth was curved upward at the corners, as she remembered from her scrutiny of him two days before, but his eyes were grave. And she felt a nasty lurching in the area of her heart when she looked into those eyes. They were wide and gray and had great depth. She could easily drown in those eyes if she ever focused on them for too long. They reminded her a little of Vera's. His hair was disheveled again. She felt an uncharacteristically maternal urge to reach up to smooth it into place. Dear God, she was staring at him.

"No," she said, looking down hastily at his silver buttons again. "I do not believe I could make a better choice than that of my parents, my lord."

Her left hand was still clasped in his right, she realized when he squeezed it a little tighter.

"Then you have made me very happy," he said. There was an awkward pause before he lifted her hand rather jerkily to his lips and kissed it briefly.

Georgiana looked up at him again as he did so. "When do you expect the wedding to be, my lord?" she asked.

He smiled at her with the whole of his face. She was fascinated. He was going to suffer from numerous laugh lines by the time he reached middle age, she thought.

"My wish is to marry you as soon as possible," he said. "But I am your servant, Miss Burton. I shall quite understand if you wish to delay until we are better acquainted."

"No," she said almost in a whisper. "I believe Papa wants the nuptials to be very soon."

"I shall discuss the matter with him," the Earl of Chartleigh said. "I am sorry if your family is rushing you, Miss Burton. I shall not, you know. You will not find me a demanding husband. You are not to be afraid of me. I shall give you all the time you need to feel comfortable with me after we are wed."

She should be feeling like bursting into giggles, not into tears, Georgiana thought in some surprise. He was talking as if he had all the age and wisdom of Solomon. And as if he had never blushed with shyness in his life. But she could not laugh, even inwardly. He was so obviously in earnest. And dammit, she thought in most unfeminine fashion, the beautiful boy was also a kind boy.

"Thank you," she said. She looked into his eyes again.

He laughed, a sound of great relief, and his face was transformed by that total smile again. "Do you know?" he said. "I was very nervous about coming here this afternoon. I did not know how you would receive me. You are very sweet. I do believe we will deal well together. I look forward to getting to know you."

Georgiana bit her lower lip. She felt decidedly guilty and quite distinctly contrite about the deception she was deliberately acting out. Poor boy!

His eyes followed her movement and remained on her lips. "You are very beautiful," he said, and Georgiana thought for one shocked moment that he was going to kiss her.

It seemed that the thought had occurred to him too. He let go of her hand suddenly, looked quickly back up into her eyes, flushed deeply, and turned abruptly away.

To the relief of both, Lord Lansbury and his wife chose that moment to return to the salon and the two young people could hide whatever they were feeling of embarrassment or guilt behind the general air of heartiness that followed Chartleigh's announcement that his proposal had been accepted.

He left fifteen minutes later, having promised to return the next day to discuss details of the wedding with the viscount.

3

THE WEDDING of the Honorable Georgiana Burton and Ralph Middleton, Earl of Chartleigh, took place at St. George's one month after the proposal was made and accepted. A surprising number of prominent families attended, considering the fact that it was August and most of them had to come from Brighton or one of the spas, or from their country homes. It seemed to most a celebration worth returning to London for. The bride had become a familiar figure during her one Season in town. The groom was unknown to most, but all had been aware that a young and unmarried earl was about to be launched on the market. A pity, several hopeful females thought, that he had made his choice so precipitately, without waiting to view the next year's crop of debutantes.

Ralph felt that he knew his bride no better at the end of the month than he had at the start. There was so much to be done in preparation for a wedding, he discovered, that there was little time for the unimportant matter of allowing the betrothed couple some time to themselves. He had not seen a great deal of Georgiana, and when he had, they had been surrounded by family. Under such circumstances they had conversed with each other very little.

But he did not feel nearly as nervous about the wedding as he had expected to feel. And he felt no aversion to it at all. He had fallen in love with Georgiana during his second visit to her. And he looked forward with some eagerness to being married to her so that they could be alone together at least and begin to get to know each other. She was so shy, so sweetly willing to obey her parents and to give her life into his hands that he had totally forgotten his usual lack of self-confidence with females. He felt protective, very masculine. Clearly he was growing up in this respect, though he realized that he was doing so somewhat later than was usual. Stanley, he had heard, was already into the muslin company.

And Georgiana was beautiful. She was small and slim and graceful. The masses of shining dark ringlets that usually surrounded her face, her heart-shaped face itself, and her enormous dark blue eyes gave her a fragile appearance. He felt large and virile when close to her. And she was so timid, so afraid even to look at him when he spoke to her. During that second visit, he had forgotten his own nervousness as soon as his eyes fell on her slim hands, fingers clenched together or twisting the blue fabric of her gown. He had wanted to kneel before her, gather those hands into his, and assure her that it was only he. There was nothing to be afraid of.

Finally he had mustered the courage to touch her. Her hand had felt very small and trusting in his. He had kissed it. He had never taken such liberties with any female outside his own family before. He had almost done worse. He had almost kissed her lips when she had caught the lower one between her teeth. She could not have known how provocative the unconscious gesture had been. He had wanted very badly to kiss her. He had stopped himself only just in time and had been very thankful for the return of her parents to the scene. What would she have thought of him if he had given in to the urge?

In the weeks since, his love for Georgiana had grown. What had he ever done to deserve such sweet innocence? he asked himself on numerous occasions, as he observed the shy demeanor of his betrothed. Ralph had no particular interest in the grand wedding that his mother and Georgiana's parents planned with such fevered thoroughness. The countess had even put off her mourning for the occasion. What he looked forward to was driving off with his bride after the ceremony. They were to go to Chartleigh for two weeks. He had rejected the idea of taking her abroad. The political situation there was too unsettled for a lady. He would take her home, and they could get to know each other at their leisure. It was true that Gloria was coming with them, but she would not intrude. They would, in effect, be alone.

For her part, Georgiana was quite glad that the wedding was to be delayed for only one month and that in the meantime she saw very little of her betrothed. Acting a part could be an amusing challenge, but it was a boring part she played, and she was not sure she could keep it up convincingly for very long. She still hated the thought of having to marry, but she was in many ways a practical young lady. Marry she must, and the situation could be a great deal worse. She could be marrying an old man whom she would find repulsive or an overbearing man who would demand unquestioned obedience. At least she was likely to have the sort of husband whose very existence she would be able to forget for large segments of her day.

Reaction to her betrothal had not been as embarrassing as she had dreaded. In fact, she had found the dismay of Ben and Warren decidedly flattering. Neither had teased or ridiculed her about the identity of her betrothed. Neither knew much about him.

Georgiana could almost persuade herself that she would be happier once she was married. Mama was quite indulgent. She appeared to understand that one needed some freedom and some excitement in life. She did not become unduly agitated if one laughed rather too loudly at an assembly or threw one's hat down and pulled the pins out of one's hair for a gallop through Hyde Park because one could enjoy the wind better that way. But Papa was a different matter altogether. He expected one to behave like a lady all the time, even though one was only eighteen years old. And he scolded and scolded.

Chartleigh would not be like that. He had said himself that he would be an indulgent husband. And she would have known as much without his saying so. The boy was a weakling. he was quiet and gentle and kind. She would be able to get away with murder if she wished. She supposed that she would have liked a more masterful manly husband. All girls dreamed of such a man as a lover. But really, if one considered the matter practically, one must admit that it might be tedious to be tied for life to such a man. What would happen to one's freedom?

She despised Ralph a little for his apparent weakesses, but she found that she did not dislike him as much as she had expected to do. She had stopped labeling him the beautiful boy after the afternoon of his proposal. His good looks almost invited the description, but there was nothing effeminate about his appearance. "Handsome" was not the right word to describe him. She could not think of the right word. There was a great kindliness and good nature about his face. She did not like to dwell too deeply on those attributes. If she did, she felt uncomfortably guilty about the deception she was perpetrating against him. He was going to have an awfully nasty shock when he discovered what she was really like.

His eyes! Her heart always did an uncomfortable little flip-flop on the occasions when she accidentally looked into them. It did not happen often. She did not see him often, and when she did, she continued to play the part of the meek, shrinking maiden, looking demurely at the toes of her slippers. They were dreamy eyes, wide eyes, eyes that seemed to look on the world without defenses. Most people had barriers somewhere close behind the surface of their eyes. Ralph did not.

She wished he had kissed her that afternoon. It would have been vastly amusing to witness his confusion afterward and to act out the part of the vaporish maiden. But not just that. She was curious about how he would do it. Georgiana had vast experience in the art. She had been kissed at home by a stablehand when she was fifteen, and had never reported him. The slap across his face that she had administered was punishment enough, she had decided indulgently. Besides, he had been an extremely handsome lad. And since then she had been kissed by three separate men, by Ben Creeley twice. All had been brief kisses, stolen in a darkened alcove of a hallway or an unlit corner of a garden. But she considered herself an authority.

The Earl of Chartleigh had a very kissable mouth. It was a smiling, generous mouth and, more important, a sensitive mouth. He would kiss with closed lips, of course. So did most of the others, though Ben liked to nibble her lips with his teeth. Perhaps that was why she had allowed him to trap her a second time. When would her betrothed kiss her for the first time? At the church? On their wedding night?

The bottom fell out of Georgiana's stomach at that prospect. A wedding night with the Earl of Chartleigh, a mere boy! The thought was absurd. Also a little frightening. Also just a little exciting.

As the wedding day approached, Georgiana could not decide when she should drop her mask and let the poor boy discover that he had allied himself with a talkative, restless, rebellious, bad-tempered, unladylike, vulgar hoyden. Oh dear, had Papa really used all those words to describe her? Yes, he had, and probably plenty more too if she were to think a little more carefully. She must keep up the pretense until the wedding. Papa would be in a thundering bad mood if she did anything in character before that occasion. After the wedding she would no longer be his concern. She would be answerable to her husband. Poor boy. Oh, poor boy! She felt quite sorry for him. He was really very sweet.

It had been decided—by the parents of the bride and by the groom's mother—that the couple would leave for

Chartleigh immediately after the church ceremony. The wedding breakfast would proceed without their presence. Perhaps the countess felt that her elder son would not show to advantage at such a gathering, where he would be very much a focus of attention and where he might be called upon to speak in public. Perhaps the viscount felt that his daughter would not show to advantage for a very different reason. The attention focused her way might tempt her to say or do something outrageous. And though her behavior would no longer be his concern, he would feel the full shame of any vulgar display.

Gloria wanted to travel with the earl's valet and Georgiana's maid in the baggage coach, but neither her brother nor his new wife would hear of her doing so.

"One would almost think they did not wish to be alone together," Gloria said as she kissed her brother Stanley on the cheek before he handed her into the Chartleigh traveling carriage.

Stanley chuckled and bent his head to whisper in her ear. "I wouldn't be surprised if you have not hit on the truth," he said. "See if they don't invite you to share their bedchamber tonight, sis."

Gloria blushed hotly and scrambled into the carriage almost without the assistance of his hand.

Georgiana and Ralph were being kissed by what seemed to be a whole host of people. Georgiana was enjoying the ordeal hugely. Lord Stanley Middleton actually had the effrontery to kiss her on the cheek, when her husband had not even kissed her face yet! She had met the younger brother only the day before. Dark like his sister, he was totally different from Chartleigh. He was three years younger—her age, in fact—but he had a great deal of swagger that made him seem older. He had eyed her appreciatively when being presented to her.

She was kissed on the hand by Cousin Roger, Lord Beauchamp, whom she was just meeting for the first time. Not that she would have particularly noticed his gesture under the circumstances. But there was the way he looked at her—one eyebrow raised, something that was not exactly a smile raising one corner of his mouth. A handsome devil. Familiar, too. Yes, of course. He had given her just such a look when she had emerged from the bushes with Ben a couple of months before at some ball or other and come face-to-face with him and another female, obviously bent on the same clandestine business. Georgiana grinned at this kindred spirit, the first public slipping of her mask for a whole month.

Finally they were in the carriage and on their way. What a relief it was to have Gloria with them, Georgiana thought. She did not wish a private three-hour *tête-a-tête* with her husband just yet. It would take three hours to reach Chartleigh, she had been told. She settled herself meekly into one corner of the seat on which she sat beside her husband, careful not to touch him, careful that her profile was half-hidden from him behind the large poke of the pink frothy bonnet that Mama had insisted was perfect for the occasion. She made polite conversation with her two companions, reliving every minute detail of the wedding, wringing every possible comment out of the weather, exclaiming over every stone and blade of grass outside the windows, and generally working herself into a state of near-screaming boredom.

She did not know if she was going to like her sister-in-law. Gloria was much older than Ralph and very severe-looking. Her mouth was a mere thin line on her face. She was faultless in her manners and there was a fond-ness in her eyes when she looked at her brother. But Georgiana could not imagine finding much in common with the older woman. And she knew for a certain fact that Gloria would not like her. She was just the sort of female who would be all thin-lipped disapproval when Georgiana stepped out of line. And that was bound to happen soon. She could not play this demure part for much longer. She would burst.

She was beginning to feel decidedly uncomfortable as

well as bored. What was this marriage going to be like? She had never expected a wedding trip into the country. Somehow she had assumed that they would remain in London. She was going to be thrown into Chartleigh's company rather a lot in the next two weeks. And there was still this bother of a wedding night coming up. She really did not feel up to it. Now, if he were Ben Creeley or even Dennis Vaughan, she could have talked quite openly about her virginity and lack of experience. They could have laughed and joked about her nervousness. One of those men could have jollied her along until she would have been over the nasty experience of the first bedding almost without realizing that it had happened.

It was all going to be very formal and very earnest with Chartleigh. She could see that now. And she would die of humiliation if she were nervous and fumbling. She was not even quite sure what she was to do. He would kiss her first, of course. She could handle that with no trouble at all. But after that? Well, she thought in some agitation, replying mechanically to some comment Gloria made about the passing scenery, it would all be over in so many hours. This time tomorrow she would be past the only real hurdle she could see between herself and a comfortable existence, free of a nasty, disapproving father, free to live in any manner she chose.

Ralph had offered his sister a place in his traveling carriage out of courtesy. He really could not consider allowing her to ride with the servants and the baggage. But it was irksome to know that three hours that he might have spent alone with his bride were to be spent instead in meaningless social conversation. He would have liked the opportunity to set Georgiana at her ease before they reached Chartleigh. She spoke during the journey, but only when spoken to. He noticed that she sat as far to the right of the seat as she could so that she would not touch him. He noticed that she hid her face behind her bonnet.

Poor girl. She must be feeling very strange, alone with a husband she scarcely knew and a sister-in-law who was still a stranger to her. He longed to take her hand in his and squeeze it reassuringly. Instead, he talked more than was his custom in order to remove some of the obligation from her shoulders.

In the familiar surroundings of his own carriage, with his sister sitting opposite him, Ralph nevertheless felt very strange. There was something very unreal about the fact that a girl who was now his wife sat next to him, that this was his wedding day, that he was taking his bride to his ancestral home to get to know her and to consummate the marriage. He felt a quickening of his breath at the thought—part excitement, part apprehension. He could scarcely wait to be alone with Georgiana. He longed to touch her, to quieten her fears. He wanted her. He did not believe his courage would fail him. He swallowed and turned away from her to look out at the passing countryside.

Gloria had the tact to plead fatigue soon after dinner that evening. She retired to her own apartment, leaving her brother and his bride alone with their tea in the drawing room. Georgiana followed her upstairs a mere five minutes later at the suggestion of her husband, who told her, his eyes on the teacup that he held in his hand, that he would join her a little later.

Georgiana was impressed with what she had seen of the house. From the outside it looked rather heavy, though definitely imposing, being almost square in shape and built of red brick in a Georgian design. But there was nothing heavy about the interior. The tiled hallway and the curving marble stairway that rose to the second floor and the main living apartments were large, light, and airy, and the few rooms she had seen gave the same impression.

Her bedchamber was square and high, exquisitely decorated. Wallpaper, curtains, bed hangings, cushions: all were varying shades of pink. It was not nor-

mally Georgiana's favorite color, but the rich tones of
these pinks defied insipidity. She would have liked to
explore the rest of the house. She was not at all tired.
But of course, she thought, releasing a self-conscious
giggle into the quiet emptiness of the room, she was not
supposed to be tired. Sleep was not the purpose of this
early retiring hour.

She examined the large dressing room attached to her
bedchamber and tried the handle of the second door in
the room. It opened into another dressing room of
similar size, decorated in blue. Through the open door
of that room, she saw another bedchamber. Her
husband's. She suddenly felt her essential lack of
privacy. Her room had always been somewhere she
could go to be alone. She no longer had the right to be
alone whenever she wished to be. There were not even
any locks on either of the dressing room doors.

Georgiana felt suddenly as if someone had punched
her hard beneath the ribs. She rang for her maid.

When Ralph tapped on the door between his wife's
dressing room and bedchamber and opened it, it was to
find her standing at the window, holding back the heavy
curtain with one hand and leaning forward, her nose
pressed against the windowpane. He was somewhat
taken aback. He had expected to find her in bed, all but
one or two of the candles extinguished. She wore a
frothy white wrap that fell loosely from neck to
hemline, but even so it suggested slimness and feminine
curves. Her dark hair had been brushed out and fell in
shiny waves halfway to her waist. She wore no nightcap.

"It is difficult to see anything outside at night," he
said, coming into the room and closing the door behind
him. "Tomorrow I shall be pleased to take you riding
around the park and farther into the estate if you wish,
Georgiana."

She let the curtain fall into place again and turned to
face him. "Everyone but Papa calls me 'Georgie,' " she
said.

"Oh, no," he protested, smiling and coming toward

her. " 'Georgiana' is too pretty a name to shorten. And the other makes you sound like a boy. It does not suit you at all."

She smiled at him, her eyes sparkling for a moment. They gave a glowing life to her face that he had not seen before.

"At least your name cannot be shortened," she said. "Do you wish me to use it, or would you prefer that I call you 'Chartleigh' or 'my lord'?"

"Oh, please," he said, reaching out and taking her hand, "you must call me by my given name. You are my wife."

She smiled that almost impish smile again. "So I am," she said. "Lady Georgiana Middleton, Countess of Chartleigh. It does sound grand. I do not recognize myself."

She was enchanting. She must be covering up great nervousness. Her hand shook slightly in his and was very cold. He lifted it to his lips.

"Nevertheless, it is true," he said.

He released her hand and put his arms around her. He drew her against him and was instantly aware of the softness of her body and the fullness of her breasts against his chest. He was having difficulty with his breathing. He bent his head and kissed her.

He did not know that he was holding her too tightly. He did not realize that the pressure of his lips was bruising hers against her teeth. He was embracing a woman for the first time, and that woman was his wife, whom he loved. He became aware only gradually that she was pushing urgently against his shoulders.

"Not like that, Ralph!" she scolded. She seemed quite in command of herself. "Softly, so that we can feel each other's mouths. Like so." Her lips came against his again, softly parted, barely touching, caressing, teasing.

Ralph inhaled sharply, and pulled his head back. "You have done this before?" he asked.

"Of course, silly!" Her eyes laughed into his and then

looked down at his li again with some eagerness. Then she pulled sharply away from him and her hand flew to her mouth. "Oh!" she said, her eyes looking stricken. "You have not?"

He looked back at her, his newfound confidence and protectiveness badly shaken. He did not answer.

"Well, it is no matter," she said with practical cheerfulness, grasping his hand and drawing him toward the bed. "They were just stupid kisses anyway, and did not signify. Do you extinguish the candles, Ralph, and I shall get into bed."

He did as he was bidden, blowing out the last candle as he sat on the edge of the bed. He took off his dressing gown and climbed under the bedclothes beside his wife. She was lying on her side. Her arms came around him.

"I have been very nervous about this, you know," she said candidly. "One looks at all the married couples around one and knows that it is the most natural deed in the world. But there is still something very embarrassing about lying with one's husband for the very first time. I am not even quite sure how it is done, you see. You must just bear with me if I am very awkward. I shall try, at least, to lie still and not to cry or scream. Would not that be a dreadful humiliation? All the household would know the exact moment at which you deflowered me. Oh, I am prattling. I always do that when I am frightened, though as for that, I sometimes prattle even when I am not. I am not scared very often, really, as you will discover when you know me better. It is only the unknown that sometimes unnerves me. Oh, Ralph, *do* something!"

She was frightened after all, he realized. She had been kissed before, but she really did not know any more than he. She needed calming, reassuring. Ralph turned onto his side and pulled her body against his. She wore now only a thin nightgown. Her body felt almost naked against his, and very warm. He felt heat surge through his own body and the blood pulse through him. He reached down, grasped a handful of the froth that was her nightgown, and pulled it up. She lifted her hips from the bed until the material was bunched around her waist.

She turned onto her back as he lifted himself above her and lowered his weight. His head was buzzing. His blood sounded like the pounding of drums in his ears. Her legs parted as soon as his own came down on them. He lay between her thighs and obeyed a blind instinct to thrust upward and into her. He felt soft, warm flesh, brought down shaking hands to hold her, and pushed urgently against the softness.

"Oh, do have a care, Ralph," a distressed voice said over the drumming in one ear. "You are hurting me."

He lifted his head immediately, pulling his hands from beneath her to brace his weight above her. He looked, stricken, into her face, which he could dimly see below him.

"Georgiana," he said, "I am sorry. I am sorry, love. I do not mean to hurt you."

"Well," she said matter-of-factly," I daresay you didn't mean to. I should have kept my wretched mouth closed. I am so very afraid, you see. I daresay you do not know any better than I how this is best done. Do let us get finished with it. I shall not say another word, and I shall merely clamp my teeth together if you hurt me. I have heard it said that it does not hurt after the first time. Do continue."

Ralph lowered his weight onto her again and buried his face against her hair. He was burning with distress for her, and with shame at his own fumbling inadequacy. He must try to proceed without giving her any more pain. But the determination brought with it the sure and humiliating knowledge that it was no longer possible for him to proceed.

He lay still on her for agonized minutes and finally lifted himself away and off the bed. He bent and found his dressing gown in the darkness.

"I am sorry, Georgiana," he said. "I . . . We both need rest, I think. You must be very tired. I . . . Please forgive me. Good night."

He left her room, finding his way in the darkness with the instinct of near-panic.

4

A STUFFY NOSE awoke Georgiana the following morning. Her mouth was dry, her face stiff. Goodness, she had slept after all. She had given up trying to fall asleep when dawn was already making a lightened square behind the curtains. What time was it now? she wondered. She did not feel as if she had slept for long. Her head was aching. And she doubtless looked a positive fright. She had not even got up during the night to bathe away the effects of her tears. She probably had puffy red eyes, at the very least. But there was no knowing. She never cried.

She had not cried at first. When Ralph had stumbled from the room, she was bursting with anger and contempt. How dare he leave her like that, the deed undone, the embarrassment to live through all over again the next night! She had been hurt and humiliated. What a wedding night! How her friends would laugh if they knew.

She had been perfectly right about him the first time she set eyes on him. He was a boy merely, a weakling. He had never even kissed before! And he had not the slightest inkling of how it was to be done. She had been forced to wrestle him away from her in order to protect her ribs from being crushed and the inside of her mouth from being cut to ribbons by the pressure of her teeth. And she had almost fainted; her nose had somehow become trapped against his cheek.

And that performance in the bed—or, rather, Georgiana thought with indignation, the lack of performance! She had no objection to the haste with which he had tried to come to her. She had been decidedly jittery herself and merely wanted the awful deed at an end. She had not been looking for a grand sensual experience. She had wanted only to know what exactly the dreaded act was and what her part in its accomplishment was to be.

But he had hurt and hurt her, and he had not even broken her virginity. That, at least, would have been pain in a good cause. And then, when she had pointed out his clumsiness to him in the most reasonable manner, he had stopped altogether, lain still on her until she was about to scream at him to get the business over with, and then got up and left her. No, he had got up muttering abject apologies and rushed from the room like a frightened schoolboy.

And that was just what he was. She had married a scared little boy who displayed not one spark of manliness. Oh, this was going to be a martyr's game of a marriage, she decided. She would be fortunate if she did not end up going to her grave at the age of eighty-two or thereabouts as virgin as the day she was born. He would be eighty-five, if he lived that long—and he probably would—just to spite her.

Georgiana threw herself back against her pillows, folded her arms belligerently across her chest, and scowled at the darkened canopy over her head. She hated him! He had made a fool of her. Ignorant little boy. Clumsy, awkward, blushing, timid, weak, unmanly little boy!

And, oh dear, she thought, sitting upright suddenly and clasping her knees, what a shrew of a wife he had! It was no crime, surely for a man to come to his bride untouched himself. It was not obligatory for a man to have associated with high fliers, opera dancers, lightskirts, whores, or whatever types of women most men apparently did associate with. And she had criticized him. What could she have possibly done that would be more humiliating for him?

Not like that, Ralph!

Her own voice came back to her with uncomfortable clarity. And she had then proceeded to explain to him exactly how he should kiss. And she had even demonstrated! Georgiana put one hand tightly across her mouth. Oh, how could she have? What a brazen hussy! Papa would die of rage if he knew.

And she had prattled on when they had got into bed. She could not remember a word she had said, but it seemed to her that she had talked for a long time, instead of lying like a demure bride and waiting for her husband to do whatever it was he was supposed to do. Oh mercy! The hand tightened over her mouth and she shut her eyes very tightly. Had she not said something about all the house knowing the exact moment of the deflowering? Had she really used that eact word? Was there any chance that she imagined it? What on earth had led her to that dreadfully vulgar expression? In her bridal bed!

She did not know exactly how it was done, did she, for all her boasted experience with kisses? How could she expect Ralph to do so? If she had just lain patient for a few more seconds, all would doubtless have been well. She would be a wife by now. Whether he would have stayed in her bed or retired to his own, she could be lying here now, satisfied and relieved that the marriage had been consummated. She could have been planning her own future, content that she was now well versed in what would, for a while at least, be her main duty as a married lady.

As it was, she had totally embarrassed herself and frightened her husband away. And did she dare blame him? She had been terrified herself. She, who had never been afraid of anything. Or almost never. She certainly had not expected to be quite so fearful of a perfectly normal experience such as being bedded by her husband. Especially such a kindly, unthreatening sort of husband as Chartleigh. She thoroughly despised herself.

Indeed, she concluded, opening her eyes again and

removing her hand from her mouth, this disaster of a night was far more her fault than his. Most of the time she did not even wish to be like other young ladies. She considered their lives insipid in the extreme. But just sometimes, just on the rare occasion, she wished she could behave in a more acceptable manner. She had ruined her wedding night and probably made a hopeless embarrassment out of tomorrow night too.

Georgiana threw back the bedclothes and stepped resolutely out onto the carpet. The very best thing to do with fear and embarrassment, she had found from experience, was to grab them by the throat and throttle them to death. She would go to Ralph immediately, be suitably meek and contrite, and offer to climb into his bed beside him. And she would lie there quiet and yielding all night if need be, allowing him to do what he would with her in his own time and his own way.

She moved resolutely through her dressing room and into his, groping her way because there were no windows in these rooms to give even some dim light. She knocked on his bedroom door—three times. Finally she opened the door and stepped hesitantly inside.

"Ralph?" she whispered.

Silence.

"Ralph? My lord? Are you asleep?"

She picked her way over to the bed, which was indisputably empty and unslept-in. She scurried back to her own room.

And that was when she had started crying. At first it was an itch and a gurgle in the back of her throat and behind her nose. Then her facial muscles started behaving with a will of their own. The tears came next, first a few trickles down her cheeks and then a raging waterfall. The sobs came last, and they were the most painful. She did not try to stop or to stifle the sound. But she did not know why she cried.

It was doubtless self-pity at first. Here she was, a bride on her wedding night, alone in a strange bed in a strange house, her marriage unconsummated, her husband goodness knew where, and her mother far away and probably fast asleep and not even dreaming of her.

But soon enough it was for Ralph she wept, and it was at this stage of the crying session that her sobs tore most painfully at her chest. What had she done to him? It was true that he was a young, unassertive, inexperienced boy. But did those facts make him automatically despicable? Did they give her the right to scold and humiliate him? And she had done both. He had been nervous, but then, so had she. And he had been so gentle with her earlier that day and for the last month, believing her to be a shy young girl.

He was a kind and a gentle man. She was sure of it. She could almost imagine how he would have behaved had she allowed him to complete that act he had begun earlier. His inexperience might have caused him to hurt her, but afterward he would have held her and soothed her. He probably would have stayed in her bed for the rest of the night, sheltering her and comforting her. If only she were the sort of girl he had thought her! He would make a wonderful husband to such a girl. He would be loving and protective and considerate. And there was nothing unmanly about such qualities.

And the poor boy was shackled to her. Poor Ralph. She would destroy his manhood with her impatience and her incautious tongue and her thoughtless, hoydenish behavior. She would make him feel inadequate. He would have no one on whom to lavish the love and the care that he was full of. They had been married for fewer than twenty-four hours and already she had gone a good way toward destroying him. How must a man feel when his wife's criticisms and complaints rendered him incapable? And she had done that to him. On his wedding night.

Georgiana was not used to such introspection. She had developed the habit of believing that people who did not behave boldly and with an unconcern for the conventions were weak and of no account. She was accustomed to laughing at such people with her friends. She could not laugh at Ralph. He did not deserve scorn. She wept for him, long and painfully.

Poor Ralph. He deserved so much better than she. Oh, poor boy!

And thus she awoke the following morning, after only four hours of sleep, feeling as if her head had been replaced by a pumpkin. She rang for her maid.

Both Ralph and Gloria were in the breakfast room when Georgiana finally came downstairs and found the room with the help of a footman. Her heart sank. She had hoped that she was late enough to have avoided them. Gloria did not rise. She merely smiled and bade her sister-in-law good morning. Ralph jumped to his feet and came striding toward her. He was looking very pale, Georgiana noticed in one hasty glance, and very youthful. He looked as if he might have been wearing his riding clothes all night. His hair was more rumpled than usual.

"Good morning, Georgiana," he said, taking her hand in his. His face flushed as he spoke to her, but he did not avoid contact with her eyes. "Did you find your way easily enough? I should have come to fetch you. But I did not wish to awake you."

Memories of the night before crowded between them like a fiery wall.

"Have you been riding, Ralph?" Georgiana asked as cheerfully as she was able. "I should have liked to come with you. I need some fresh air after spending most of yesterday cooped up inside a carriage."

"But of course we will go riding," he said, squeezing her hand and smiling down at her. "I promised yesterday, did I not, that I would show you the grounds and the estate today?"

He had said it when he first entered her room the night before. They both remembered as he spoke the words, and their eyes slid away from each other.

"Perhaps you do not feel like doing anything quite as

strenuous as riding, Georgiana,'' Gloria said into the silence, unconsciously winning the undying gratitude of her brother and his wife. ''I shall be walking over to the vicarage later with some flowers for the church. Would you care to join me?''

Georgiana withdrew her hand from Ralph's with careful unconcern and went to sit beside her sister-in-law at the breakfast table. ''Perhaps some other time, Gloria,'' she said. ''I want to ride with Ralph this morning.'' She frowned with discomfort when Gloria colored, smiled, and looked down at her empty plate.

It would have been a great deal easier to have gone with Gloria, Georgiana thought an hour later as she adjusted her riding hat to her liking over her smooth hair, which had been tied loosely at the nape of her neck. The last thing she wished to do this morning was to have to face Ralph. His night had clearly been more sleepless than hers. He had looked downright haggard in the breakfast room. She was still feeling guilt-ridden even after some sleep. She was also feeling a little angry. Why should she find herself in the position of feeling responsible for the feelings of a sensitive boy? She had not asked for this marriage. She had not forced him into it. Was it her fault that his confidence in himself was such a fragile thing?

She made a face at herself before turning away from the mirror and drawing on her leather gloves. The fact was that she did feel guilty. She was going to have to do something to restore her husband's sense of manhood, though she could not for the life of her think how she was going to do it. It was an unpleasant task she was setting herself, and she had much rather not have to face him this morning and make conversation with him. But she was never one to shirk something that must be done. The embarrassment of being alone with him again would only grow worse if it were postponed. She picked up her riding crop and left the room.

''I have had Flora saddled for you,'' Ralph said a few minutes later when she joined him in the stables. ''She is

quiet and will not fuss at a stranger on her back. You
need have no fear.''

Georgiana looked with disgust and indignation at the
plump little mare with the sidesaddle.

"Well," she said, hands on hips, "yours makes her
look like a pregnant cow. I would deem it a cruelty to
ride such a sorry creature."

Ralph laughed. "Have I offended you?" he asked. "I
really did not know if you were an accomplished rider or
not. You seem so small and so shy, Georgiana, that I
guessed you were not. I am wrong, am I not? And I
might have known it. Quiet people usually like to get
away on their own, and what better way to do it than on
a horse's back. Am I right?"

Georgiana leveled a thoughtful look at him. "Yes,
you are right about one thing," she said. "I was shockingly rude just now, was I not?"

He laughed again and his whole face lit up with
delight, she noticed with interest. "You must always say
what you feel with me," he said. "Only so we can grow
close as a husband and wife should."

The smile faded during the awkward little pause that
followed his words, and he turned away to summon a
groom to return Flora to her stall and bring out a more
mettlesome mount.

Georgiana had planned to bring up the topic of the
night before as soon as their ride began. Since it so
obviously loomed large in the consciousness of both,
she might as well bring it out into the open. But Ralph
had clearly planned the conversation too. From the
moment they left the stableyard he did not stop talking.
He pointed out to her everything there was to see in the
extensive grounds around the house. She soon knew the
name of every variety of bloom that grew in the formal
gardens throughout the year. It seemed to her that she
was given the history of every tree within sight and a
description of how each had been used in childhood
games. Soon they were beyond the gardens and riding

along a dirt road between fields that were almost ready to be harvested.

For once in her life Georgiana kept quiet. It was almost as if her behavior of the last month had become a habit. She let him talk. Let them be well beyond the house before she forced him to discuss what was uppermost in both their minds. But, she thought ruefully a few minutes later, she had always been right to believe that if one did not tackle an embarrassing topic immediately, it became very much harder to do so later. When Ralph suggested that he take her to meet some of his laborers in the village, she readily agreed.

It was immediately apparent that only the women and children were at home in the small cottages clustered together in a rough circle around a well. The harvest had begun early on one of the distant fields, Ralph explained. Children, in various stages of undress and grubbiness, were playing intensely in the dirt outside their doors. A small group of women was gathered at the well. A few more appeared in the doorways as the sound of horses' hooves drew their attention.

Georgiana was surprised to note that all of the women smiled at their approach. Some of them called greetings. On her father's estate she always stayed as far away from the workers as possible. It was not that they were openly hostile. Rather, they lacked all expression whenever she was forced to be close to them. But she had always sensed hostility. The children here stopped their play to gaze curiously at the new arrivals. One child ran up to Ralph, grinned up at him to reveal two missing front teeth, and shyly stroked the toe of his boot.

"Hello, Will," Ralph said, smiling down at the child. "Now did I imagine it, or did you really run all the way over here without once limping?"

"I ain't limping, y'r lordship," the boy said. "See? It's all better." He lifted one skinny bare leg off the ground.

Ralph leaned down from his horse's back and tousled the boy's hair. "Do you want to hold my horse's head while I get down and talk to your grandmama?" he asked. "And . . ." he looked around the group of eager faces and frantically waving hands of children who had gathered close. "Colin. Yes, you. Colin. Will you look after the countess's horse?"

Georgiana watched in fascination. What had happened to her shy boy? Ralph had soon swung himself down from his horse's back and was stooping on his haunches examining with serious attention the string of gaudy beads that a scruffy urchin of a child had held up from her neck for his inspection.

He touched the child's cheek and straightened up, turning a brightly smiling face in her direction. "Do let me lift you down, Georgiana," he said. "The horse will be quite safe. You can be sure that Colin here would die rather than let harm come to one hair of its body. And I assure you that Mrs. Harris will be mortally offended if we do not sample her cider. She has been plying me with it ever since I was too old to drink warm milk."

Mrs. Harris turned out to be a withered little old lady whose face was so full of wrinkles that Georgiana wondered if she had ever been a girl. She was the grandmother of Will, the boy who had first approached Ralph, and lived with her son and his family in a tiny but immaculately tidy cottage. There were two mugs of cider and two small cakes on the table already when Ralph led his wife inside.

Georgiana for once felt genuinely shy. She had never associated with the lower classes. The closest she had ever come to talking with any of them was in giving orders to house servants. She did not know how to behave or what to say. She clung to Ralph's arm and allowed him to lead her to a bench.

"Mrs. Harris," Ralph said, "I had to bring my wife to meet my oldest friend almost as soon as we arrived home, you see. She cannot know Chartleigh without knowing you, now, can she? And without sampling your cider? Mrs. Harris used to spoil me shamefully when I was a boy, Georgiana. She could never let me pass without feeding me."

The old lady chuckled. "Such a little dab of a boy you was too, Master Ralph," she said. "You always looked as if you would blow away in the wind. But look at you now. As handsome a lord as the king and all the dukes, I dare swear. And as pretty a wife as a queen or a princess."

Ralph grinned.

"Y'r lordship, y'r lordship," the urgent voice of Will Harris called, first from outside the house and then from Ralph's elbow. "Judy had her pups last week. Six of 'em. The prettiest little things. Susie's pa was going to drownd them, but me and Harold and Ellie's going to take one each and the others is to be let live. Will you come and see them, y'r lordship? They are ever such little pups and we ain't let take them out of their box. Else we would bring them here to show you."

"William!" a woman hissed from the doorway, and Georgiana recognized one of the women who had been standing at the well when they arrived. "Leave his lordship be! He don't want to be looking at no puppies."

"On the contrary!" Ralph said, laughing and getting to his feet. "How could I possibly miss the treat of seeing six newborns? Lead the way, Will, and show me which one is to be yours. Georgiana?" He turned a laughing face and held out a hand for hers.

"Oh, go on with you, Master Ralph," Mrs. Harris said, "Your young countess will stay here and have another cake. Such a pretty little thing don't want to be poking around a smelly old dog box."

Ralph was dragged away by an excited Will.

Mrs. Harris put another cake on Georgiana's plate. "Such a fine young lord," she said. "It was a glorious day for us when he became the Earl of Chartleigh. Not that I mean any disrespect to his dead lordship."

Georgiana felt tense without Ralph to stand between

her and exposure to this old lady who belonged to a
class of which she knew nothing. "You knew him as a
child?" she asked politely.

"And such a sweet little lost soul!" the old lady said.
"As different from his pa as day and night. I think he
used to like being here, y'r lordship, more than he liked
being at the house. He used to laugh here."

"I am glad he had you to turn to," Georgiana said
hesitantly. She was feeling decidedly self-conscious and
uncomfortable.

"Bless his dear heart!" Mrs. Harris continued,
picking up the jug of cider and adding more to
Georgiana's mug. "Going to build us all new houses, he
is, because he says these cottages ain't fit for hogs to live
in and there ain't no use doing more repairs to them,
else we will be adding repairs to repairs, if you know
what I mean, y'r ladyship."

"Ralph is going to build a whole new village?"
Georgiana asked in some surprise.

"Right after the harvest, we may begin," the old lady
said, "and our dear Master Ralph will pay for it all. He
hasn't told you, y'r ladyship? You don't know the half
of the goodness of that young man, I'll bet my life on it.
You have a treasure there, let me tell you. There's
nobody like our earl. His pa always said there was no
money even for repairs."

"Oh?" Georgiana said.

"Our Will fair worships him," Mrs. Harris said with
a chuckle. "Poaching for rabbits he was when he broke
his leg in the woods at Eastertime. His lordship was the
one to find him. The poor little mite expected a good
thrashing if he was lucky. Instead Master Ralph carried
him to the big house, called a physician, had his bones
set, sent word to my son, and kept the boy at the house
for a whole week. In a feather bed, if you please!
'That's not the way to learn the boy what's right and
wrong,' I says to him. And do you know what he said,
y'r ladyship? He says, 'P'raps I'm the one what's
learned something, Mrs. Harris. I've talked to your

son,' he says, 'and I've told him that from now on anyone from the village can hunt in the woods for food, though not just for fun, mind,' he says. 'This land is as much yours as mine.' "

Mrs. Harris nodded sagely, her eyes on Georgiana. "I am certainly glad he has married himself a pretty young wife," she said.

Georgiana smiled. "I can see why Ralph keeps coming back for more of your cider," she said, looking down at her empty mug and plate. "Thank you, Mrs. Harris."

She was relieved to hear the returning noise of the group of children and to find that Ralph was in their midst. He took her away immediately afterward. They had been in the village for no longer than fifteen minutes. To Georgiana it had seemed more like fifteen hours.

5

"HOW CAN YOU be so friendly with those people?"
Georgiana asked when they had ridden out of earshot of
the villagers. "How do you know what to say to them?"

Ralph looked across at her in some surprise. "But it is
so easy," he said. "They are so open and so willing to
share their possessions and themselves. I have always
been most at ease with people of the lower classes.
Don't you find that our own class is so hemmed in by
rules and conventions that one is not free to be oneself?
It is with my own class that I find myself stiff and
tongue-tied."

"Pooh, there is no need," Georgiana said. "If I do
not like a rule or a convention, I just do not follow it.
There is nothing more simple."

Ralph laughed. "You are so very sweet, Georgiana,"
he said. "I thought you were very shy. But you are not
entirely so, are you? You have the courage sometimes to
speak what is on your mind. But I cannot believe you to
be as bold as you pretend. And you need not pretend
with me, you know. With me you must always be
yourself. I like you as you are."

Heaven help the poor boy, Georgiana thought, if she
should be herself at that moment. Yes, she would say,
and how are we going to get over this nasty and
humiliating hurdle of an unconsummated marriage? Let
us talk about what happened, or did not happen, last
night, Ralph. Let us talk about it and look at each other
and try to overcome the embarrassment of the whole
thing.

That is what she would have said. That is what Georgiana Burton would have said. Georgiana Middleton did not speak what was on her mind. She turned craven. She said, "Are you really going to rebuild the laborers' village, Ralph?"

The smile faded from his face. He flushed and looked extremely uncomfortable. "Did Mrs. Harris tell you that?" he asked. "I wish she had not. She seems to think there is something heroic about my having agreed to do so."

"And you do not think so?" Georgiana asked.

"Oh, no," he said. "I realize that you will see it as a great weakness in me to have said they may go ahead with the building."

"Why?" she asked. "Can you not afford the expense?"

"I imagine your papa has told you that I am extremely wealthy," Ralph said. "This will not reduce us to poverty, dear. Perhaps it will mean that we cannot do anything very extravagant, like spend a few months in Europe for the next year or so, but I do not wish to expose you to the dangers of Europe at present, anyway. It is just that you must think a really strong man would not allow himself to be affected by the feelings or the comfort of his servants."

"That is what Papa always says," she said, frowning slightly. "Your father too?"

"Oh, yes," he agreed. "But I am afraid I have had to accept the fact that I can never be strong and forceful as most people see those qualities."

"Do you wish to be, Ralph?"

He flashed her a grin. "No," he said, "I am afraid I do not. I would prefer to be myself, even though I will never be respected as my father was. I am sorry, Georgiana. You have married what many people must consider a poor excuse for a man."

"I have been under the impression in the last hour that many people respect and even love you, my lord of Chartleigh," she said.

"Does it count to be loved by the lower classes?" he asked with a smile.

"Well, does it?" she asked, challenge in her eyes.

He looked steadily back at her. "Yes, to me it does," he said. "You see, I love them. I am sorry, Georgiana. You will have a hard time making an acceptable nobleman out of me. You will learn to sympathize with my mother. It makes her very unhappy that she can scold and scold until I seem to agree with her but then go my own way anyway. She may be right. With all the education of my upbringing, I feel she is right. But I have too tender a conscience to live up to my upbringing. Perhaps too unmanly a conscience." He looked at her as if expecting a comment.

Georgiana opened her mouth but found that she did not know what she wished to say. Strength? Weakness? They were opposites, were they not? She had never worried over the differences between them. It had always been perfectly obvious to her who were the strong people and who were the weak. Ralph was crowding her head with new notions, and she was not at all sure that she liked his doing so. She was unaccustomed to thinking, and resentful of anyone who tried to make her do so. She liked a simple life, a life given over entirely to the amusement of self. It was not at all amusing to find herself trying to judge if Ralph were right or wrong in what he was doing, weak or strong.

"You are very quiet," Ralph said. They were riding along a grassy avenue between two lines of poplar trees. It was very peaceful. "Shall we dismount and walk for a while?"

He did not wait for her answer but swung himself from the saddle and came across to lift her down from hers. He did not immediately release his hold on her waist when she touched the ground.

"Do you feel very strange here?" he asked. "Are you homesick, Georgiana? I do sympathize with you. It does not seem entirely fair that after marriage it is the wife who has to leave her home and all its familiar faces.

Will you think of me as a friend? Believe me, there is nothing you need be apprehensive about. I will make no demands on you. I will not force you into anything for which you are not ready. You may relax. And I will be very honored if you will talk to me and come to me with your loneliness and your troubles. Will you, dear?"

His face was full of tender concern, his eyes full of kindness when she looked up at him. She had felt the urge to laugh when he began, to tell him what an idiot he was making of himself, believing still that she was a tender, wilting little creature. Why was it, then, that his face suddenly swam before her eyes? Heavens, she was not crying again, was she? She must be sickening for something deadly. Smallpox? Did one become a watering pot when one was contracting smallpox?

His hands were resting very gently along the sides of her face. "Poor Georgiana," he said, "taken away from your family at such a young age. Once you get used to me, you will feel better, I promise. I shall take care of you."

He bent his head and kissed her softly on the lips. He did not draw her body against his. His eyes were twinkling when he lifted his head again. "There," he said. "Was not that a better kiss than the last? You were quite right, you know. I thought it much more effective."

"Oh, Ralph," she said in a voice that sounded despicably unsteady, "what a horrid beast I am!"

He laughed and turned away to catch his horse's bridle before beginning to walk along the avenue, holding the hand of an unusually subdued Georgiana. She was feeling almost angry with him. His gentle kindness was proving to be a formidable weapon against her scorn. And if that was not a paradox, she did not know what was.

When they arrived home for a late luncheon, it was to find that Gloria still had not made her planned visit to the vicarage. The gardener had promised to make up a special bouquet for her of the late blooms in the garden and she had decided to wait. Georgiana eagerly agreed to accompany her. She needed to be away from the uncomfortable thoughts and feelings that Ralph's presence aroused in her.

Ralph too was almost glad at the prospect of an afternoon alone. Although this was his honeymoon and no one would expect him to exert himself about estate business, nevertheless he wished to spend some time learning more about the working of his lands. He had come to Chartleigh at Easter for that express purpose. His father had never made an effort to explain anything to the son who would succeed him and, indeed, it was doubtful that the late earl had known everything there was to know himself. Why pay servants if one had to constantly be overseeing their work? Ralph remembered his saying. Provided the income had not declined, he was satisfied.

But Ralph found that he could not feel the same way. He needed to understand his inheritance. The money he received from the lands, a handsome enough income, was not satisfying in itself. He wanted to know where the money came from, for what his land was used, how his workers were recompensed, what improvements, if any, could be made. He had spent his Easter holiday walking and riding over his land, talking to everyone who lived and worked on it, poring over the estate books.

And he had loved every moment. He was surprised. He had always dreamed of an academic career. He had never realized how close to the land his deepest feelings really were. He knew that he was peculiar. He even felt very self-conscious about admitting his interest to anyone outside Chartleigh. If he were a normal gentleman, he would not be concerned about such matters. He would be in London enjoying the Season, filling his days with card-playing, gossiping and shopping for new clothes, horses, and conveyances.

He did not now want to forget what he had learned in

the spring. After his wife and his sister had left to make their visit, he shut himself into the library and succeeded for a whole hour in concentrating on the books he had had his bailiff bring in for him during the morning.

It was a heroic achievement. He was very tired, having had a sleepless night. And it was very difficult to keep his mind from personal matters that were trying to claim his attention. Finally he pushed the books away with a sigh, got up from his desk, and stood at the window looking out along the poplar grove down which he and Georgiana had led their horses a few hours before.

This was the day after his wedding day. He should be in a state of ecstasy. He should be with his wife, inseparable from her during the days of their honeymoon. He had made such a disaster of the whole business. He loved Georgiana. He wanted to be with her, beginning a friendship with her. They were still virtual strangers. These days at Chartleigh should give them the perfect opportunity. But within a day of their marriage he had given her every reason to despise, even hate him. It said a great deal for the sweetness of her character that she had agreed to ride with him that morning and had behaved with such courtesy toward him.

He had made a dreadful ruin of their wedding night. He felt hot with embarrassment and humiliation at the memory. He had been unable to quieten her fears, unable to control his own desire long enough for her to relax in his arms and be ready for his invasion, and finally incapable of consummating the marriage. And he had left her like a small boy in disgrace, to hide his head in shame, instead of waiting until they were both ready to proceed. He hated to imagine the kind of distress in which he must have left Georgiana.

He was a man, in years anyway. And he had begun recently to feel confident in his own maturity and ability to run his life as he saw fit. Yet in this one area of his life he seemed quite incapable of acting like a man. His

main responsibility the night before had been to
reassure a shy and frightened bride, to make her his wife
while giving her as little pain as possible. And he had
failed miserably. There was little point, he supposed, in
going over the facts yet again. He had thought of
nothing else during the long night, which he had spent
out-of-doors wandering around he knew not where. But
he had still not come to any conclusions. What was to be
done about the situation?

He had never really wanted any woman before,
except perhaps that little barmaid for a few mad
minutes. But he wanted Georgiana. He was thoroughly
enchanted with her. Much of the time she seemed so shy
that he wanted to fold her in his arms and protect her
from all the threats of the world. But there were
surprising little flashes of spirit that made him think
that there was a very interesting character behind the
shyness. He wanted to get to know that character and
help her to develop it. And there was occasionally a
directness about her that he found surprising. This
morning, for example, she had not said whether she
disapproved of his strange theories on estate
management. But she had quite skillfully drawn from
him an admission that he was satisfied with his own
ideas, unconventional though they were. She had made
him feel good about himself. She could be a good
friend, he suspected.

Perhaps he could still cultivate her friendship.
Perhaps it was not too late for that. She had been
willing to ride and walk with him and had not avoided
talking to him. But he had to admit that his desire for
her went beyond the need for friendship. He felt a
sexual desire for her. Her small, light figure made him
feel protective and excited him. Yet she had a shapely
body. Ralph's cheeks grew hot at the memory of her
breasts pressing against his chest, her thighs soft against
his. He could remember, though with some humiliation,
how small and feminine she had felt beneath him on the
bed.

He wanted her. He wanted to go to her again that night and make love to her in a manner that would erase her fears and perhaps bring pleasure to her as well as to himself. He wanted to be fully married to Georgiana. He wanted to put his seed inside her.

But he dared not. He had decided that the night before. He could not go to her tonight and risk the same outcome. He would not do that to her. He remembered unwillingly just how very frightened she had been, prattling away to him in bed, yet obviously not knowing what she said. And it was so out of character for Georgiana to prattle. He wondered if she was blaming herself for what had happened. Perhaps she thought she was not desirable enough to attract him. His behavior must have gone a long way to destroy any confidence in herself that she might have. If he repeated the failure tonight, he might destroy entirely her faith in her own femininity.

And he had hurt her. Ralph closed his eyes and rested his forehead against the cool pane of the window. God, he had hurt her. She had cried out to him that he was hurting her. He shuddered. Poor little girl! She deserved so much better. She deserved a husband who could at least make love to her without hurting her.

He had decided the night before that he must try to win her trust and her friendship. Perhaps in time, when they grew accustomed to each other, when they came to like each other, and to be relaxed in each other's presence, their relationship could take on a physical dimension. He would not hesitate to touch her: hold her hand sometimes, touch her cheek, even kiss her—that brief kiss this morning had been achingly sweet. But he would not rush her into deeper intimacies. Those would come when they were both ready for them—he hoped! He dreaded to think of what would happen if he found himself forever incapable of being a man for her.

Georgiana came bouncing into the house an hour later looking anything but the shy, homesick girl that

Ralph pictured to himself. She threw her bonnet and
gloves in the general direction of an oak chest that stood
in the hallway, called to the butler to ask where his
lordship was, and strode toward the library, calling over
her shoulder for Gloria to follow her. She threw open
the door to the library before the butler could scurry
across the hallway to perform the honors for her.

"Ralph," she said as soon as she saw that he was
indeed in the room. He was seated in a deep leather
chair beside the fireplace, reading. "Such an afternoon!
We met three of our neighbors: a Mrs. Horsley and her
daughter and Lady Quentin. Gloria presented me and
they declared their intention of calling on me tomorrow.
They would have come today, they said, but they
thought that perhaps we needed a day to rest after our
journey from London. Was not that foolish? And we
went into the milliner's shop, where there was a chip
bonnet that looks just perfect on Gloria, but she would
not buy it because she said she does not need more
bonnets. You must persuade her to purchase it, Ralph.
It was just made for her. The vicar's housekeeper made
us some tea when we called. And you did not tell me
that Gloria and the Reverend Boscome are betrothed. I
was never more surprised in my life, especially to know
that they have been betrothed for six years." She paused
for breath.

Ralph had jumped up in surprise when his wife first
entered the room without a knock or a footman to
announce her arrival. He watched her and listened with
growing enchantment as she spoke. Her face was alight,
her eyes sparkling and her cheeks flushed from the
walk. He was smiling by the time she paused.

"You seem to have enjoyed your afternoon," he said.
"Hello, Gloria. Does that betrothal still exist, by the
way? I thought it had been forgotten about a long time
ago. I have heard no mention of it."

"It still exists, Ralph," his sister replied gravely. "It
is just that with Papa dying last year and Mama being

left alone while you were at university, it did not seem appropriate to talk about nuptials.''

"But that is absurd now, is it not, Ralph?'' Georgiana said, turning to him in appeal. "I have been telling Gloria so all the way home. Why, if we can get married little more than a year after the death of your papa, there is nothing improper about her and the Reverend Boscome doing the same. And it has been six years, Ralph! Why, Gloria will be too old to bear children if she waits any longer.''

Both brother and sister flushed. Gloria looked away and busied herself with folding her shawl.

"Perhaps that is for Boscome and Gloria to decide,'' Ralph said gently.

"Yes,'' Georgiana persisted, "but they have wanted to marry these six years past. It is your mama who has always found reason to put off the wedding. That is not really fair, is it, Ralph?''

Ralph put down his book and took his wife by the elbow. "Let us go upstairs to the drawing room for tea,'' he said. "You must be thirsty after your walk. If Mama has advised Gloria to wait, dear, I am sure she has a good reason.''

"But six years, Ralph!'' Georgiana trotted along beside him as he led her across the hall and up the stairs. Gloria came quietly behind them. "You could permit them to marry. You are the head of the family. The Reverend Boscome is almost old already.''

"Only four-and-thirty, Georgiana,'' Gloria protested from behind her.

"He will be too old to romp with his children if he does not have them very soon,'' Georgiana said severely, preceding her husband into the drawing room. She appeared not to have noticed the embarrassment of her companions at her earlier mention of children.

"Just a cup of tea for me, Ralph,'' Gloria said. "We ate at the vicarage, and I am not hungry.''

"Me either,'' Georgiana said absently. "Ralph, I

have had a famous notion. Do let us give a dinner party for your neighbors. We could have cards and music afterward, and perhaps even some charades or dancing. This room would be quite splendid for the dancing if the carpet were rolled up. It is big enough, and I would not think there are a great many people to invite, are there? Oh, do let's, Ralph. I have never had a chance to have my very own evening party before.'' She was almost dancing around the room, viewing its possibilities from various angles.

Ralph looked inquiringly at his sister and then smiled warmly at his wife. ''I cannot think of a better way of introducing my countess to the neighborhood,'' he said. ''It is many years since Chartleigh was used for parties. Papa used to have hunt dinners, but the guests were almost exclusively male.''

Georgiana clapped her hands. ''Oh, splendid!'' she said. ''We shall have such fun. I shall go right now to confer with the cook on the menu. You must tell me how to reach the kitchen, Ralph.''

His smile had turned to a grin. ''I think Cook might have an apoplexy if you rushed at her with such a proposition at the moment,'' he said. ''Cook is a very excitable person, and I am sure that at this time of day she is very busy preparing our dinner. Perhaps later tonight, Georgiana, or tomorrow morning? I shall take you down myself and introduce you to her. She is an old friend of mine.''

Georgiana had stopped bouncing around. She came to sit demurely in a chair across from her husband's. ''Oh, very well,'' she said. ''I shall wait. Though it is very provoking to have to do so when one's mind is once set on something. I suppose the cook also fed you shamelessly between meals when you were a child. I believe you must have had all the servants wrapped around your little finger, Ralph.''

He looked sheepish. ''I was such a puny little boy, you see,'' he said. ''Everyone thought I needed fattening up. Georgiana, are you sure you are up to giving a party? You will be expected to entertain a large number of people and will be very much on display. No one will expect such an event from a new bride. Would it be better to wait until we return to London, when Mama can help you and perhaps be official hostess?''

Georgiana stared at him. ''What nonsense!'' she said. ''What is so difficult about conversing with a dozen or so people who are no different from you and me? I do not need to shelter behind your mama or anyone else, Ralph.''

He smiled warmly at her. ''What a brave girl you are, Georgiana,'' he said. ''I do admire your spirit. And I shall be at your side to help you, you know.''

''Of course you will,'' she said. ''Gloria, I have just had an inspired thought. I shall buy you that chip bonnet as a gift because I have just become your new sister-in-law.'' She beamed with delight at her own ingenuity.

6

THE DINNER PARTY was set for an evening nine days after Georgiana conceived the idea. She found herself very busy during those days. There was all the planning to do for this, her first party. Not that there was really very much to be done. Once she and the cook had decided on the menu, there was nothing else she could do about the food, and once the gardener had informed her of what flowers would be available to decorate the dining room and drawing room, there was little she could do until the day, when she planned to make the floral arrangements herself.

But Georgiana was excited at the prospect of entertaining guests. She planned her wardrobe with care and changed her mind about it every day. She planned the entertainments and decided definitely that there must be dancing as soon as she learned that Miss Dobb, unmarried sister of Mrs. Horsley, played the pianoforte with some skill and that Mr. Chester, a gentleman farmer, enjoyed some local fame as a violinist. She planned seating arrangements for the dinner table, the arrangement of furniture in the drawing room, even the topics of conversation that would be introduced during the meal.

But it was not just her party that filled her days. She was visited by all the prominent matrons for miles around and returned their visits with Ralph. She walked several times into the village with Gloria as a type of youthful chaperone to permit her sister-in-law to call at the vicarage. She attended church. She spent hours with the housekeeper, the cook, and the gardener, getting acquainted with the home of which she was now mistress. She rode with Ralph each day and soon became familiar with every corner of the estate and every soul living on it. She wrote letters to her parents and to Vera.

In fact, she decided at the end of the first week of her marriage, she had been busy doing all the kinds of things that she would have found a horrid bore just a few weeks before. Even the party that she was planning with such minute care was the sort she would have avoided like the plague back in London. What real enjoyment could be expected from a gathering of country people who probably had no particular elegance and no very amusing conversation?

She dismissed her thoughts with a shrug. This life was a novelty. That was why she was enjoying it. There was something exhilarating about finding oneself suddenly a countess and the center of local attention. It was only now after all the fuss of the wedding was over that she was fully realizing the fact that she was the Countess of Chartleigh, mistress of one of the grandest estates in southern England. Although she was only eighteen, and in fact nowhere near nineteen, she was suddenly no longer treated like a very young girl, with either impatience or an amused tolerance. She was a married lady, and a very important one at that, and she was deferred to as such, her opinions on all matters listened to seriously.

Georgiana was enjoying herself. She had been somewhat horrified to know that they were to come here for the wedding trip. She would literally die of boredom in the country, she had thought, especially with such a boy for a companion. There could not possibly be any enjoyment in being with such a shy young innocent. At least if he had taken her to the Continent, there would have been so much to see that she could have ignored his presence.

Now she was surprised to discover that her days were

not boring at all. Not yet, anyway. Once the party was over and the novelty of her situation wore off, she supposed, she would be very ready to get back to London. But really, so far, the days were just not long enough.

Something else that surprised her a great deal was that she almost enjoyed Ralph's company. He was not at all her type of man. His age was against him. He was too young to interest her to any great degree. And he was always very gentle and agreeable. There was nothing wrong with that, but sometimes she did enjoy a good sparring match with a male companion, if not an out-and-out quarrel. And there was no mischief in Ralph. She often wondered with inward hilarity how he would react if she suggested doing something quite outrageous like putting a lidded saucepan full of grasshoppers on the kitchen table for Cook to discover, or having a race down the elm grove by swinging from tree to tree.

No, he was really not her type of man. But granted that she was stuck with him, whether she wished to be or not, she had to admit that she was not finding his company or his person repulsive. And she could no longer think of him as weak. He might not be what she had always considered manly, but he had a great deal of character. He had a library brimful of books and had awed her by admitting, when she asked, that he had read most of them. She did not see how the contents of all those volumes could be stored in one brain, but she knew he was not a liar. He had an intimate knowledge of his estate. There was not a question of hers that he could not answer, and she asked a great many. And everybody on the estate loved him. Everybody. He had an almost awesome patience and kindness with other people, herself included.

He had never once spoken unkindly to her or looked frowningly at her. Even when she pestered him about Gloria and the Reverend Boscome's marriage. And she did pester him about that. She could see very well—it was as plain as the nose on her face—that those two

were very well-matched and that they were drifting
perilously close to middle age. She had made it her
crusade to see that they were allowed to marry soon.
Ralph would only smile at her and tell her gently that
Gloria was of age and must herself come to some
arrangement with Mr. Boscome and her mother. He
would speak to the latter when they returned to
London, he said. And that was the only concession he
would make to her nagging. It was annoying, but then,
Papa would have roared at her long since to hold her
tongue and mind her manners.

There was, in fact, only one unpleasant fact to mar
Georgiana's happiness. And that was the fact that her
marriage was still unconsummated. Ralph had made no
attempt to come to her since that first night and had
made no reference to his absence. She had expected him
on the second night. She had brushed her hair and
perfumed herself with special care and had arranged
herself in her bed as invitingly as she knew how. But he
had not come, and finally she had been forced to blow
out the candles and try as best she could to go to sleep.
She had prepared herself with less hope the following
night. Since then she had tried not to expect him at all.

She was not happy with the situation. Mainly, she
persuaded herself, she felt guilty. If only she had
behaved herself like a well-bred young lady on her
wedding night, all would have been well. Ralph would
not have lost his courage. By now she would have been
able to receive him in her bed with unconcern. She
would know exactly what she was to do and would be
past the embarrassment of having to allow him such
intimacies. She was terribly afraid that he might never
again have enough courage to try what he had failed to
do that night. Perhaps she had destroyed his manhood
for all time.

Georgiana did not like to admit to herself that there
was some personal disappointment in her unhappiness
too. She had decided with such certainty that Ralph was
not her type of man, that he was too young, too boyish

in physique, too sweetly good-looking, too shy, too
good to attract her in the least, that she was almost
unaware of the fact that she stared at him frequently, at
his tall, slender figure, his thick, wavy, always unruly
hair, his long, slim hands, and his smiling eyes and
mouth, and imagined her own body in contact with his.
On their wedding night he had been nervous and
clumsy. But if he were not nervous, she thought sometimes, if he were relaxed and bent on giving them both
pleasure, how would those hands feel—on her naked
breasts, for example? If ever she did catch herself in
these daydreams, she would always shake them off with
a shudder and a grimace.

And she was so accustomed to believing that she did
not want him physically that she was unaware of the
fact that she made no effort to avoid his touch. Sometimes he would hold her hand—if she was talking to him
when they sat side by side on a sofa, perhaps, without
the presence of Gloria, or when they had dismounted
from their horses and were walking together over part
of the estate. She was never the one to break the
contact. Sometimes, in fact, she would unconsciously
move closer so that their arms and shoulders were in
contact too.

And he had kissed her twice since their wedding night,
once the morning after in the poplar grove, once in the
library after he had told her that he would speak with
his mother about Gloria. Both kisses had been brief and
very gentle—not by any means of earth-shattering
sensuality. But she found herself sometimes looking at
that good-humored mouth with a slight breathlessness
and a shudder, which she took to be of distaste, and
remembering how warm and reassuring it had felt on
her own. How would it feel to trace the line of his lips
with her finger? With her tongue? She had recoiled with
hot disgust at herself on the one occasion when she had
become conscious of this deviant desire.

On the whole, Georgiana was a great deal better
pleased with her marriage after nine days than she had

expected to be. If only she were a wife in deed as well as in name, she would consider herself no worse off than hundreds of other women of her class who had been persuaded into marriages with partners not of their own choosing. There was even a good chance, she felt, of a mild affection developing between her and her husband. If only he would bed her soon!

The party at Chartleigh was seen as a big occasion by the gentry for miles around. All of them had heard with deep interest the news of the marriage of the young earl to a viscount's daughter. They remembered the earl as a thin, shy, but sweetly cheerful young boy who had shot to a tall and gangly young manhood before leaving for university. They had seen little of him since then. His father's death and funeral had brought him home briefly, but the family had stayed at the house most of the time. They found it hard to believe that the new Lord Chartleigh could be grown up enough to have taken a bride.

After visits at the house had been eagerly made and had been returned, not only by the countess, but by her husband too, opinion was mixed. Several of the older men lamented the days when the house had been open to them during hunting season, the liquor flowing free. This quiet, polite stripling could not be more different from his father if he tried.

Almost all the ladies, except perhaps the very young, saw the young couple as unutterably romantic. The countess was extremely youthful—little more than a schoolgirl. But she was pretty and sprightly. There was nothing affected about her manners, though all of her visitors were her inferiors in rank. The earl, too, still looked younger than his one-and-twenty years, but he had matured since the days when they had known him well. He was still quiet, still flushed easily. But there was a charm about his manner that won their female hearts. And what lady could resist a man who was so obviously devoted to his wife?

The very young ladies, perhaps, could do so. Ralph—and even Georgiana—would have been surprised to know how many of these girls looked at his lean height, his fair hair, and his smiling face with quickened heartbeats. Georgiana was a figure of envy to these females.

Thirty-four people sat down to dinner at Chartleigh. It was a prodigious crowd, Georgiana admitted when the cook repeated the number with some incredulity, but one had to invite all the guests to dinner. Even those who lived closest had a few miles to drive, and it would be unreasonable to expect any of them to travel the distance merely for the evening's entertainment. Ralph had fully agreed with her.

Georgiana, from her place at the foot of the table, gazed down the vast length of tablecloth to Ralph and felt a thrill of satisfaction. Everyone was engaged in conversation. Ralph did not seem to be unduly daunted by the presence of Lady Quentin on his right and Mrs. Hadleigh on his left. Georgiana was free of the conversation of Sir Harold Quentin for the moment. Mr. Hadleigh, on her other side, had an ear bent to some observation of his other neighbor. She had a free moment in which to admire the fruits of her own careful planning. The two floral arrangements on the table looked quite superb, even if she did say so herself. And Cook had excelled herself. She must remember to make a personal visit to the kitchen tomorrow to tell her so.

She did wish that she could have seated Gloria and the Reverend Boscome together. She had fully intended to do so, but Gloria had looked over the first seating plan and asked that it not be so.

"But why?" Georgiana had asked.

"It would look too contrived," Gloria had replied. "I believe some people have an inkling of our understanding, but it has never been announced. I would not wish to start any gossip."

All Georgiana's protestations of the utter foolishness of this idea had not changed her sister-in-law's mind.

She was beginning to lose a little patience with the situation. She had decided that she liked Gloria, who was gentle, sensible, and affectionate, despite her rather severe appearance. But she could not imagine that anyone could be so spiritless. In Gloria's situation she would have grabbed her man and headed for Gretna a long time ago and been done with the whole business. At the rate the betrothal was progressing, it might be another six years before the banns were called.

And Ralph was no help. She caught his eye across the length of the table for a moment and returned his smile. He would do nothing to cross his mother, who was clearly opposed to this marriage. Those two lovers needed a helping hand. It would have to be hers. No one else in this family had any gumption. A wild plan was already forming in Georgiana's head when Mr. Hadleigh turned toward her.

It was many hours later before she had a chance to put her plan into effect. She had had so little time to think about it in the meantime that there had been no opportunity to deliberate on its wisdom. But Georgiana had never been strong on forethought. Enough to have conceived an idea. It must immediately be acted upon. One would find out later if one had been wise or not.

When all her guests had served themselves with supper and were seated, Georgiana looked about her with flushed pleasure. The dancing had been a great success, though most of the older people had disappeared into the card salon. Miss Caroline Horsley had told her that it was an age since there had been a dance anywhere near. For some reason dancing in the country was considered a winter entertainment, unless it were around a maypole out-of-doors.

Georgiana had danced so much that she had not had a chance to see if everything was going smoothly in the card room. But Ralph had reassured her during the one set in which he had partnered her. And that had been a pleasant surprise. She had expected Ralph to be one of those men who had two left feet when it came to dancing. But he was a very good dancer. She had never had a more graceful partner.

Now the evening was almost over. After supper the card players would probably play another rubber, and the young people would dance a few more sets. The party had been a great success. And would be an even greater one. She drew in a deep breath and rose to her feet.

Ralph looked up in astonishment from the conversation he was having with a group of his neighbors. What was it that Georgiana had to say that made it necessary for her to call the attention of the whole gathering? She looked very flushed and very determined. And extremely pretty. He had been very proud of her all evening. She was the perfect hostess: sparkling with life, smiling at and talking to everyone. His fears that her shyness would make her unequal to the task of being hostess had very quickly been put to rest. Her training and her experience during the past Season in London had given her a poise in public that he had not expected. But what was she about now?

She wanted to make an announcement, she said, and what better time than now when they were surrounded by all their friends and neighbors? Ralph's eyes on her sharpened.

"Lord Chartleigh and I wish to announce officially the betrothal of Lady Gloria Middleton and the Reverend David Boscome," Georgiana said very clearly. "Now that her year of mourning is at an end, my sister-in-law is ready to proceed with the wedding plans. I believe you may all expect to hear the banns before Christmas."

She had no chance to say more. Delighted murmurings quickly developed into loud congratulations to the prospective bride and groom. Ralph did not look at either. He gazed, mesmerized, at his wife, who was smiling, her hands clasped against her chest. What, in heaven's name, had possessed her?

He was allowed to think no more. Sir Harold was pumping his hand and declaring that it was about time that marriage took place. Most of the vicar's parishioners were despairing of ever seeing Lady Gloria established at the vicarage. Ralph smiled and concentrated on saying everything that seemed appropriate for the next twenty minutes, until he deemed it time to begin the activities that would close the evening's entertainment. He withdrew to the library as soon as he decently could. He hoped no one would remark his absence but would merely assume that he was with the guests in the other room.

He slumped into his favorite leather chair and passed one hand across his eyes. He had a feeling of uncontrollable disaster, such as he had known occasionally as a child. Sometimes one did something so wrong that one could not put it right again but just had to prepare oneself for the consequences. There was that time, for example, when he had forgotten to close a gate that he had been warned about numerous times, and all the cows got out into the corn. The worst of it had been that he was the one to discover the fact, yet had been totally unable to round up all the animals and herd them back into the field where they belonged. That particular thrashing he had received from his father had been all the worse for the long anticipation he had had to suffer.

There would be no thrashing for this. But in fact it was many times worse than letting out cows from a field. An announcement had been made in an appallingly public manner and it would affect the lives of several people quite drastically. Gloria and Boscome would now be almost forced into matrimony whether they truly wished it or not. He believed that they did, but that was quite beside the point at the moment. Everyone for miles around Chartleigh now knew about the impending marriage. Yet Mama in London knew nothing. She would be furious! Ralph remembered the opposition she had put up against the betrothal in the first place. The daughter of an earl was simply throwing

herself away by marrying a vicar, a mere younger son.
She had succeeded in postponing the wedding for so
long that he had assumed that the engagement no longer
existed.

How would poor Gloria break the news to her? He
must do it himself, of course. Now that the deed was
done, he must assume responsibility for it. It had been
his idea. Clearly Gloria was determined either to marry
Boscome or to die an old maid. She was six-and-twenty
already. She did not need anyone's permission to marry,
but the truth was that duty to their mother had held her
back from her own happiness. Well, he was Chartleigh
now, head of the family, as Georgiana had pointed out
to him a week or so ago. He must convince both Gloria
and his mother that the initiative had been his, that he
was asserting his headship of the family.

It was an appalling thought. He had always found it
hard to confront his mother face-to-face. On those
occasions when he had been determined to defy her,
such as on the topic of the rebuilding of the laborers'
cottages, he had done so quietly, leaving her to assume
that she had won the victory. Well, perhaps it was time
that he learned to assert himself more openly. His love
and respect for his mother did not blind him to the fact
that she was on occasion quite selfish. Most parents
would have recognized by this time that Gloria's attachment to Boscome was no trivial matter. Perhaps it really
was a situation in which he had every right, even a duty,
to assert his position.

In fact, perhaps Georgiana had done him a favor. She
had certainly forced him into taking matters into his
own hands. And thinking about Georgiana, what on
earth had possessed her to do such a thing? He was quite
certain that Gloria had expected the announcement as
little as he. It had been such an indiscreet announcement, yet it had obviously been deliberate. She had
stood before the whole gathering and called everyone's
attention.

It seemed so out of character for his sweet little

Georgiana to be so bold. And bold about such a matter!
If the announcement was to be made at all, it was he or
Boscome who should have made it. Surely all his guests
must be thinking it quite peculiar that his bride had been
the one chosen to make public such news. Why had she
done so?

Ralph pondered the matter for several minutes before
getting to his feet. He was smiling when he did so. He
left the room with some reluctance. His guests would be
beginning to leave soon. He could not allow the
discourtesy of his absence to be noticed.

7

GEORGIANA MEANWHILE had been suffering agonies since supper. She had noticed Ralph slip away to the library and consequently decided to play the hostess more conscientiously than she had done all evening. She moved from card salon to drawing room, making sure that everyone was occupied and happy. She did not dance. And now, when she no longer wanted the leisure in which to think, she found that she had plenty of it. And the thoughts came thick and fast.

And not one of them pleasant!

What, in heaven's name, had she done now? It had seemed such a famous idea when she had had it at the dinner table, to force everyone's hand by making a public announcement. It was only as she was making it that she had realized just how irrevocable it was. What if Gloria did not truly wish for the match? What if the six-year delay had really been of her own making? What if the Reverend Boscome did not really wish it? What if he was secretly quite comfortable with his bachelor existence? She had really left them little choice now but to marry. She might have just doomed them to eternal unhappiness.

That was nonsense, of course, she told herself briskly. Of course they wished to be wed. One had only to look at them to see how devoted they were. They were not by any means a handsome pair. Gloria's features were somewhat harsh; she certainly did not share her brother's beauty. And Mr. Boscome was a very ordinary man, his sandy hair already thinning on top.

But they loved each other. She must not begin doubting that.

But would they be very angry at what she had done? Would they feel humiliated at having the organizing of their affairs taken from their hands?

And what must all these people around her be thinking? They had all seemed genuinely delighted by her announcement. In fact, even Gloria and the vicar had not looked outwardly displeased or discomposed. They had come together after her words and received the congratulations of the guests with composure. But would not those guests already be wondering why she, a new and young bride, should have been entrusted with so momentous an announcement? Would they not be considering how improper it was that it had not been Ralph who had spoken?

And how, in the name of heaven, had she had the nerve to get up in front of all those strangers, who were to be her neighbors for the rest of her life, and tell such an out-and-out lie? Oh, she was a hopeless case. Papa was perfectly right about her. All those horrid names he had ever called her were true. She could at least have waited for another occasion, given herself time to think out the implications of what she was going to do. Papa would surely beat her in earnest if he were here now and had witnessed the very improper and embarrassing spectacle she had made of herself.

What would the countess have to say when they returned to London next week? The dowager countess, that was. Georgiana herself was now the countess. Everyone seemed to stand in such awe of her mother-in-law. Georgiana had had an impression of an overweight, self-indulgent complainer before the wedding, but both Ralph and Gloria seemed to find it difficult to stand up to her. And Georgiana was to be part of her household when she returned to London. She would have to account for this night's work. No, Georgiana thought defiantly, smiling at Miss Dobb and nodding that yes, indeed, there was time for just one more set, she would not be a part of her mother-in-law's household. The dowager would be part of hers. She had not cringed before anyone in her life. She was not about to start now.

Her eyes alighted on Ralph as this thought was passing through her mind. Fortunately, the whole width of the drawing room was between them, and he walked on past toward the salon. It was of Ralph she should be thinking most. Now what had she done to him? She had set herself more than a week before to try to restore his sense of manhood. And what had she done? She had gone right over his head and done something that only he had a right to do. She had made a public announcement, a family announcement, in the name of Lord Chartleigh. And she had probably made him look quite foolish in the eyes of his neighbors, who might think that he did not have the courage to speak for himself but must engage his wife to do so. She had done it again!

He must be very furious with her! What would he do when everyone had left? He was far too well-bred to reprimand her publicly, of course. But afterward. Would he yell at her as Papa always did? Threaten to beat her? Actually beat her? She could not imagine Ralph angry. She certainly could not picture him being violent. But the provocation had been great. At the very least, he would doubtless tell her that he had been deceived in her and was sorry that he had married her. She did not want him to be sorry.

Well, she thought, if he was so mean-spirited as to say that, she would stick her chin in the air and tell him quite coolly that she was disappointed in him and was sorry she had married him. After all, if he were a real man, he would have insisted long ago that his sister be allowed to marry the man of her choice. And he would have told his mother where she might take her whinings and complainings. She was indeed sorry to be married to such a meek and mild man. What would all these people think if they knew the true state of her marriage: unconsummated because the Earl of Chartleigh had taken fright in her bedchamber on their wedding night?

By the time the dancing came to an end a few minutes later, Georgiana had worked herself into a comforting indignation against the whole of the Middleton family, Ralph in particular. Even so, she slipped away guiltily to bed after bidding the last of her guests good night. Ralph was still busy instructing the butler and the footmen to leave the tidying up of the drawing room and salon until the morning. She was relieved to note that Gloria had not lingered to be confronted that night. Perhaps it would be easier to face them both after a half-night's sleep.

Georgiana was standing before the mirror in her room, humming tunelessly to herself as she brushed her hair, when Ralph came into her room. He did knock but did not wait for an answer. She had no time to compose herself. She faced him with jaw hanging and brush dangling from one limp hand.

"Am I disturbing you, Georgiana?" he asked cautiously.

Georgiana snapped her jaws together. She peered suspiciously at her husband. Papa sometimes began on her that way too, with deceptive mildness. Well, she certainly was not about to play cat and mouse with Ralph. He was not nearly such a formidable adversary as Papa.

"I was about ready for bed," she replied, "but you may as well say your piece now, Ralph. About the announcement I made regarding Gloria and the Reverend Boscome, I believe?" Her chin went up. There was a martial gleam in her eye.

Ralph came across the room and took both her hands in his. He smiled down at her. "Dear Georgiana," he said. "Putting the welfare of others before your own comfort.'

"Eh?" Georgiana was surprised into extreme inelegance.

"What a brave wife I have," he continued. "You

quite put me to shame, Georgiana. It must have taken you days to gather the courage to do what you did this evening.''

"You are not angry?" she asked, frowning suspiciously.

"I am very proud of you," he said, squeezing her hands tightly. "You have seen in the last week and a half how unsatisfactory is the situation between Gloria and David Boscome. And you saw that the only remedy was to force the issue. It must have been very dreadful for you to get up as you did before all our neighbors, dear, and say what you did. I am deeply touched at the love you have shown for my sister."

"Oh," Georgiana said. What he said was all true. But he made her sound so heroic. Had her deed really been so splendidly selfless? Perhaps it had. Yes, it really had taken some courage to do what she had done. She smiled tentatively at Ralph, who had had the intelligence to recognize the truth.

"Come and sit down for a while," he said very gently, releasing one hand and leading her to the daybed. He sat down beside her, retaining his hold on her other hand. "I do wish you had come to me before the party, Georgiana, and taken me into your confidence."

"You would have stopped me," she said. "It was because no one seemed to want to do anything that I acted as I did."

"We could have talked to Gloria and Boscome and asked if they wished for such an announcement," he said. "They might well have said yes. And they would have been better prepared for the flood of congratulations."

"Oh, Ralph, you know that Gloria would have felt it necessary to consult your mother first, and the Reverend Boscome would have bowed to her wishes, and you would have been afraid to offend the countess —the dowager," Georgiana said.

Ralph frowned briefly. "Perhaps you are right," he said, "and I certainly meant it when I said that I am proud of you. But you are very young, Georgiana. So am I. Is it right of us, do you suppose, to presume that we know what is right for others and to try to organize their lives so that they have little choice about the course they take?''

"Oh!" Georgiana shook off his hand and rose indignantly to her feet. "I see what you are about, Ralph Middleton. You are just like Papa, only worse. At least Papa yells and shows his disapproval in no uncertain terms. I know where I stand with him. You think to lull me like a child with your soft words of approval. But you are scolding me just the same. You are telling me that what I did was wrong and thoughtless. Why do you not at least be honest about it? Shout at me. Threaten to beat me.''

"Georgiana!" Ralph was on his feet too, his face pale and clearly distressed. "Please. I did not mean to hurt you. I do not feel at all angry with you. And how could I threaten you even if I did? You are a person, and my wife. I would never offer violence to any person, especially not to a woman, and to the very woman I have undertaken to protect and cherish for the rest of my life.''

"You see!" she accused. To her annoyance she felt hot tears blurring her eyes. "You are doing it again. You think that because you use gentle words you will not hurt. But it is just through your gentleness that you wound the most. One feels a fiend in opposing you. You make me feel wretched. Here I am, quite overwrought and speaking far too loudly, and all you do is stand there and look . . ." Her hand circled the air. "Dismayed.''

She turned away sharply, breathing deeply in an attempt to bring herself under control and to prevent the tears from spilling over. She felt foolish. How could one argue satisfactorily with a man who refused to get angry and yell back? She felt two warm hands take her by the shoulders and draw her back against a lean body.

"Georgiana," he said very quietly into her ear. "I am sorry, my dear. Indeed I am. I did not intend to make you feel guilty about what you did tonight. You were so wonderfully brave and unselfish. I merely wished to point out that you are young and eager and impulsive. I love those qualities in you. But sometimes they can get one into trouble. I am very unfeeling and clumsy with words. I did not mean at all to accuse. Please believe me.''

Georgiana sniffed. ''I know I should not have made that stupid announcement,'' she said. ''It was just that . . . Oh, I know I was wrong, Ralph. I didn't need you to point that out to me.'' Her voice sounded appallingly high and thin to her own ears.

He turned her in his arms. Concern made his face look even more gentle than usual, Georgiana noticed as she scrubbed impatiently at her eyes with a handkerchief.

''Oh, my dear,'' he said, looking deep into her eyes, ''I have not made you cry, have I? I am very angry with myself. I have been so very proud all this evening to know that you are my wife. I wanted to tell you that. I truly do not deserve you, Georgiana.''

''Who could be proud of me?'' Georgiana sniffed against her handkerchief. She was suffering from a very satisfying attack of self-pity. ''I can never do the right thing. I always get into the horridest scrapes. But I think this one is worse than usual.''

''Georgiana!'' he said softly. ''Oh, my sweetest love. Don't do this to yourself. Hush now.'' He cupped her face in his hands and gazed searchingly into her eyes. ''Come. Smile at me. Don't punish me with these tears.''

Georgiana laughed a little shakily. ''I never cry!'' she announced. ''You have such an effect on me, Ralph.''

''Do I?'' he asked.

And he kissed her softly on the lips. He still held her face in his hands. Georgiana grasped the lapels of his evening coat and kissed him back. She was so wretched with remorse she needed the comfort of his mouth on hers, of his arms that soon encircled her and held her protectively against his body. And slender as he was, he was certainly not frail, she thought, relaxing her weight and the burden of her guilt against him. She slipped her arms up around his neck so that she could feel him with her breasts.

Ralph held her slim figure wrapped within his arms. He moved his head and parted his lips over hers so that he was suddenly aware of the taste of her. He felt her breasts press against him as her arms twined around his neck. He wanted to touch those breasts with his hands. He wanted to have his hands beneath her nightgown so that he could feel their warm softness. He wanted her. He could feel the blood pounding through his head. He could feel the excitement and near-pain of arousal. He lifted his head to look down at his wife.

She looked troubled as soon as the contact of their mouths was broken. "It is so easy to hurt people when really we intend just the opposite," she said.

He froze. She might as well have thrown a pitcher of cold water in his face. He completely forgot about Gloria and Georgiana's perhaps indiscreet attempt to help her. He could think only of his wife and of the way he had hurt her almost two weeks before. When he had been trying to love her.

She was afraid of him.

She was afraid he would hurt her again.

Could he be sure that he would not?

He loved her. He wanted to make love to her. He wanted to love her and love her until she cried out with pleasure.

Would he hurt her instead?

He smiled down at her and kissed her gently on the lips again. "I am keeping you from your sleep," he said. "Thank you, Georgiana, for this evening. You are a good wife, and you have shown me tonight an example of courage that I will try to emulate. Good night, dear."

Georgiana's jaw had dropped when he came into her room. It dropped as he left. A full minute passed before she recovered herself sufficiently to pick up her evening slippers one at a time and hurl them furiously at the

dressing-room door through which he had disappeared.
A few choice epithets, learned from some of her male
London friends, followed the slippers.

How dared he? How dared he . . . play with her like
that! She hated him. Unfeeling, cowardly, self-
righteous, spineless . . . boy! She hated him. Just let him
try to climb into her bed at any time in the future. She
would tell him a thing or two. She wanted a man in her
bed, not a stupid boy who had probably not even
realized what a fool she had just made of herself, sur-
rendering her body to him, almost begging him to pick
her up and carry her to the bed and ravish her. Good
night, indeed! She hated him.

Georgiana strode over to her dressing table, picked up
her ivory-backed hairbrush, and hurled that too at the
dressing-room door.

She burst into tears.

Five days later the Chartleigh traveling carriage was
on its way back to London. For much of the journey
very little sound came from inside, though there were
three occupants. Each seemed more content to be left
with private thoughts than to indulge in conversation.

Gloria had said a final farewell to her betrothed when
the carriage passed the vicarage. She did not find this
parting as painful as she had the last, because it was
likely that it would not last so long. Even so, it is a
dreary business to be leaving a loved one behind. And
the future was not as full of certainties as the previous
few days had lulled her into believing. There was still
her mother to face.

Ralph was finding it difficult to shake off the mood
of depression that had oppressed him since the night of
the dinner party. He had made an effort to be cheerful
and to carry on with his daily living as before, but he
seemed to be permanently blue-deviled. His opinion of
himself was at a very low ebb. His marriage was in a
mess. And he did not know how to turn things around.

He had been so happy just two weeks before when he
married Georgiana, and so full of hope. He had offered

for her to please his mother and to fulfill a sense of duty. But he had discovered that he loved his bride. She had seemed to be the perfect wife for him. She shared his extreme youth, his quietness. And she had added to those qualities a sweetness and an air of innocence that had made him feel older than his years, that had given him a determination to protect her. And he had looked forward to two weeks with her at Chartleigh, alone except for the unthreatening presence of Gloria. It had seemed like a fairy-tale beginning to a happy marriage.

Yet somehow nothing had worked out as he had imagined. And none of it was Georgiana's fault. She was everything he could wish for, and more. She was different from what he had expected, it was true. She had a liveliness of manner and a forthrightness of address that denoted a strong character. And he would never have suspected that she would be capable of showing so much courage. But he had not been mistaken about her basic sweetness of character. She had shown an affection for his family that could not have been expected after less than two weeks of marriage. He still marveled at the way in which she had laid herself open to all kinds of censure on the night of the dinner party in her determination to help his sister.

No, it was entirely his fault that the marriage had gone wrong. He had married a sweet and loving young girl and he had made her afraid of him. He loved her, and he could not come near her. He had resolved after their wedding night to be patient, to win her trust and her affection before trying again to consummate the marriage. Yet his own selfishness and uncontrolled desires had prevailed. He had not been able to resist his need for her when he had been foolish enough to visit her in her bedchamber. He had tried to make love to her long before she was ready for such intimacy, and he had frightened her again. She had told him so as delicately as she could.

He knew that he had to begin all over again to become her friend, to win her confidence. He had to renew his hope that eventually she would trust him sufficiently to allow him to touch her and to make her his wife. But it would be a long process. He did not think he had the patience, not, that is, unless he could feel confident that all would turn out well in the end. But he was not convinced. Perhaps the time would never come. Perhaps the rift between them would only widen with time. Perhaps she already felt a distaste for him that would turn to revulsion.

Ralph turned his head to look at his wife. She was sitting quietly beside him, her hands folded in her lap, her face turned toward the window. So small and so fragile-looking. So lovely. And so courageous. Except about that one thing. She was afraid of his touch. And he could do nothing about it. He wanted to take her hand in his and smile reassuringly at her when she turned. But how could he be sure that she would not cringe at even that much contact? He had not touched her since that night. He had been afraid to do so.

And now they were on their way back to London, where they would be joining Mama at Middleton House. Her family would wish to spend time with her. Her friends and his would take some of their time. They would have less chance now to get to know each other. They would surely drift apart until only a name held them together. Ralph turned back to his window as he felt panic catch at his breathing.

Georgiana was feeling very tense. She was conscious of Ralph beside her with every nerve ending in her body. She was aware that he turned and looked at her for perhaps two minutes. The urge to look back at him turned her neck muscles so rigid that finally she did not think she could have moved if she had tried. She could not look him in the eye. She could not speak to him. She would have to do both if she turned her head. She was just too close to him. It would be too intimate a moment. Gloria, on the seat opposite, was asleep.

The last few days had been dreadful. They had hardly spoken. They had hardly looked at each other. At least, she had not looked at him. She could not speak for him because she had not been looking to observe if he looked at her. They had not touched. Even this morning, it was a footman who had handed her into the carriage. If the lack of contact had been caused by absence of interest, it would have been bearable. But the air between them positively bristled with tension and unspoken words.

If this state of affairs lasted much longer she would positively scream and start throwing things again. She hated him. She despised him. The words had been repeated to herself so many times that they had become like a sort of catechism, words without meaning droning away somewhere in the back of her mind. The truth was that she did care. Ralph was rather a sweet boy. She had had much evidence in the last two weeks that he was kind and considerate.

And he was unhappy. Of that there could not be any doubt. And there could be only one reason. It could not be that she had treated him badly or made him feel unwanted. Heaven knew, she had made her availability mortifyingly obvious to him a few nights before. No, it must be that he just could not consummate their marriage. Georgiana knew that such things happened to men. Someone must have told her so, though she could not remember who it was or how that person had come to confide such a shocking fact to a girl of such tender age. Anyway, the fact remained that Ralph must be incapable of making love to her. It had not been so on their wedding night. Clumsy as he had been, he could have done so if she had only kept her infernal mouth shut.

And so the whole thing came back to her again. It was her fault. She had destroyed his confidence to such a degree on that night that she had made him impotent. Yes, that was the word. And what a shocking burden it was to have on one's conscience. Poor Ralph. She wished he would touch her. She would like to curl up against him and try to make him feel protective and manly again. And her motives were not entirely selfless, she admitted. She was finding Ralph increasingly attractive and really quite handsome. It must be that

eternal human tendency to want what we know we
cannot have, she decided. Georgiana was starting to feel
annoying physical frustrations at being close to her
husband, married to him, yet unable to enjoy his
embraces.

She should, of course, just turn to him, take his hand
and draw it around her shoulders, lay her head against
him, and tell him right out that she was disappointed
that he did not come to her bed. The old Georgiana
would have done that. Why on earth was she suddenly a
new Georgiana just at the time when she needed all her
courage and brazenness? Somehow she found that she
could not take the initiative.

But she would have to do so if she were not going to
go mad, she decided. As it was, she was not looking
forward at all to returning to London. She dreaded
meeting Ralph's mother again. She would be living in
the same house as the woman. And her mother-in-law
did not yet know about her terrible interference in
Gloria's betrothal. She had really been very fortunate so
far, but the worst was yet to come. As it happened,
Gloria had been almost pathetically grateful to Ralph
for taking such a firm and public stand in favor of her
marriage. And the Reverend Boscome had been
delighted that finally the head of the family had put a
stop to the endless delays. Ralph had taken full
responsibility for what had happened, of course. It was
just like him to show such quiet courage. If there was to
be any accusation of interference or impropriety, he
would bear the blame and protect the name of his wife.

Something would have to be done. The closer they got
to London, the more determined Georgiana became not
to tolerate the present state of her marriage with quiet
resignation. Ralph had to regain his confidence. He had
to have his sense of manhood restored. She had
destroyed it. She must see that it was rebuilt.

But how?

How could an eighteen-year-old girl, and a rather
pitifully ignorant virgin at that, go about restoring to a
man his ability to make love? It was a daunting task

even for her. Perhaps Dennis Vaughan or Ben Creeley or Warren Haines could help her? She suddenly had an appalling vision of herself seated at the edge of a ballroom with one of them, or waltzing around a room confiding with a bright smile the fascinating news that her husband was impotent and she still unbedded, and what was she to do about it, please? The vision was too horrifying even to be amusing.

She would have to devise some plan, some way of getting satisfactory answers without divulging to a living soul the mortifying truth of her husband's disability and her own unsatisfied yearnings.

She would think of something. She always did. Suddenly Georgiana felt almost cheerful. A good challenge was always the best remedy for the dismals, she reflected.

8

THE HONORABLE VERA BURTON was walking in the park with her sister. It was a chill day. They were both wrapped in warm pelisses, their hands thrust into fur-lined muffs. One would hardly know that it was only September, Georgiana complained, except that the park was so empty. She sighed with regret. At this time of the afternoon during the Season Rotten Row would be so crowded with carriages, horses, and pedestrians that one would be scarcely able to move. And there would be so many acquaintances and admirers that one would not really wish to move. But at this time of the year there was positively no one in London.

Georgiana was finding her sister a great comfort. The return to town two weeks before had proved every bit as dreadful as she had expected. There was very little entertainment; none of her special cronies was in town, even Dennis Vaughan, who had told her he would be back by the end of August; Ralph spent a great deal of time away from home, having taken his seat in the House of Lords; Gloria lived in her mother's shadow; Lord Stanley, who was her age and who might have brightened her home life, merely tried to flirt with her; and the dowager countess was the crowning horror.

Georgiana could quite see why everyone within her sphere of influence lived in awe of the dowager. She did not order people around. There was no obvious domineering against which one could set one's will. All was complaints, whines, hints, and sly suggestions. She would give up her room at Middleton House to Georgiana, she had said on their return, of course she would. It was only right that the Countess of Chartleigh should occupy the best set of rooms in the house. She, after all, was relegated now to the position of dowager countess. She merely hoped that Georgiana would be as happy in the rooms as she had been. The dear departed Chartleigh would be sorely grieved if he could see her now having to carry all her belongings to another suite. He had taken her to those rooms on their marriage and told her that that was where she would reside forever after when they were in town. She had pulled out a lace handkerchief at that point in her recital.

"Heavens!" Georgiana had declared. "I have no wish to turn you out of your room, Mother. You can put me anywhere. I shan't mind."

"We will share the rose apartments, Georgiana," Ralph had said with a smile. "They are smaller than Mama's, but I have always thought them far more lovely."

That had happened only an hour after their return from the country. It was seemingly a very minor incident. But it set a pattern, Georgiana had discovered. Her mother-in-law got her way in everything. She totally ruled the house and everyone in it. Everyone gave in to her because that course led to the easiest existence. Had Georgiana realized these facts on that first evening, she was convinced, she would merely have offered to help the dowager carry her belongings to her new room—as if the woman would have been called upon to carry one pin for herself anyway. Not that Georgiana had any interest in occupying the largest apartments in the house. But she should have shown right from the start that she intended to be the mistress of her new home.

It was quite ludicrous really to think that she was mistress of Middleton House. She felt more like a nuisance of a little girl intruding on a well-established routine. It was his mother who suggested that Ralph eat

larger breakfasts to ward off chills and that he spend
less time in the library reading in order to preserve his
eyesight, and, and, and . . . She was constantly nagging
at him about something. Georgiana fumed. He never
argued with his mother or told her to hold her tongue.
He always favored her with that annoying, affectionate
smile. She noticed that he still ate only one slice of toast
for breakfast and spent as much time reading as before.
But even so! Could he not openly assert himself?
Georgiana did not think she would be able to keep her
mouth shut much longer.

The dowager had received the news of Gloria's
approaching nuptials with ominous sweetness. She had
kissed her daughter and commended Ralph for his
kindness in granting his permission for the banns to be
read—Georgiana's part in granting that permission had
not been mentioned. But somehow in the two weeks that
had passed since their return, she had made them all feel
that the marriage would be a disaster to the two
principals and especially to her in the rawness of her
grief and her present low state of health. Georgiana was
terribly afraid that, after all, the wedding would be
postponed yet again.

She had turned to Vera for companionship. The two
sisters had always been surprisingly close. There was a
five-year difference in their ages, and a larger difference
in their temperaments. Vera was the very antithesis of
Georgiana. She was serious and thoughtful. She took
little pleasure in the social round and had only a few
close friends, all of them female. She was not a beauty,
at least not to anyone who knew her less intimately than
Georgiana. The latter was always loud to proclaim, in
fact, that she had a sweetness and a depth of character
that gave her beauty to those who knew her well. That
beauty showed particularly in her eyes, which were large
and almost always calm. But it showed too in her face
on the rare occasions when it was animated.

Vera was offering comfort during this walk in the
park.

"I can understand just how difficult it must be to find suddenly that your home is with near-strangers," she said. "And it is doubly difficult when Lady Chartleigh has been mistress of the house for so long and must now step down in your favor. But I am sure, Georgie, that if you have patience you will find that it will become easier as time passes. Both you and your mother-in-law will adjust to the new situation. And she cannot but love you once she gets to know you."

Georgiana looked doubtful. "Patience is something I have very little of," she said.

They both paused to nod in the direction of a passing carriage, from which one of their acquaintances waved to them.

"I am sure his lordship will help you," Vera said. "He seems a very kindly man, Georgiana. You have been very fortunate in your choice, I believe."

"Oh yes," Georgiana agreed, "very fortunate. I rarely even see him."

Vera looked sharply at her sister, alerted by her tone. "Is something wrong between you?" she asked.

Georgiana did not immediately reply. "Oh, everything!" she blurted at last. "And it is all my fault, Vera, as usual. I think I must have said something when we were at Chartleigh that hurt Ralph in some way. And since then it has been as if there were a huge barrier between us. We cannot communicate at all."

"Oh," Vera said. "I did not know. I am so sorry, Georgie. Can you not go to him and say you are sorry?"

"No," Georgiana said, coloring slightly. "It is not as simple as that. Ralph is very quiet and sensitive, you see. I believe I did more than hurt him. I think I destroyed his confidence in himself. And just saying something to him will not restore that. I have been trying to think of some way of making him believe in himself again."

Vera stared at her for a few silent moments. "I cannot think that you could have said or done anything so dreadful, Georgie," she said. "You were ever mischievous and impulsive, but you have always had a good heart. His lordship is fond of you, I am sure. I don't believe the situation can be as bad as you think.''

Georgiana had been watching her shoes with a frown. Else she would certainly have noticed the rider approaching them, especially as he was a particularly handsome young man mounted on a quite magnificent stallion. But she did not see him until he was drawing rein before them and sweeping his beaver hat from his head.

''Well, if it is not my newest cousin, the Countess of Chartleigh,'' he said as she looked up startled.

Georgiana recognized him immediately and dimpled. ''Lord Beauchamp,'' she said. ''How glad I am to see a familiar face.''

''What?'' he said. ''Never tell me you are admitting to boredom, ma'am, and you a four weeks' bride?''

''Well, I am nonetheless, sir,'' she said candidly. ''There is positively nothing to do in London at this season of the year.''

''My cousin Ralph must be a poor-spirited creature if he is not finding amusement for his bride,'' Roger Beauchamp said. ''I must take the matter in hand myself. You will be hearing from me, ma'am.''

''Oh,'' Georgiana said, delighted, ''you mean there are entertainments to which we may procure invitations? Then I do wish you will exert yourself on my behalf, sir.''

He grinned. ''At your service, my dear Lady Chartleigh,'' he said. ''May I have the honor of being presented to your charming companion?''

When Georgiana made the introductions, Lord Beauchamp leaned down from his horse's back and extended a hand to Vera. ''Charmed, Miss Burton,'' he said. ''We were not introduced at the wedding, though I recall seeing you there.''

He held on to Vera's hand rather longer than she seemed to think necessary. She colored. ''I am pleased to make your acquaintance, my lord,'' she said, looking up at him.

"I shall look forward to hearing from you," Georgiana said as he replaced his beaver hat on his head and made to ride away. He touched his hat with his riding whip, grinned at her, and rode on.

"Well, what do you think of that?" Georgiana said, looking after him thoughtfully. "Do you think he will keep his promise, Vera?"

"Probably not," her sister replied. "Lord Beauchamp is a notorious women's man, Georgie. Even I know that. Ella Carver calls him a rake, and I would not be at all surprised if she is right. He has a way of looking at one and holding one's hand that is meant to make one think that he finds one more interesting than any woman he has ever met."

"You do not like him?" Georgiana asked in some surprise.

"No, I do not," Vera said firmly. "When a man tries those tactics on me, I know that he is insincere. Do have a care of him, Georgie."

"Why?" her sister asked. "Do you think Ralph will become jealous?"

A close observer would have noticed that she was paying no attention to her sister's reply. There was a deeply thoughtful look on her face.

Ralph was sitting in the reading room at White's Club, perusing the newspapers halfheartedly. He had eaten dinner there after spending the morning in the Upper House, and was feeling guilty about not having gone home. This was the third day since his return home from the country two weeks before that he had stayed away from morning until almost dinnertime. He really had been busy. There was much to learn about his new position as a member of the Lords, and many new and important men with whom to become acquainted. And he had several matters to settle with Parker, his man of business. But he had to admit to himself that perhaps he had been welcoming reasons to stay away from home.

The truth was that the state of his marriage had gone

from bad to worse since their return from the country. They seemed always to be surrounded by other people. They were almost never alone. And he still could not bring himself to go to Georgiana at night. He had been unable to carry through his resolve to build a friendship with her. On the two afternoons when he had suggested a drive with her, they had ended up having company. His mother had decided the first time that an airing would do her no harm. Georgiana's sister had arrived at the moment of their departure on the other occasion and had been persuaded to go with them. He had not tried again.

He should be at home now, he knew, with Georgiana. She was living in a new and strange home, and he knew that life with his mother would not be easy for her.

Through the years he had learned that the best way to handle his mother was to humor her, to let her have her way over unimportant matters and to let her think she was having her way over more important ones. He was not in the habit of confronting her. But he had the uncomfortable feeling that he was going to have to do so soon. He could not expect Georgiana to be as docile as he. She did not have the deep-seated affection for his mother that made all her annoying traits bearable to him.

Georgiana was now the Countess of Chartleigh. Middleton House and Chartleigh were her domains. By rights his mother should retire quietly into the background. Most women in her situation would move to their own establishments. There was a dower house at Chartleigh. It would be a simple matter to lease or rent a suitable house in London. But she had made no mention of any such plans and in the meantime succeeded in imposing her will on the running of their lives.

Georgiana was taking the whole matter very well. She had refused to turn his mother out of her apartments, though Ralph had never planned any such upheaval anyway. And she had not said or done anything that suggested to him that she was finding the situation intolerable. Perhaps he had not been home enough to discover her real feelings. But he found the state of affairs impossible. He remembered with some wistfulness the enthusiasm with which his wife had made preparations for the dinner party at Chartleigh. He had begun to feel like a married man with a home and family of his own. He wanted her as the mistress of his home here in London too.

And what was he doing about it? he asked himself glumly. He was staying away from home, busying himself over matters that were really not as important at the moment as was the solving of his personal problems. It would not do. He was not being fair to his wife—or to himself, for that matter. He wanted to spend more time with her. He must do something. And that something was going to have to be confronting his mother. He grimaced at the thought.

"Ah, if it is not the happy groom himself," a voice said from the doorway. "Ralph, my lad, you look the picture of marital bliss. I was talking to your wife just half an hour ago."

Ralph put down his newspaper and rose to his feet to shake hands with his cousin.

"How are you, Roger?" he asked. "I didn't know you were in town."

"I cannot imagine why I am," his cousin said. "There really is not much doing here these days. The trouble is, dear boy, that I cannot think of anywhere else where life may be more exciting. Your wife seems to be suffering from the same *ennui*."

"Georgiana?" Ralph said with a frown. "She said she was bored? Where did you see her?"

"Strolling in the park," Roger Beauchamp said. "She brightened my day, I tell you, Ralph, my boy. The only pretty female I have seen today."

"She was alone?" asked Ralph.

"Oh no," his cousin said. "She had her sister with her. The little countess certainly was blessed with all the beauty in that family, eh?"

"Vera has character," Ralph said.

Roger laughed. "Trust you, my boy, to find some redeeming feature in a poor dab of a female. She has fine eyes, though."

"Yes," Ralph agreed absently.

"Now, why would a bridegroom of a month be sitting reading newspapers at his club when he might be with his bride . . . er, amusing himself?" Roger asked, seating himself on a wing chair and hooking one booted leg carelessly over one of the arms. There were no other occupants of the room.

It was not the sort of question Ralph was adept at answering. He colored and stared uncomfortably at his companion.

"Of course," Lord Beauchamp continued, swinging the suspended leg and viewing the tassel of his boot swaying back and forth, "I've never been married, though Mama is beginning to make ominous noises on the topic now that my thirtieth birthday is looming on the horizon. Perhaps such afternoon amusements lose some of their charm when the female is one's wife. Do they, Ralph, my lad?"

Ralph grinned despite some feeling of discomfort. "I wouldn't know, Rog," he said. "I am your very much younger cousin, if you will remember. You plagued me with the fact throughout my growing years."

"Did I?" Roger asked. "But you were such a sweet innocent, little cousin. Are you still? Are you a very proper husband, Ralph, enjoying the little countess's favors just once a day, at a respectable hour of the night, with all the candles doused? How very dull! No wonder the poor lady is suffering from *ennui*."

"You are getting a little personal, Rog," Ralph said quietly. "I do not like to hear Georgiana spoken of in such a way."

"Oh, quite," his cousin agreed. "I meant no offense, you know. What I suspect, Ralph, my lad, is that you do not know how to enjoy yourself. I'll wager you have never kept a high flier. Am I right?"

"I think you know you are," Ralph said. "And I make no apology for the fact."

"Yes, yes," Roger said, waving energetically in the direction of a passing waiter and directing him to bring some claret to the reading room. "You always were high-principled. I remember your throwing yourself at me once, both fists flying, when you were the merest stripling, because I wouldn't release one of those village maidens of yours without first claiming a kiss. If you had had an ounce of wisdom, my lad, you would have known that the wench was panting for her kiss even more than I was."

"Well, I seem to remember getting much the worse of that encounter anyway," Ralph said with a grin. "A bloody nose, if I remember correctly. And Ginny Moore had her kiss."

"The point is, my young innocent," Roger said, "that one learns from such females. When I do marry, you see, I shall be able to enslave my bride with the pleasure I know how to give her. Women are fools when they frown on their men indulging in amorous adventures. We would be the clumsiest dolts if we did not, and quite incapable of offering them any compensation for the services they must render. And we must be the ones to offer the experience, my lad. The type of female we must marry knows precisely nothing."

"You are undoubtedly right, Rog," Ralph agreed amiably. "But it is a trifle late to try to convert me to your philosophy now, is it not?"

Roger swung his leg to the floor and leaned forward in his chair as the waiter entered with a tray and glasses. "Ah, the end to a long drought," he commented, drinking from his glass until he and Ralph were alone again. "I'm not so sure of that, my boy," he said. "You look blue-deviled, and the little countess looked positively out of sorts. She needs parties and theaters. You need a mistress."

Ralph laughed. "Would you not think it a little out of

character, Rog?'' he said. ''Can you imagine me with a mistress?''

''Let me find you someone,'' Roger offered magnanimously. ''It won't be difficult. There are always dozens of women in search of rich, titled protectors. And they would fall over themselves if he were also young and handsome. And you are turning out to be quite well-endowed in that last department, Ralph. Surprising, really. You used to be quite a puny lad. In a few years' time, you will probably be putting us all in the shadow. What say you?''

''I say good day to you, I must be getting home,'' Ralph said with a laugh. He got to his feet and held out a hand to his cousin again.

''I have promised the little countess to try to sniff out some entertainments for her,'' Roger said. ''I shall see that some invitations are sent your way, my lad. Even at this godforsaken time of year there are some similarly desperate people organizing parties. And you think of what I have said. It is time you started enjoying the life to which you were born, my serious young scholar. And what better way to begin than with a hot little affair, eh?''

He took the proffered hand, and Ralph left the room. Roger yawned, picked up his drink, and went in search of companionship.

Ralph took his wife to the theater that night. The outing had not been planned. His thoughts of the afternoon and his meeting with his cousin had combined to make him feel actively guilty about his neglect of her. And she reacted with almost pathetic eagerness when he suggested taking her out. He did not extend the invitation to anyone else, though he knew that his private box at the theater would comfortably hold a sizable party. He shut his mind to the possible disappointment his mother or Gloria might be feeling at being excluded.

They did not speak a great deal either during the carriage ride or at the theater. He watched her covertly.

Was she unhappy? Roger's words suggested that she might be. She was quiet. Before his marriage and during the first few days afterward, he would have thought this quite characteristic of her. But during the days at Chartleigh he had become aware of a vitality in her and even a tendency to become talkative at times. Her face could be alight with animation and doubly beautiful. All of these facets of her character were absent now.

If she were not actively unhappy at the moment, there was a strong possibility that she would be soon. She could not be happy with the state of their marriage. He knew that women did not crave sexual activity as men did, but even so, she must wish for a normal marriage. She would wish for a child eventually.

Yet he was terribly afraid to make theirs a normal marriage. He mentally cursed himself now that he had not gone to her on the second night of their marriage and asserted his rights. Even if he had caused her pain, it would have passed. He knew that a woman felt real pain only when she was still virgin. The same held true now, of course. He could go to her tonight, and by tomorrow the pain would be gone forever.

But it becomes so much more difficult to do something positive when one has once procrastinated. He could not just go to Georgiana's bed. If only he did not love her so much! He watched her as her attention was on the stage. She was so small and slender. And so very dear. He wanted to protect her from all the pain and unhappiness that life might throw her way. How could he be the one to hurt her?

Unbidden, his conversation with Roger came back to his mind. If he were to take his cousin at his word and take a mistress, he could learn not only how to give pleasure to a woman but also how to make love without the clumsiness that his present inexperience made inevitable. It was a mad thought, of course. How could he deliberately be unfaithful to the wife he loved and to the principles by which he had always lived? He blanked the memories from his mind.

Georgiana, for her part, was also covertly observing her husband. Why had he suddenly decided to bring her out? It had been a pleasant surprise. And she despised herself for feeling so. It said little for the state of her life that she could be grateful to a poor-spirited boy like Ralph for an outing. Yet the truth was that she was feeling annoyingly pleased to be seen with him. He really did look almost splendid in his dark blue satin evening clothes. His valet had done fascinating things with his neckcloth.

He was not happy, though. He was always quiet, of course. That was nothing to signify. But his laughter-filled eyes and upward-curving mouth seemed to have been left behind at Chartleigh. Oh dear, it was all her fault. She had wrought this change in such a little time. And the plan that had struck her like a lightning bolt that afternoon recurred to her mind. It might work. Something had to work. And yet for some stupid reason she could not do the obvious thing and just talk the matter out with Ralph.

Roger Beauchamp was handsome enough. In fact, he was quite devastatingly handsome: tall, slim, dark, self-possessed. He was older, too, undoubtedly a real man. She could even remember that for one moment on the occasion when she and Ben on their way out of the bushes had met him and a young lady on their way in, she had wished that they might all change partners. He would undoubtedly know all there was to know about kissing, she had felt sure then.

He was a man framed by heaven for the express purpose of making other men tear their hair in jealousy. That much was perfectly obvious. What woman could look at Lord Beauchamp without even the smallest thrill of admiration? She was going to flirt with him, that's what she was going to do. Just a little, of course. She was not going to arouse any major scandal. But she was going to drive poor Ralph wild with jealousy. She was going to make him angry, furious at her. So angry that he would . . . Georgiana felt a lurch of excitement somewhere low down in her anatomy.

She chattered in quite animated fashion about the play during the carriage ride home and was somewhat cheered to find her hand in her husband's for the second half of the journey. She had certainly not put it there. She even noticed with some gratification when they entered Middleton House that the smile was back in his eyes.

But miracles do not happen in a flash, she discovered a few minutes later, as she entered her lonely bedchamber, the imprint of a gentle kiss on the back of the hand that she held against her cheek.

9

LORD TIMOTHY BOOTHBY and his lady were giving an evening party in honor of their five-and-twentieth wedding anniversary. They did not dignify the occasion by the title of "ball" because there were so few families in town to attend it. They were able to send out only one hundred and twenty invitations. Nevertheless, their ballroom was to be thrown open to their guests, and an orchestra hired to play background music if no one seemed inclined to dance, and a variety of country dances, quadrilles, and waltzes if anyone did.

Three of the invitations found their way to Middleton House, one for the Earl and Countess of Chartleigh, another for the dowager countess and her daughter, Lady Gloria Middleton, and the third for Lord Stanley Middleton. Georgiana danced around the morning room with delight when she opened hers. She could see the hand of Lord Beauchamp in this happy turn of events. She was even more gratified later in the day to find that her parents and Vera had also received invitations.

"You see?" she said to Vera. "He did not forget us. That proves that he is not an entirely selfish man. And he was kind enough to procure you an invitation too, Vera."

"I find the very fact that he acted so soon ominous," Vera replied calmly. "Do have a care, Georgie. That man is dangerous."

Georgiana prepared with special care for the evening. With the exception of the dinner party at Chartleigh, it was a positive age since she had been to any very glittering entertainment. Making one's debut during the Season really did spoil one, she reflected. One assumed that life for a girl past schoolroom age was always like that, a constant round of exciting activities.

She had her hair cropped and curled close to her head. She had a new gown of peach satin and lace made and spent a whole morning on Bond Street with Gloria choosing slippers and gloves and a fan. She was going to be quite dazzling, she decided, even if there were very few people to see her.

Ralph liked her new hairstyle. He looked a little dubious when he first saw it. She was in the drawing room drinking tea with his mother.

"Georgiana!" he said. "All your lovely hair is gone."

"Don't you like it?" she asked. "It is very fashionable, you know."

"Let me have a good look," he said, crossing the room to her and taking her chin in his hand. He spent several moments examining her head. "Yes," he said at last with a smile, "it does suit you, dear. I like it."

"I almost fainted dead away when I saw what she had done," his mother said from behind him. "Such a boyish look might be passable for a very young and foolish girl, but perhaps a countess should cultivate a more dignified image, would you not say, Ralph? Chartleigh would never have tolerated any unladylike appearance in me."

Georgiana kept her eyes on Ralph's. They smiled back at her. His hand was still beneath her chin.

"Boyish?" he said. "No, I think not, Mama. Elfin, perhaps. And very pretty. And remember that my wife is indeed very young, though not, I think, foolish. And this Chartleigh will not tolerate her being made to feel obliged to behave older than her years."

He spoke very pleasantly and quietly. Yet Georgiana's eyes widened in surprise. It was the closest she had ever heard him come to defying his mother.

And he had done it in her defense. A few minutes later
Ralph was obliged to ring for the dowager's maid to
help her to her room. She had one of her frequent head-
aches.

Ralph came to her room when she was ready to leave
for the party. She was turning in front of the pier glass,
trying to see how the scalloped hem of her gown would
look if she were twirling in the dance. She stopped in
some confusion when he entered. She had not expected
him. He rarely entered her room.

"You do look lovely," he said as she was
appreciating his own appearance, quite resplendent in
gold and brown. "I had hoped your gown would be a
suitable color."

As Georgiana raised her eyebrows in inquiry, he drew
a long box from behind his back and held it out to her.

"For me?" she asked.

"I bought it for you this afternoon," he said. "I do
hope you like it."

Georgiana found a single strand of pearls inside the
box. She looked up at the eager, boyish face close to her
own. "They are lovely, Ralph," she said. "Thank you.
Whatever made you think of buying them for me?"

"I realized that I had not bought you a gift since our
wedding," he said. "It was remiss of me. I am not used
to pleasing a lady."

She held the box out to him and turned her back when
he lifted the pearls from their satin resting place. He put
the pearls around her neck and she bent her head for
him to secure the clasp. He rested his hands on the bare
skin of her shoulders after completing the task.
Georgiana put up her own hands and patted his lightly.
He put his arms right around her from behind and drew
her against him.

Georgiana was touched by the gift. She felt a rush of
warm affection for her husband. But she was on her
way to a party with a new gown and a new hairstyle. She
was not at that moment thinking of love or passion or
even the lamentably sexless state of her marriage.

"Oh, do have a care, Ralph," she said quite good-humoredly. "You will crease my sash, and I shall ruin that neckcloth your valet must have sweated over for half an hour."

He let her go immediately and without a word. She examined her pearls eagerly in the mirror, fingering them in admiration, turned to pick up her wrap and her fan from a chair, and gave Ralph a smile bright with affection as she preceded him from the room. By that time he had erased his expression of deep hurt. She was quite unaware of the way he had winced as he released his hold on her.

The party turned out to be not nearly the squeeze that Georgiana was used to, but nevertheless she found herself flushed with enjoyment after the first hour. There was dancing, and Georgiana loved to dance. Ralph partnered her for the opening set of country dances, and she found as she had at Chartleigh that he was a graceful partner. She felt almost regretful when Stanley came to claim her for the second set.

Georgiana found her brother-in-law quite a trial. He was actually older than she by four months, but he seemed years younger. She did not doubt that in a few years' time he would be quite a gay young blade, but his attempts now to be worldly-wise were merely ludicrous. At least he no longer made a fool of himself by trying to flirt with her as he had at first. She had given the poor boy a freezing set-down four days after their return from Chartleigh and felt sorry for him all of an hour afterward.

She waited with some impatience for the arrival of Lord Beauchamp. She might have known that he would be fashionably late, she thought as she saw him finally, standing with languid grace in the doorway, surveying the gathering. And she noted with some glee that he put all the other men quite in the shade, except perhaps Ralph, his ice-blue satin coat and knee breeches and snowy white linen and lace in marked contrast to the darkness of his hair. Georgiana noticed these facts with almost clinical detachment. She did not feel a tremor. She was not at all interested in falling in love with the man.

He crossed the ballroom to talk to Ralph, who was in conversation with two other men, and then to the dowager, over whose hand he bowed with grace. Finally he approached Georgiana. She had been waiting impatiently. Another set was about to form, and she had been hoping that no one else would solicit her hand.

"Ah," he said, bowing elegantly before her, "my cousin, the little countess. And easily the most lovely lady to grace this ballroon tonight."

Georgiana smiled dazzlingly. "You flatter, sir," she said. "Have you come to dance with me? I do hope so. I should hate to be a wallflower. And there is a shortage of men here. I fear the lure of cards has drawn some of them away."

"How could anyone be so ungallant and so blind to the charm they have abandoned?" Roger Beauchamp said. "May I have the honor, ma'am?"

Georgiana smiled and chattered and fluttered her eyelashes for the next twenty minutes, until her husband's cousin danced with a half-smile on his face, a strange gleam in his eyes.

"La," Georgiana said, fanning her face vigorously as the music drew to a close, "I am as dry as a desert stream. I have not stopped dancing in an hour."

"May I have the honor of procuring a glass of lemonade for you?" Roger asked, the gleam deepening.

"I shall come with you," Georgiana declared, placing her hand on his arm unbidden. "Perhaps it will be cooler in the refreshment room."

They found an open alcove at one side of the ballroom in which she might drink her lemonade. They watched the dancers for a few minutes.

"And are you enjoying yourself, my dear Lady Chartleigh?" Roger asked.

"Oh yes," she said with enthusiasm, "and I do thank

you, sir, for making someone aware that my husband's family is ready to go into society again. You may call me by my given name, you know. We are cousins of a sort, are we not?''

"And so we are," he said, "Georgiana."

"All my friends call me 'Georgie'," she confided, looking archly at him over the top of her waving fan.

"Do they indeed?" he said. "And do I take it that I am being invited to join their ranks—Georgie?"

She smiled dazzlingly and leaned a little closer to him. "And will you return the compliment?" she asked. "Am I to call you 'Roger'?"

He grinned back at her and touched a finger to the tip of her nose. "I hope you will," he said. "But I tell you what, Georgie. I believe I have something of a reputation with the ladies. But I do not specialize in flirtations with married ladies, my dear, especially when they happen to be married to my favorite young cousin.''

"Oh," she said, mortified, sitting quite upright again.

He laughed lightly. "Not that you are not an extremely tempting morsel, Georgie. I can see that Ralph is going to have his hands full. Is it no good, my dear?''

"Is what no good?" she asked stiffly.

"Your marriage," he said. "Is it not working out?"

"I think he is afraid of me," she almost whispered.

Roger schooled his features to remain serious. "Ralph?" he said. "Afraid of you? Do you bite?"

"Are you laughing at me?" she asked suspiciously. "I wish you would not. I am serious."

"What leads you to think he fears you, pray?" Roger asked, fascinated. He was waiting for this unusual little creature beside him to realize the glaring impropriety of this conversation and hoping that it would not be soon.

Georgiana shrugged. "I think he has not known a large number of women," she said. "I think he is afraid. . . . I think he . . ."

Good God, Roger Beauchamp thought, fascinated,

does she realize how much she is saying during the pauses in her speech? The full uncomfortable truth was glaringly obvious to him.

"Georgie," he said severely, "were you trying to flirt with me just now so that Ralph would feel honor-bound to challenge me and overcome his . . . er . . . fear by putting a bullet between my eyes?"

"Something like that," Georgiana admitted, spreading her fan in her lap and examining its design.

"I am honored beyond speech to think you would have chosen me for the sacrifice," he said.

"Oh," she assured him, looking up in some concern, "I did not imagine a duel or anything stupid like that. I merely thought that if Ralph saw another man interested in me, he might become angry and . . . and . . ."

He smiled at her. "You are quite out there, you know," he said. "I believe I know Ralph better than you do, Georgie. It would be much more like my noble cousin to offer you your freedom if he felt your feelings were engaged somewhere else."

"Yes," she said with a sigh, "he is very sweet and kind, is he not? And not at all selfish."

"Do I detect a note of affection for my young cousin, Georgie?" he asked.

"Oh," she said, sounding almost annoyed, "who could not feel affection for Ralph?"

"What we need is some plan," Roger said to her bowed head.

"We?" she asked, looking up sharply.

He ignored her query. He was looking thoughtful. "A flirtation won't do, though," he said. "I shall need to think. Give me a day or two. Now, if we are not inadvertently to be accused of that flirtation, I think I had better leave you, my dear little cousin. As it is, I have been sitting here through one whole set, and another is already beginning. May I convey you to anyone's side?"

"No," she said, "I shall stay here."

Roger favored her with a bow, looked assessingly around the floor, and crossed the room to repeat his bow before Vera, who was sitting with her mother and some other older ladies. She had not danced.

"Ah, the divine Miss Burton," he said. "And how are you this evening, ma'am?"

"I would feel very much better if I did not have to listen to ridiculous flattery, my lord," she replied quietly.

He looked somewhat taken aback, but the gleam was back in his eye. "Will you dance?" he asked. "It is a waltz and has only just started."

She looked as if she would refuse, but she seemed to realize that such refusal would serve only to draw attention to herself. She rose to her feet and placed her hand in his.

"You do not look to be the sort of female to have claws," he said thoughtfully as they began to waltz.

"I did not mean to be rude, my lord," she said, "but I hate hypocrisy."

"And do you consider yourself such an antidote that any man who expresses pleasure in the sight of you must be lying?" he asked, amusement in his voice.

"I know I am no beauty, my lord," she said firmly, "and I am not fishing for a compliment."

"Let me see," he said, holding her a little farther away from him and surveying her with lazy eyes. "Yes, you are right. You are not as shapely as your sister. Of course, you are taller than she and could achieve a slender grace. Your hair is unfortunately neither brown nor blond. But it is thick and shiny and would look quite delightful if you allowed it to frame your face instead of scooping it back as if you meant to drag it from its roots. Your cheeks lack some bloom but your features are good and your face would be more than attractive if you relaxed and smiled more. Indeed, now I look more closely, I find that your annoyance has added some quite becoming color to your cheeks. Your eyes, of course, could not be improved upon. I am sure you

keep them lowered only because you know very well
what effect they might have on a notorious rake like
me.''

Those eyes flew upward to meet his. "Sir, you are
impertinent,'' Vera said.

"Very,'' he agreed. "But you are the one who drew
swords. Can you blame me for retaliating? And you
would be advised to lower those eyes, ma'am, especially
when they are flashing as they are now. They are doing
alarming things to my heartbeat and making me notice
that your mouth is by no means your worst feature
either. Decidedly kissable, in fact.''

Vera's eyes continued to glare. Her nostrils flared.
Her cheeks flushed an even deeper shade with hot
indignation. All of which reactions caused Lord
Beauchamp to smile broadly.

"Are you contented now that you have succeeded in
giving me a thorough set-down?'' she asked icily.

"Quite contented,'' he agreed, "for the present, Miss
Burton. The transformation in your appearance over
the last minute has been worth witnessing.''

When Ralph returned home the following afternoon,
it was to find his mother sitting alone in the drawing
room, sewing.''

'How do you do, Mama?'' he said, crossing the room
and kissing her on the cheek. "Where are Georgiana
and Gloria?''

"Your wife is in her apartments, as far as I know,''
the dowager replied, not lifting her eyes from her work,
"and Gloria is in the morning room writing a letter to
the Reverend Boscome. If she is following my advice,
she is suggesting to him that their nuptials be postponed
until the summer. It would be a shame for her to miss
the Season, when she was forced to miss the last.''

"And what does Gloria think of the suggestion?''
Ralph asked.

"Oh, the foolish girl believes that she would prefer
life in a village vicarage to the pleasures of town,'' his

mother replied. "Will she never meet a more suitable husband? The daughter of my dear Chartleigh to be thrown away on a mere vicar, a younger son, Ralph. The prospect is intolerable."

"Mama." Ralph seated himself on a chair close to his mother's. "Gloria is six-and-twenty. She is old enough to make her own choice. Indeed, she is already well past the usual age of marriage. Do you not think that after six years of constancy to David Boscome she has proved that she has a lasting attachment to him?"

"Attachment!" the dowager said contemptuously. "What has that to say to anything? The girl is just too obstinate to consider someone more eligible, that is all. She has had any number of chances to fix the interest of more suitable gentlemen."

Ralph was silent for a minute while he watched his mother make angry stabs at her work with the needle. "I shall go to Gloria," he said quietly then, "and urge her most strongly to obey the dictates of her own heart. She has considered the feelings of others for too long. It is time she pleased herself."

"Ralph!" His mother looked up at him at last, in shocked disbelief. "Have you taken leave of your senses, my boy? Since when have you spoken to your own mother with such disrespect? Chartleigh would never have allowed such impertinence. You can be thankful that he is no longer here to deal with you."

Ralph turned very pale, but he did not flinch from his mother's wrath. "Mama," he said, "I am Chartleigh now. I am head of the family. I love you deeply and I respect you for the firmness with which you have brought us up to know our duty. But I must assume the responsibilities of my position. At the moment the happiness of my sister needs to be assured, and I shall do all I can to see that it is done."

His mother looked down again and began to sew furiously. "I might have known that marriage would do you no good," she said. "You are too young and too impressionable, Ralph. I should have taken you in hand for another few years. You are becoming as wild and as headstrong as your wife.''

Ralph went very still. ''As my wife?'' he said. ''What has Georgiana done?''

''What has she done!'' she repeated contemptuously. ''Sometimes, Ralph, you are the merest child. Everyone else noticed. Stanley certainly did, and Gloria must have, though she will not say anything. Your wife behaved in a most disgraceful manner last night, flirting quite openly with Roger. She was with him for a whole hour and danced with him for only part of that time. I thought I would faint quite away when she disappeared with him into the refreshment room, and I was never so mortified in my life as when she sat alone with him in that alcove for fully half an hour, making eyes at him. Everyone knows what a dreadful rake Roger is.''

Ralph was on his feet. His face was paler than before, though his mother did not look up to observe the fact. ''You have said enough, Mama,'' he said, his voice agitated rather than angry. ''Pray, no more. I will not hear any more against Georgiana. Roger is her cousin now too. Of course she will show him civility. She danced with any number of men last night. It would have been quite unseemly if she had been unwilling to leave my side. I saw nothing indecorous in her behavior, and I would thank Stanley to keep such insulting suggestions to himself. I will talk to him.''

''You would do better to have words with your wife, Ralph,'' she said. ''She will be making a fool of you, and heaven knows it is easy enough to do. I am beginning to wish that I had gone into society for a while and found out about her myself instead of taking Eugenia's word for her respectability.''

Ralph, who had been pacing the room, came to a stop before her chair. ''Mama,'' he said, ''I will answer for the respectability of my wife. I will not allow even you to call her honor into question. I do not wish to hear you talk about her in this way ever again. Or to her. I presume it is because of what you have said to her that she is in her own rooms?''

The dowager countess bundled her sewing onto a table beside her and got to her feet, her hands to her cheeks. "I never thought to hear any of my own offspring speak so undutifully to their own mother," she said. "And it is all on account of that dreadful girl. Oh, if Chartleigh were only here still! You will oblige me by sending my maid up to me. I am too distraught to ring for her myself. I am deeply, deeply hurt."

She stumbled from the room. Ralph made as if to go to her support, but he held himself back. He stood looking at the door, which his mother had closed behind her, for several minutes before following her out and ascending the stairs to his wife's apartments.

Georgiana was in her sitting room, curled up on a chaise lounge, a book open on her lap. She was not reading it. She was torn between rebellion and remorse. It had been bad enough to have Stanley at the breakfast table asking how she liked their rakish cousin and inquiring how Ralph had approved of her spending so much time with him the night before. She had handled him with dispatch by replying that she liked his cousin quite well enough since he had conversation that consisted of more than unpleasant innuendo. She had added, as she got to her feet and dropped her napkin onto the table, that he might ask Ralph himself the second question, as she could not be expected to speak for him.

But her mother-in-law! The woman almost never came out with an open attack. Georgiana had noticed that. She would know how to deal with that approach. She occasionally enjoyed a good verbal battle, especially since she had been blessed with a ready wit and a caustic tongue. But how could one fight against hints and suggestions, all very kindly meant, according to the dowager herself? How could one hold an adult discussion with a woman who treated one as a child, and a rather naughty, rebellious child at that?

She was the Countess of Chartleigh, Georgiana reminded herself crossly, and she had let herself be forced into retreating to her own room just as if she really were still a child. And she knew just what would happen next. Ralph would come home and his mother would fill his ears with her poison. Then he would come to her—he was probably on the way right at that moment—and he too would have a talk with her. He also would be very kind and assure her that he was not angry with her at all. And then he would go on to hint and suggest that perhaps she had been indiscreet and that perhaps she should not be seen with Cousin Roger in future. It suddenly struck her how like his mother Ralph was, once one got to know the two of them.

She would love to have a raging, screaming row with him. She would love to throw things at his head. The only trouble was that she was not quite conscience-free. She *had* been flirting with Roger Beauchamp until he put a stop to it. And as usual, she had done quite the wrong thing and got herself into a public scrape. The flirtation scheme had seemed to be a good one. What she had not once considered, of course—so typical of her, she thought ruefully—was that if she were to flirt enough for Ralph to notice, she would be doing so for everyone else's eyes too. At least, she thought, she had considered the possibility. She had decided not to go so far as to cause a scandal. But how could one flirt just a little bit, just enough to arouse one's husband's jealousy, but not enough for anyone else even to notice? She must be quite mad.

So now she had won everyone's disapproval. Plus she had probably made Ralph look a little foolish. And she could not give herself the satisfaction of ripping up at him when he came to scold her. In fact, he might have some of the less-pleasant characteristics of his mother, but even so she was quite unworthy to be his wife. He never got into scrapes. He would never flirt with another woman. Of that she was convinced.

Georgiana sighed and tried yet again to concentrate on her book. But she put it down with a resigned air of gloom when a soft knock sounded on the door.

"Do come in, Ralph," she called.

10

RALPH OPENED the door and smiled at his wife. "Hello, Georgiana," he said. "How did you know it was I?"

"Oh," she said airily, closing her book and tossing it onto the cushion beside her, "I have been expecting you."

"Have you?" he asked, closing the door and crossing the room to sit in a chair close to her. "I hope I have not interrupted your reading."

"Not at all," she said. "I have been all of one hour trying to read through a single paragraph. I am not in the mood for books."

"Are you upset?" he asked. "I gather Mama has been talking to you."

"Of course she has," Georgiana said. "And she has really said everything that could possibly be said, Ralph. I do not believe that she has left one single word for you to add."

"She has upset you," he said, concerned. "I am very vexed that she should have done so, Georgiana. I wish you will not let her words prey on your mind."

"Why?" she asked curtly, swinging her feet to the floor and smoothing the muslin of her day dress over her knees. "Did you wish to have a clear field, Ralph?"

"I am not at all angry with you," he said. "I know you were not flirting with Roger last evening. I trust you more than to believe that of you. You have a good heart, and you are a good wife to me. Better than I deserve, I think."

"But you would still like it if I were just a little more

discreet,'' Georgiana said, looking up into his face and staring at him with stony eyes. "Lord Beauchamp, after all, has something of a reputation as far as ladies are concerned, and one has to be doubly careful not to encourage him, or who knows what sort of a wrong impression one might give to the gossipmongers? And I have the illustrious name of Chartleigh to uphold now. I cannot behave with the same careless freedom as when I was merely Georgiana Burton. Not that you are at all suspicious of me, of course. But still and all—''

"Good God!'' Ralph leapt to his feet and looked down into his wife's cold eyes in some horror. "Is that what Mama said? Georgiana, they are not my words or my sentiments. I trust you. And I trust Roger. He is my cousin. We have always been very close despite our age difference.''

"Well,'' Georgiana said, "am I not fortunate to have chosen to flirt in such a vulgar manner with your cousin? Perhaps you would be less trusting had I spent as much time last evening with a stranger.''

"No,'' he said, coming and kneeling in front of her, the better to see her face. "That makes no difference, dear. I have seen nothing to disapprove of in your behavior. Please do not upset yourself. Come, smile at me and let me see the sparkle in your eyes again. I do not like to see you look so unhappy.''

He smiled warmly up at her and held out a hand for hers. She did not respond to either invitation. She kept her hands folded in her lap and looked down at them.

"You are a fool, Ralph,'' she said quietly, "if you believe my behavior was blameless last night. I *was* flirting with Lord Beauchamp, and everyone was aware of the fact except you.''

His hand remained stretched out toward her. There was a momentary silence.

"No,'' he said gently, "that is not so, Georgiana. Why would you do such a thing?''

"Because . . .'' She looked up at him again, her eyes blazing. Because I wanted to make you jealous so that you would *do* something, she had been going to say. But those wide-open, vulnerable eyes were looking back at her, full of trust still. And she was suddenly overwhelmed by the urge to hurt him quite viciously. She was hurting so badly herself. Let someone share her pain.

"Because I am bored!" she almost yelled at him. "Bored, bored, bored! Do you understand, Ralph? You bore me. Always so quiet and so gentle and so . . . so damned proper! Why should I not turn to other men for company and some excitement? Why should I not even take a lover, perhaps? Can you give me a reason? You are not even capable of making me your wife!"

And then she gazed, frozen with horror, into his eyes, which had lost their vulnerability. They had become opaque, dull. His hand was still held out before him, palm upward. He got to his feet and closed his eyes for a moment.

"Ralph," she said shakily. "Oh, please. I did not mean it. My wretched tongue! I have been in a devilish bad mood and have said what I did not mean."

He opened his eyes and looked down at her. His face was chalky white, even his lips, Georgiana noted in dismay. "You are right," he said, and she could tell what an effort it cost him to keep his voice steady. "I have not been a husband to you at all. And I am turning all your sweetness to bitterness. I wanted you as my wife. I loved you. But I had no business marrying you. I do not know the first thing about making a woman happy. I wanted to bring you happiness, and I have brought you misery. I . . ."

He drew a shuddering breath, but no more words would come. He stared at her in agonized silence.

"Ralph," she said, "it is not true. It is I who have been at fault."

"No!" he said harshly. "Never say that, Georgiana. I will not have you blame yourself. I must . . . I will . . ." He paused and sighed in frustration. "I have to leave. Just do not feel guilty, please. There really is no need.

You did not behave with any impropriety last night."

He turned and left the room hurriedly, even as she jumped to her feet and reached out her arms for him.

Lord Beauchamp arrived at Middleton House the following afternoon just as Georgiana was about to leave. The butler, as she came down the stairs to the hallway in her pelisse and bonnet, bowed and informed her ladyship that the visitor had been shown into the drawing room but had asked specifically for her.

"Oh, bother," Georgiana muttered. "Is there anyone in the drawing room?"

"Her ladyship, ma'am," the butler replied.

By which title Georgiana guessed him to mean her mother-in-law. Gloria had gone out with her aunt in the morning to shop for her trousseau and was not expected to return before dinner. Her mother had been indisposed and unable to accompany her. But she had obviously decided that she was un-indisposed, Georgiana thought nastily. Probably the recovery had been made when she heard that her daughter-in-law was on her way out to visit her parents.

Georgiana considered continuing on her way out of the house, but she sighed and turned to climb the stairs again to the drawing room. She continued to pull on her gloves as a footman opened the double doors for her.

"Good afternoon, Mother," she said. "Is your headache better? Good day, Roger."

Lord Beauchamp was on his feet and bowing to her. "Good afternoon, Georgie," he said. "I see I have come calling at an inopportune moment. May I see you to your carriage?"

"I am going to Papa's," she said, "on foot."

"On foot? Georgiana! That will never do," the dowager said, surprised out of the icy silence with which she had received her daughter-in-law's greeting. "Would you have all our acquaintances believe that Chartleigh is too miserly to allow you the carriage?"

"By no means, Mother," Georgiana said calmly. "It is a mere ten-minute walk. By the time I order out the carriage, I shall be there already."

"You are taking your maid, my dear?"

"I had not planned to," Georgiana said.

"Then allow me to escort you, ma'am," Roger said. "It will set Aunt Hilda's mind at rest to know that you are properly accompanied."

Georgiana did not look to see how the dowager had received this dubious reassurance. She smiled at Lord Beauchamp.

"I had not thought that walking would be in your line, Roger," she said. "But I shall not refuse your offer Shall we go?"

A few minutes later they were walking along the street, her arm linked through his.

"Well, Georgie," he said, breaking the silence, "you are looking remarkably elegant. But a trifle out of sorts?"

"Oh, no, sir," she said. "Whatever makes you say so?"

"Nothing at all except a certain absence of inclination to talk," he said. "I believe that to be out of character."

"Oh," she said, "but then, it is not always easy to chatter away to a virtual stranger."

"A stranger?" he said, looking at her sideways, amusement on his face. "Do I take it that I must drop 'Georgie' and address you as 'Countess of Chartleigh' again?"

"Oh, of course not," she said, dimpling. "What an absurd idea."

"I thought only your friends called you 'Georgie'," he said.

"And so they do," she replied.

"And how can I be both a stranger and your friend?" he asked.

She laughed lightly. "Ah," she said. "There you have

me, Roger. It is just that I was very indiscreet the other night. It puts me to the blush just to recall how freely I talked to you.''

"I was honored to be so confided in," he said. "And I have put my brains to work to quite an extraordinary degree in your behalf. I think I have the solution to your little problem."

"Indeed?" she asked guardedly.

"Assuredly," he said. "You wish to have a bolder, more assertive husband. Am I right?"

"Well," she said, "it is not that I do not like Ralph as he is."

"Oh, quite," he agreed. "But ladies, I have found, like to be able to relax in the knowledge that their men have . . . er, some little experience, shall we say?"

Georgiana blushed and stared straight ahead.

"I have thought that perhaps I can help my young cousin to gain that experience," Roger Beauchamp explained.

"What?" Georgiana squeaked. "You mean as in mistresses and such?"

"It cannot do Ralph any harm to sow some wild oats, can it, Georgie?" he asked. "And you stand only to gain, my dear, considering the present lamentable state of your marriage."

"I fail to see how I would gain from my husband's taking up with a mistress, sir," Georgiana said caustically. "And what do you know of the state of my marriage, pray?"

"Oh, come now, Georgie," Roger said, laughing down at her. "You admitted to me at the Boothby's party that you are—shall we say?—in your maidenly innocence still."

"I said no such thing!" Georgiana said indignantly. "And how dare you speak to me of such a matter, sir!"

Roger stopped walking, threw back his head, and roared with laughter. "I really do not know how I dare," he said. "I could never have imagined myself having such a conversation with any lady, let alone the very young and very innocent wife of my cousin. But you started it all, you know, Georgie. You are the one who flirted quite outrageously with me and succeeded in arousing my interest in your affairs. 'Affairs' being not quite the word, of course.''

"Well, I have never heard anything so outrageous in my life," Georgiana said. "Do you really have the nerve to suggest to me that I permit you to find my husband a mistress so that he may prove to be a better husband to me?"

Roger patted her hand on his arm and started walking again. "In short, yes," he said.

"I will not hear of it," she said.

They walked a few paces in silence. Around the next corner, they would be able to see her father's house.

"And did you have anyone in mind, pray?" Georgiana sked sharply.

"Certainly," he said. "When I think, Georgie, I think in practicalities."

"What is she like?" Georgiana asked.

"Are you sure you wish to know?" Roger said. He looked at her indignant face and laughed. "She is small and slim. A dancer."

"I don't like her," she said.

"You do not have to," Roger replied. "She is not unlike you in size, Georgie, but no match for you in looks or breeding. You need not be afraid that Ralph will become attached to her."

"I am not at all afraid of any such thing," she said. "He will never even see her."

"Oh, he has already done so," Roger said. "Did he not tell you that he attended the opera with me last night?"

"Roger," she said with ominous calm, "has this affair already begun? Is that what this insane conversation is all about?"

"Oh, by no means," Roger said. "He has seen her on the stage, you will understand, but he has not met her."

"You are to see to it that he never does meet her,"

Georgiana said. "Or any other . . . female. Do you understand me, Roger? If Ralph is ever unfaithful to me, I shall hold you personally responsible."

He laughed and patted her hand again. "This begins to look more and more interesting," he said. "You know, Georgie, I think you are a fair way to being in love with my young cousin."

"Nonsense," she said. "But Ralph is a sweet innocent. He needs to be protected from the world of mistresses and ladybirds. He would not know how to cope."

Roger roared with laughter again. "And you know everything there is to know about that world," he said. "Georgie! You are a veritable delight. I could almost find it in me to envy Ralph. I wonder if he will ever learn to cope with you."

"Hush," she said, "and pray do behave in a more seemly fashion. We are approaching my father's house and must already be visible from the windows."

"I am all gentlemanly decorum, ma'am," he said.

"Will you be leaving me at the door?" she asked.

"Oh, my no means," he assured her. "After walking all this great distance with you, my dear Lady Chartleigh, I shall at least come inside and pay my compliments to Miss Burton. She was gracious enough to dance with me the other evening."

Vera did not seem at all pleased with the courtesy he paid her. She was sitting in the green salon with her mother, having just bidden farewell to some other visitors. She rose and curtsied low to Lord Beauchamp, but her lips tightened and she did not raise her eyes. She sat down and picked up some embroidery.

"I walked over to see if you cared for a stroll in the park, Vera," Georgiana said. "I have not been out yesterday or today up until now and was beginning to feel as if my feet were about to send down roots. Lord Beauchamp arrived as I was about to leave and kindly offered to escort me here."

"How kind of you, sir," the viscountess said

graciously, having just been presented to Roger. "Will you take tea?"

"Perhaps one cup, ma'am," he said, "before I retrace my steps and retrieve my horse from Middleton House. What delicate stitches you do, Miss Burton. It never ceases to amaze me how you ladies find the patience to produce such beauty and to cultivate personal charms and loveliness at the same time." He crossed the room to seat himself beside Vera.

"Mama," Georgiana said, taking a chair adjacent to her mother's after carrying the cup into which the viscountess had poured tea across to Roger, "have you received an invitation to Mrs. Hoby's soiree next week? Ours came this morning, but I do not know if we are to accept it. I have not seen Ralph yet today."

"Perhaps it is because most of us do not waste our time in such idle pursuits as visiting clubs and playing cards and going to the races, sir," Vera replied, not looking up from her work.

"Ah," Roger said. "I had not thought of that. If I gave up such wild pursuits, ma'am, would you undertake to teach me skill with a needle?"

Vera looked up in astonishment, her face relaxing unwillingly into a grin of pure amusement. "What an absurd idea," she said. "You make fun of me, sir."

"On the contrary," he said, his eyes fixed on her face. "I am trying my best to be agreeable since you appeared not to enjoy my conversation a few evenings ago."

"I wish you would leave Georgiana alone," she said very quietly. Her mother and her sister were engaged in talking to each other.

"You think I should have stood on the steps of Middleton House a half-hour ago and waved my handkerchief in farewell while she set off on her lone walk here?" he asked, eyebrows raised.

She looked up in some annoyance. "Do you make a joke of everything, sir?" she asked. "I think you know very well what I mean."

"You must have a sorry opinion of your sister," he said.

"I am extremely fond of Georgie," she said indignantly. "But she is very young and impulsive and has had a tendency to get herself into innocent scrapes. I am afraid that she may be no match for a man like you."

"A man like me," he said. "And what is a man like me, pray, Miss Burton?"

"It is quite clear that you are unprincipled where ladies are concerned," she said firmly. "But you might at least confine your gallantries to someone who knows how to handle your advances."

"Ah," he said. "The voice of experience, I perceive. Are you applying for the position, ma'am?"

Her eyes flew to his face in shock. Her face was flushed, her eyes wide. "You are insufferable, sir," she said. "I should slap your face if we were alone."

"I regret the extra bodies as much as you, ma'am," he said. "When you direct those eyes my way, my mind becomes hopelessly addled with speculations on how sweet your lips would taste. If we were alone, we could both fulfill our desires."

Vera's eyes dropped involuntarily to his mouth, and she drew an audibly uneven breath. She rose abruptly to her feet, folding her embroidery with hasty hands. "If you will excuse me," she said to the room at large, "I shall go and fetch my cloak and bonnet. That walk in the park will be very welcome, Georgie."

Lord Beauchamp rose to his feet and bowed graciously as she swept past him. "I shall say good day, ma'am," he said. "I must be leaving."

Ralph decided to spend that evening at home, though he did not find the prospect a comfortable one. He had offended his mother and felt unhappy about that. Yet he could not apologize to her. He had not spoken to her in haste and had not said anything deliberately bad-mannered or disrespectful. He felt that he had been right to tell her that he would encourage Gloria to continue with her wedding plans. And he certainly felt justified in telling her to leave Georgiana to him. He could not feel sorry for a word he had said, but he was sorry for the necessity of speaking thus. He was sorry at the moment to be the Earl of Chartleigh. He felt all the loneliness that a position of authority must bring with it on occasion.

He felt even worse about having to face Georgiana. He still could not believe that that terrible quarrel had really occurred the afternoon before. He had known he was not a good husband. And he had known that his behavior to her was indecisive, that he would have to do something to try to win her trust and even her affection. But he had not known how terribly hurt she was.

He remembered her as she had appeared to him on the first two occasions he had met her, especially on the second, when he had made his offer to her. She had been so quiet, so sweet. He had learned at Chartleigh that she was not timid, that she could be talkative and lively and exceedingly brave in the cause of others. But he had seen nothing at all in her to dislike or to censure.

What a change he had wrought in her in such a short time! She had lost her temper the previous afternoon. She had even used language that he had never thought to hear on the lips of a woman. And she had admitted to flirting with Roger. Because she was bored, she had said. Because he himself was not man enough for her. And she had threatened to take a lover.

Could that have been Georgiana? What had he done to her? It did not occur to him to blame her at all. She had changed in a very short time. There could be only one cause for that change: himself. She must be right. He was a failure.

And there seemed no way to put things right. She hated and despised him now. The time when he might have gone to her and tried to make a new beginning on their marriage was past. If the rest of their married life was not to be an utter disaster, he would have to approach the problem with considerable decisiveness, skill, and knowledge. And he had none of those things where Georgiana and women in general were concerned. He was aghast at his own youth and innocence. How did one win the trust and love of a woman who hated and feared one?

He had been unable to face Georgiana for the rest of the day and most of this. He had walked around the streets of London the afternoon before and ended up calling on Roger. It was unusual to find his cousin at home, but it was close to dinnertime when he arrived. Roger had persuaded him to stay and to accompany him to the opera in the evening.

The motive for the chosen entertainment had been immediately obvious to Ralph. His cousin had seen that he was no more cheerful than he had been on an earlier occasion at White's. He took him to see a little dancer whom he had been considering bringing under his own protection but whom he was magnanimously willing to renounce in favor of his cousin.

Ralph had looked at her and felt a shiver of revulsion and something else. A feeling of inevitability, perhaps. She was small. She had a good figure and was light on her feet. She was not unlike Georgiana if one did not look at her face and her hair. But who could escape doing so? Her hair was a vivid red, in a mass of short curls around her head. The color was clearly not natural. And her face was heavily painted. Even at a distance from the stage, Ralph could see the sheen of bright red lip rouge and the rosy glow of false color on her cheeks. She was pretty, he supposed. But there was a coarseness about her that repelled him.

"Of course she wears paint," Roger said on Ralph's comment. "She is on the stage, my lad, and is in the business of attracting attention. The hair is dyed for the same purpose. Doubtless all would be suitably toned down in a boudoir. She is a pretty little armful, Ralph, my boy. Fresh from the country. I hear that Grimble has been trying to get her, but he is notoriously close-fisted."

"I cannot imagine how women can live such an existence," Ralph said, gazing at the little dancer with some sadness. "She is surely very young, Roger."

"It is probably a better existence than the workhouse," Roger said. "If she is frugal, she can probably save enough in these years to ensure a comfortable life afterward."

"Poor girl," Ralph said.

Roger laughed. "She would not thank you for your pity," he said. "Doubtless she believes she has the world at her feet at the moment. Do you want her?"

"What?" Ralph said. He looked at his cousin's raised eyebrows and flushed. It was stupid to pretend not to understand. "I don't think I could, Rog. I am a married man."

"And not too happily so," Roger pointed out. "Why not do a bit of the living you have missed in your years at university, my lad? Then perhaps you will be able to settle to a happier marriage."

Ralph looked back to the dancer. "I would not know how to go about attracting her notice," he said.

"That is the least of your problems," Roger assured him with a wave of one hand. "I shall be your ambassador, my boy. I don't think there will be any difficulty once she hears whom I represent and how much you are prepared to pay. I take it you will give me a free hand in deciding on terms? And my house in Kensington is available to you. Evelyn moved out almost a month ago and I have been enjoying my freedom too much to replace her yet. Well, what do you say, Ralph? Shall I go down after the performance and have a word with her?"

"No!" Ralph said sharply. "I really do not want to do this, you know. I must consider."

Lord Beauchamp could not induce his young cousin to make any more definite commitment for that night.

And the following evening Ralph was still confused, unhappy, undecided. He sat through an uncomfortable dinner, responding as best he could to Gloria's attempts at conversation. She talked about the shopping expedition she had made that day with Aunt Elspeth. Apparently a large number of her bride clothes had been either purchased or ordered. He was glad he had talked with her before leaving the house the previous afternoon. She seemed to be acting on the assumption that her wedding would take place before Christmas.

He sat in the drawing room after dinner, attempting to talk to both his mother and Georgiana. It was hopeless. Neither ignored him. But there was no communication. They were all worlds apart. He excused himself early and retired to his room. He was miserable with the knowledge that his wife was unhappy and that he was about to sin against her. He was about to set up an opera dancer as his mistress.

He was going to be unfaithful to Georgiana.

11

"AUNT HILDA, I have been charged by Mama to tell you that if you have recovered from your headache, you are to call out your carriage this afternoon and go to take tea with her. She is expecting other company that she believes you will enjoy." Roger Beauchamp smiled at his aunt and waited with raised eyebrows for her reply.

"I am still not in the best of health," the dowager countess said, "but perhaps I will accept dear Elspeth's invitation, Roger. Everyone in my own household is too busy to keep me company. Not that I can expect them to. They all have their own lives ahead of them. I have had mine already. Stanley is rarely at home, though of course he is a growing boy and needs to get out to meet new people and keep up with the fashions and the news. Ralph is more concerned with the affairs of the House of Lords than with his family, and Gloria has suddenly become giddy and taken to visiting friends in the afternoons. And now you have come to take Georgiana driving."

"Dear aunt!" Roger said. "May I speak to your butler about bringing around the carriage?"

"Tell him half an hour," she called as he turned to leave the room. She turned to Georgiana. "I am sure Ralph would consider it unexceptionable for you to drive in the park with my nephew, dear. But then Ralph never did have much of a notion of how to go on in society. You are fortunate indeed, Georgiana, to have such an indulgent husband. My dear Chartleigh would have called out the man who dared to so much as talk to me without his consent.''

"Yes, I am fortunate,'' Georgiana agreed, smiling warmly at her mother-in-law. "How dreadful it must be to have a husband who does not trust one's good judgment and character.''

She rose to her feet and left the room to fetch her cloak and muff for the ride in the park. How dreadful she was becoming, she thought with some remorse, digging in her claws just like a cat.

"My mother-in-law does not approve of my driving out with you, you know,'' she said to Roger a few minutes later as his phaeton was maneuvering its way in the direction of the park.

"She never did trust me after discovering me at the age of eighteen fondling one of her scullery maids in a broom closet,'' Roger said, turning to grin at Georgiana.

"How shocking!'' she said. "Did you really?''

"And she would disapprove of this outing still more if she knew that you had written to me this morning asking for it,'' he said. "Do you have no notion at all of proper behavior, Georgie?''

"Certainly,'' she said. "But if I had done the proper thing and waited until I saw you next, I might have waited for weeks.''

"Quite so,'' he said. "And I cannot imagine any female having the fortitude so to deprive herself. To what do I owe the honor, my dear little cousin?''

"I have been thinking,'' she said, "and I believe you are right. It would do Ralph the world of good to gain some experience with other women.''

"Spoken with a stiff upper lip and a breaking heart, doubtless,'' Roger said. "But I mistrust the gleam in your eye, Georgie. Out with it. What are you planning? To catch him red-handed in compromising circumstances so that you may beat him over the head with a frying pan?''

"No,'' she said, turning and looking at him with wide

eyes, "I mean it, Roger. You must persuade him to take a mistress."

"Are you relinquishing all interest in him?" Roger asked. "Or are you planning to sit back for a suitable number of months or years, patiently twiddling your thumbs until he has the experience to make an interesting husband?"

"Neither," she said. "I am going to be his mistress."

Roger gave her his full attention. A carter shouted angrily as his horses swerved toward the center of a crowded road. "I believe I have missed a step in this very fascinating and quite scandalous conversation, Georgie," he said. "Hang on a minute. Let me coax these brutes through the park gates before you continue. I have the feeling I am going to need all my concentration to listen to you."

Georgiana did as she was bidden and sat primly beside Lord Beauchamp, hands clasped inside her muff, feet in their warm half-boots set side by side on the footrest before her.

"Now then," Roger said at last, "let me hear this plan of yours, Georgie. I would wager my fortune on its being quite priceless."

"Has he met that dancer yet?" Georgiana asked. "Has he begun a liaison with her?"

"By no means," Roger said. "I do not believe he is even interested."

"And she is a little like me, you said?" Georgiana asked.

"Absolutely not!" he assured her. "Except a little in height and build, I suppose. No, she has not nearly your beauty or delicacy of feature, Georgie. And probably none of your indelicacy of tongue, either."

"That will be good enough," she said. "It will be your task, Roger, to persuade Ralph that he does want her. I shall impersonate her."

"What?" Roger began to laugh. "You would have to dye your hair bright red and smear your face with cosmetics at the very least, Georgie."

"How disgusting!" she said. "But that will be quite unnecessary, of course. I assume the assignations would be a night?"

"Probably," he conceded.

"It will be easy enough then," she said. "A darkened room, a heavy veil over my face and head, a feigned voice, and the disguise will be complete."

Roger had drawn the horses almost to a halt. He held the reins loosely in one hand and continued to laugh.

"Impossible, Georgie," he said. "Do you seriously believe that your own husband would not recognize you?"

"Yes," she said. "He would not even see me. Are you to make the arrangements? I imagine so, since I do not believe Ralph would know how to go about setting it all up. Then you must tell him that this dancer is somewhat eccentric and refuses to let herself be seen except on the stage. The room where I receive him can be quite dark, can it not? And the bedchamber can be completely without light. And I will not need to talk a great deal. I do not imagine such women talk much, do they, Roger? They are too busy with other matters."

"Georgie!" Roger said, turning a grinning face in her direction. "You are putting me to the blush. Please remember that, unlike you, I am unmarried and unversed in such matters."

"Oh, pray be serious," she said crossly. "We have much to arrange and should really not be gone from the house for longer than an hour. That would not be proper, especially as the park is virtually deserted at this time of year. You see, I do know something of propriety."

"You could have deceived me by what you have chosen as a topic of conversation for this afternoon," Roger said fervently. "How would you get out of Middleton House to keep your assignations, Georgie? And how get back home again? Have you thought of that?"

"Well, of course I have thought of that!" Georgiana

said. "Do you take me for a complete clothhead, Roger? I have a faithful maid, who used to help me escape from Papa's house all the time when I was sent to my room for various offenses. And though I was punished numerous times, it was never for one of those escapades. I was never caught. And as for getting to the rendezvous, wherever that is, why, you will escort me there and back, of course, Roger."

"Ah, of course," he said. "I have nothing better to do with my evenings than to drive mistresses around London in search of their lovers."

"Well, I imagine you will have to make some sacrifice of your time," Georgiana said kindly. "But you will do it for your favorite cousin, will you not?"

"For you?" he asked, aghast.

"No, silly," she said. "But you told me yourself that Ralph is your favorite cousin. And all this is for the sake of his happiness, you know."

Roger sighed. "Do you know, Georgie," he said, "before I met you, my life was deliciously uncomplicated. I do wish I had not seen you emerging from those bushes looking shockingly disheveled—with Creeley, was it? If I had not, you see, I might not have particularly noticed you at your wedding and I might not have even recognized you in the park with your sister afterward. And I might not be sitting here now concocting the most outrageous plot with you. You are a most degrading influence on me, you know. I have never even broached such topics with a delicately nurtured female before. You are not even supposed to know about such things as assignations and mistresses."

"I know," she said. "It comes of enjoying male company far more than female, I suppose. All my closest friends are men. And sometimes they seem to forget to whom they are talking."

"Yes," he said dryly, "I know the feeling."

"Well," she said briskly, "is everything settled?"

"You are quite mad, Georgie," he said. "You can't be serious about all this, can you?"

She gave him a speaking look. "Would I have said all I have said in jest?" she asked. "You must get everything arranged, Roger. You will let me know where and when. Only let it be soon. Once I have set my mind on a thing, I am all impatience until it is accomplished."

"Good God!" said Roger Beauchamp, giving his horses the signal to move more briskly. "I must be as mad as the lady. I am actually thinking out ways and means already."

"Of course you are," Georgiana assured him.

Ralph could not quite believe that this was actually happening. He was still close to convincing himself that he had not finally made up his mind, that he could put an end to this ridiculous scheme at any moment and forget the whole thing. He had never actually said yes to Roger, had he? Had he not merely agreed that his cousin might talk to the dancer he had seen at the opera to find out a little more about her? He had also said that Roger might discuss terms, but only so that he would know what was expected of him if he ever did decide to engage her as a mistress. And he had agreed that the house in Kensington would probably be an ideal site for a liaison. But he had not actually told Roger to prepare the house or to make any definite arrangements with the girl. Had he?

Why was it, then, that he was in his carriage on the way to Kensington at a time of night when he should be at home in his own room? Why had he told Georgiana that he was going to White's? He had gone there for a while, it was true, on Roger's advice, but he had known that he had essentially been telling a lie.

He could not go back now, however much he tried to persuade himself that he might. The girl was there waiting for him, if Roger was to be believed. This was the night. He would be there with her in no more than ten minutes' time. And he had very little wish to be. It was as if he had lived in some kind of dream for the past week.

He had made a determined effort to set his life in some sort of order again. He had continued to spend much of his time in the House of Lords. He had never taken much interest in affairs of state, but it was his duty to do so. He must learn how to play his role in society. There must be all sorts of problems to which to devote his energies. He could not justify his life of luxury and idleness. In a short time he had learned more about the deplorable conditions under which the less privileged lived than he had ever dreamed. Chimney-sweeps, factory workers, vagabonds, workhouse dwellers: all lived lives of unimaginable poverty, drudgery, and suffering. Children seemed to be especial victims of poverty.

Ralph was not at all sure yet that there was anything he could do about the situation. One man felt so helpless against such a huge national problem. But he felt that he had discovered some purpose for his life.

He had taken to attending Jackson's boxing saloon as many mornings as he could. He had never particularly enjoyed physical activity. He was a reader and a thinker rather than a doer. But he knew with his mind that physical fitness and a certain amount of physical strength were necessary. He set about building that fitness and that strength. His sparring partners were not Jackson's most talented boxers, by any means, but only that morning the great man himself had stood and watched him for a minute, laughed heartily at the end of it, and commented that in a few months' time, if his lordship continued to improve, he would take upon himself the pleasure of leveling him.

And even in his home, Ralph was trying to bring some sort of order. It was clear that there would be no peace as long as he and Georgiana lived with his mother. It had not occurred to him after the death of his father to claim Middleton House or Chartleigh for his own and to suggest that his mother move elsewhere. They were her homes, though with his head, he supposed, he had realized that they now belonged to him.

But now he began to think that his mother must make her home somewhere else. There was a dower house at Chartleigh, which was an attractive and imposing mansion in its own right. He sent a message to his bailiff to look over the house and estimate what repairs, renovations, changes, and additions might have to be made if his mother were to take up residence there. He had visited Parker to ask advice on the renting or leasing of a suitable establishment in London.

He was not at all sure how his mother would react to his plans. He must be sure to break the news to her well in advance of the move. It would be cruel to make plans behind her back, as if he were trying secretly to get rid of her. He guessed that she would be most upset at first. He also believed that once she grew accustomed to the change, she would be the happier. Part of the reason for her bad temper lately was surely her knowledge that she was no longer mistress in the house that had been her home since her marriage. It must be hard for her to step down in favor of Georgiana, who was so very young.

Gloria's future seemed well in hand. She had received a letter from Boscome the day before, confirming that the date for the wedding had been set and the bishop engaged to perform the ceremony. Gloria was in the process of drawing up a list of wedding guests.

Stanley seemed to be no particular problem, though Ralph deplored the fact that his younger brother appeared content to be an idle and fashionable young man-about-town. He flatly refused to go to university. But he seemed amiable enough, if somewhat empty-headed. Doubtless he would move in with his mother, though Ralph had no objection to his staying at home.

Finally, then, he seemed to be taking charge of his own life again. Finally he felt he was quite outgrowing his boyhood and his dependence on the decisions of other people. Except for the one area of his life that had always been his problem. Except for his marriage.

Nothing had improved in that relationship. There had

been an almost total breach of communication between him and his wife since their quarrel the week before. They usually dined together and occasionally break-fasted together. They spoke to each other enough to satisfy good manners. They had attended Mrs. Hoby's soiree together the evening before. But there was no communication whatsoever. They never looked into each other's eyes. There was never a hint of anything personal in their conversation. They never touched.

There was a tension between them that was imposing a strain on both their nerves. Georgiana was quiet. He had not seen her smile in more than a week, except at the soiree. She had smiled there at her sister and at Roger. And he found himself totally unable to relax in her presence. He would have liked to warm the atmosphere a little, to say something to her that would show that he cared. But he could never think of a single thing to say, incredible as it might seem. He loved her, but he felt that there was a huge, invisible stone wall between them.

Hence this mad journey to Kensington, Ralph thought with a sigh. He desperately needed someone with whom he could communicate, even if only on a purely physical level. He needed this girl. Not emotionally. He did not crave a relationship. All his emotions were already centered on his wife. He needed contact with a woman, with no barriers between.

He was glad that the girl appeared to be rather strange. She liked to protect the privacy of her person, Roger had explained. Roger thought it a joke that she was willing to give her body and still felt that there was some privacy to guard. But Ralph understood. The girl had chosen to make her living on the stage and in the beds of wealthy men. But there was still a person who would not be at all visible in either activity. The girl was not just a dancer. She was not just a whore. She was a person.

She did not like to be seen or heard, Roger had explained. She would receive him, heavily veiled, in a darkened room. She would speak only in a whisper. In the bedchamber she would have all light excluded. Roger had even had to have the window draperies changed so that no glimmering of light from the street outside would penetrate the room.

His cousin had been amused and apologetic about the eccentricities, but Ralph had raised no objections. In fact, he quite welcomed the conditions the girl had set down. Sally, her name was. Sally Shaw. He must think of her by name. She was a person. She had a name. He would accept her wishes. He had no real wish to see her. He had been rather repelled by her artificial appearance onstage. He had no real wish to converse with her. He wanted to touch her merely. He wanted her as a woman.

Or did he? The carriage drew to a halt, and Ralph felt a queer lurching of the stomach. He had only to make a move now, and he was irrevocably committed. He drew a deep, steadying breath and vaulted out of the carriage as soon as the postilion opened the door.

Georgiana had set the single candle on the mantel across the room from where she sat and some distance from the doorway that led from the sitting room into the bedchamber. She had had the fire piled with coal so that it gave very little light. There was no fire at all in the other room. She did not believe that her disguise was at all penetrable. She wore a black crepe gown and gloves. She had removed her wedding ring before slipping out of the house by the side entrance unbolted by her maid. Her head and face were completely covered by two heavy black veils. In fact, the room looked quite impossibly dim through them.

The chamber beyond the doorway was in readiness, the sheets turned back from the heavy four-poster bed. She wondered fleetingly how many assignations had taken place in just these two rooms. But she pushed the thought from her mind. She did not wish to speculate on Roger and his love life at the moment. He had done a really splendid job of preparing everything according to her directions. And he had conveyed her here a short while ago after ascertaining that Ralph was indeed at White's.

She wondered if Ralph would come, or if he would take fright at the last moment. Part of her wished for the latter. Her hands felt cold despite the fire. And then she heard the knock at the outer door, silence, and the sounds of the bolts being drawn back by the one servant Roger kept on the premises. Her hands felt clammy. Her heart began to thump uncomfortably against her ribs.

Georgiana rose to her feet when Ralph came into the room. He had left his hat and coat with the porter. He looked very familiar and strangely dear standing rather hesitantly in the doorway, his eyes adjusting to the dim light. She held out her gloved hands to him.

He came across the room and took them. His face looked somewhat strained, Georgiana could see now that he was close. She felt suddenly naked. How could she have expected that he would not know her? He was looking directly at her. But his expression did not change.

"Miss Shaw," he said, "how kind of you to agree to see me."

She nodded and squeezed his hands. How typical of Ralph to be so courtly in such a situation.

"Have you been dancing tonight?" he asked. "You must be very tired."

Georgiana shook her head. Her heart had begun to palpitate with alarming rapidity. Otherwise, she might have found his conversation amusing.

"I understand that you want to remain unseen," said Ralph. "I respect your wishes absolutely, Miss Shaw, and will not try to take advantage of the liaison that may develop between us. I understand your desire to retain your privacy."

She nodded and squeezed his hands again. "Thank you, my lord," she whispered.

"Shall we . . . ?" he began. "Do you wish to sit down for a while?"

"No, my lord," she whispered, and she released one

of his hands and led him by the other to the bed-chamber. She opened the door wide and stood to one side so that he could see by the dim light from the sitting room the arrangement of the furniture. Then she led him inside and shut fast the door behind them.

"I shall undress, my lord," she whispered, and crossed to the bed, which was exactly nine paces from the door, as she had discovered earlier. She felt her way around to the other side of it. She had laid a nightgown on the bed and undressed hastily now. But when she had picked up the nightgown, she hesitated and dropped it to the floor. Did men's mistresses wear anything in bed? She did not know, and it was the one thing that she had not summoned the courage to ask Roger about. She climbed onto the bed.

Ralph joined her there a few moments later. They met in the middle of the great mattress. He was warm, Georgiana felt, as her hand came in contact with his bare chest. She was shaking with the cold of nervousness. He put his arms around her and drew her against him, pulling the blankets up around them as he did so.

"You are cold," he said against her ear, and he cradled her against him, rubbing one hand along her back for several minutes until she felt warmth envelop her. She felt her body relax. Yes, this was Ralph as she knew him to be: gentle and tender, considerate of her comfort. She snuggled closer.

And then returned to her senses. She was an opera dancer engaged to provide certain services for part of the night. She feathered her fingers over his chest and twisted her hips closer to him. She suddenly felt more than just warm.

Ralph's hands moved from her back. He explored her body: her breasts, the curve of her waist and hips, her thighs. His hand was warm and gentle. She could picture it: long and slender, sensitive. She turned over onto her back.

She did not know how a practiced mistress proceeded in such matters. She knew only as much as she had learned on her wedding night. And that was not a great deal. But she would not give in to panic. After all, he knew no more. When he lifted himself across her, she moved to accommodate him, spreading her legs, raising her knees, and setting her feet flat on the bed. As he lowered his weight onto her body, she guided him until he was at the entrance of her womanhood. She closed her eyes very tightly, bit down on her lower lip, and pivoted her hips.

And then she was drawing blood from her lip. It was the only way she could keep from crying out. She did not know if the pain or the shock was the greater, but she did know after a few moments that triumph and delight were taking the place of both. She was in her husband's deepest embrace. She was becoming a wife. She held him inside her.

Georgiana threw back her head on the pillow and smiled up into the darkness as he moved in her with deep, intimate strokes that aroused no physical excitement but brought great emotional satisfaction. The moment she had awaited weeks before in some trepidation and ever since in impatience had finally come. And now she was receiving it with eagerness. She truly wanted to be Ralph's wife. She closed her eyes, still smiling. This, then, was what it felt like, the long-dreamed-of, much-feared intimacy of man and woman.

And then it was over. Much too soon. She wanted more. She wanted him to continue thrusting and thrusting into her. But he was still, warm and relaxed on top of her. She held him very close, stretching her legs alongside his, laying her cheek against his soft hair, willing him not to notice that she was having difficulty breathing beneath his weight.

And too soon again he stirred and lifted himself away from her. He lay beside her for a few minutes before reaching out a hand to find hers.

"Thank you," he said. "You are very beautiful."

It was only then that she remembered again that it was not his wife to whom he had made love. Not her.

Just a dancer. She stared up into the darkness and said nothing. She waited for him to remove his hand, for the loss of all contact again.

He got out of the bed and she could hear him dressing in the darkness. He spoke to her before he left.

"Will you come on Friday again?" he asked. "At the same time?"

"Yes, my lord," she whispered.

"Thank you," he said. "Will you be able to get home safely? Do you wish me to accompany you?"

"No, my lord," she replied.

"Good night, then," he said.

And he was gone.

Georgiana shot out of bed and dressed with feverish haste and shaking legs, throwing open the door into the sitting room so that she could see what she was doing. Roger was to return for her and see her home. If Ralph behaved according to plan, he would return to White's to meet Roger there later.

It was only as she went to leave the sitting room on hearing Lord Beauchamp arrive downstairs that she noticed the money on the table by the door. She picked it up and counted it.

"Heavenly days!" she muttered, her eyes wide. "Do they really earn this much?"

12

WHEN GEORGIANA was ushered into her mother's drawing room the following afternoon, she was surprised and a little embarrassed to find Lord Beauchamp already there. She had been wondering how she would face him again in the cold light of day after the events of the previous night. He had been very tactful. He had taken her cloak from his servant and wrapped it warmly around her before taking her outside to his carriage. She had expected to be teased mercilessly. Instead, he had sat across from her, propped one booted foot on the seat next to her, examined her face, and smiled. He had made only one comment.

"So it has been worth all the risk, Georgie," he had stated. It had not been a question.

He had looked away then and remained quiet until the carriage was drawn to a halt some distance from Middleton House. And even when he had taken her arm and escorted her to the side door of the house, he had said nothing beyond a good night greeting.

She had been grateful for his tact. She had been very aware of how rosy her cheeks must be and how bright her eyes. She had been far too excited and happy to disguise her feelings. Now, of course, it was somewhat different. It was daytime. Here she was, apparently a respectable married lady calling on her mama and her sister. And there was he, handsome and elegant, an unmarried gentleman paying an afternoon social call. And just last night he had taken her to an illicit meeting with her own husband to render services for which she had been very well paid indeed!

Georgiana almost giggled. She curtsied hastily and launched into speech. She had walked again from Middleton House, but one of the maids had been sent to accompany her, if anyone could imagine anything so tiresome. She had tried to persuade Gloria to come with her, but her sister-in-law was so busy with wedding preparations that she did not even have time for an afternoon visit. Did everyone like her new bonnet? She had not meant to purchase it at all, but when she had been on Bond Street looking for new gloves, she had seen it and fallen in love with it. Was it not a sin to be buying things one did not really need? But how dull to have only the necessities.

"Georgie, dear, do sit down," her mother said, "and hear our news. The builders have finally finished the repairs on the house, and Papa says that we are to go home within the month. I never thought to say so, dear, but I shall be most awfully glad to get away from town for a while. I had no idea that life could be so dull with so many people away."

"Oh, but I shall miss you," Georgiana cried. "Cannot Papa go alone, Mama, to see that the work has been properly carried out? Does he need to drag you and Vera along with him?"

"I was just trying to persuade Miss Burton to walk with me when you arrived, Georgie," Lord Beauchamp said. "She was murmuring some fears about the wind, which is reputed to bite right through to the bone. Can you confirm such a report? I must say the only evidence of cold I can see in you is the rosiness of your cheeks."

"Oh, it is windy," Georgiana said, "but very bracing. A lovely day for a gallop."

"Galloping is not an extremely elegant way to move around on foot," his lordship commented, "but if a more sedate walk would suit you, Georgie, perhaps you and your sister will accompany me? I have two arms and can hardly think of a better use to which to put them."

"I shall certainly come," Georgiana said, leaping to her feet. "I cannot speak for Vera."

Her sister frowned at her, unseen by Lord Beauchamp. "I shall be delighted to come too," she said, the tone of her voice contradicting her words. "But do sit down again, Georgie. I shall have to change into walking clothes and I hate to know that someone is standing impatiently down here waiting for me."

"I shall come up with you," Georgiana announced, "and make sure that you wear a suitable color. You have a dreadful tendency to choose yellow or gray or some other shade that is all wrong for you."

She followed her sister upstairs and into her room and curled up on the bed while Vera began to get ready. "Wear the green," she said. "It is very dashing with the frogged buttons and epaulets. I wish I had one similar. And I do admire the new way you have of dressing your hair, Vera. It looks far more becoming looped down over your ears like that. In fact, it vastly improves your whole appearance."

"Why did you agree to go walking?" Vera asked. "You have only just arrived, Georgie, and Mama has had scarcely a chance to exchange a word with you."

Georgiana sat up. "Have I offended her, do you think?" she asked. "I did not think of that. I am so used to doing exactly as I please with Mama. She is so easygoing."

"No," Vera said. "I do not suppose Mama will mind. But Lord Beauchamp, Georgie! I really cannot like your association with him."

"Why not?" Georgiana's eyes were wide. "He is Ralph's cousin."

"And an unprincipled man and a rake," Vera said. "He does not even behave like a gentleman."

Georgiana frowned. "How can you say that?" she said. "I have always found him perfectly friendly. And he has always been polite to you, Vera. He has danced with you and I have seen him conversing with you on several occasions. Why, he even came here today to take you walking. I believe if I were in your position, I should feel flattered."

"You mean if you were three-and-twenty and unattached and very plain," Vera said, "you would welcome the attentions of a handsome, charming rake."

Georgiana looked at her sister in surprise. Vera was always so placid, so sensible. Now she sounded cross, almost spiteful. "You have such a low opinion of yourself, Vera," she said. "I have always told you that you are not plain at all. And your single state is of your own choosing. I know for a fact that you have turned down at least two offers. And Roger is not a conceited man. He cannot help the fact that he has been blessed with extraordinary good looks."

"He treats you with too great a familiarity," Vera persisted. "He calls you 'Georgie.' Why, even your husband does not call you that. I believe his intentions toward you are not honorable."

"Stuff!" Georgiana was shocked enough to say. "Roger does not flirt with married ladies. He told me so himself."

"You see what I mean?" Vera said, pausing in the process of pinning her hat to her hair. "What on earth was he about, to even mention such a thing to you? I hate to say this, Georgie, but I love you and I shall say it anyway. I think you are rather struck with Lord Beauchamp. And it is a shame. You have a husband whom I believe to be a fine young man. I am disappointed to see your eye roving already."

Georgiana jumped down from the bed and smoothed out her skirts with angry hands. "It is not so," she said. "I am true to my husband and I appreciate his good qualities quite as much as you, Vera. Roger is merely a friend. I had not expected you to accuse me. It is bad enough to have Ralph's mother and brother insinuating such things."

"Oh, Georgie," Vera said, her face full of concern. "Have they noticed too? Do have a care. You know how thoughtless you can be sometimes and what scrapes you can get into as a result. But this would be much worse than usual, you know."

"We are keeping Roger waiting," her sister said stiffly.

Lord Beauchamp appeared to notice nothing amiss in the atmosphere around him as he took a lady on each arm and led them in the direction of the park. He conversed amiably with both and soon restored Georgiana at least to good spirits. She was strolling along the edge of the grass beside the main pathway, swinging her reticule, when she suddenly stopped, pulled her arm from Roger's, and shrieked in most unladylike fashion.

"Dennis!" she yelled, and picking up her skirts, she began to run toward a curricle which was approaching from some distance. The driver stopped his vehicle, swung himself down from the high seat while flinging the ribbons to his tiger, and broke her headlong flight by catching her in his arms and swinging her around.

"Dennis Vaughan, you are back!" Georgiana announced rather unnecessarily. "You have been gone this age. And I have so much to tell you."

"So I gather," the young man replied, doffing his hat to reveal a shock of bright red hair. "Not the least item being that you have got yourself married since I left, Georgie. Most unsporting of you, you know, without giving the rest of your admirers fair warning so that they might have made their own counteroffers."

"Oh, nonsense!" she said. "You know you would not have offered for me, Dennis. You have said yourself that you will not marry until you are well past thirty, and you are only seven-and-twenty now."

"Eight," he corrected her.

"And anyway, we would make a dreadful match," she told him cheerfully. "We do not have a sensible or stable thought between us. We both need someone to control our madder impulses."

He grinned and chucked her under the chin. "And is that what you have found in Lord Chartleigh?" he asked. "I confess I have never met him, though I have heard that he is bookish and indecently young."

"You must not say anything about Ralph that even borders on criticism, you know," she said, "or you will have my wrath to deal with."

"Dreadful!" he said, cringing back from her. "A love match, is it, Georgie? Pardon me, Miss Burton. I am being dreadfully ill-mannered. How d' ye do, ma'am? Beauchamp?"

Bows and greetings were exchanged.

"If you are walking, I might as well join you for a while," Dennis said. "I need the exercise."

He gave directions to his tiger to take his curricle to the gate and wait for him there. He offered his arm to Georgiana and the two of them strolled on ahead.

"So, Miss Burton," Lord Beauchamp said, taking Vera's hand and setting it inside his arm again, "you find yourself trapped into being alone with me after all. My commiseration, ma'am."

"Thank you," she said, "but I find walking in the park with another couple quite respectable exercise, sir."

"Ah," he said, patting her hand, "I see. It was to walking alone with me here that you objected when I first made the suggestion, was it? Did you fear that I would give into my baser passions and take you behind a tree to taste of your lips, perhaps? You malign me, ma'am. I shall choose a far warmer and more comfortable setting in which to do that when the time comes."

"Do you talk to all ladies this way?" she asked in a suffocated voice. "I find your conversation quite shocking and insulting."

"No," he said, "in fact, I do not. Now, what is it about you that gives me the irresistible urge to shock? You have an air of great calmness and self-control. Admirable qualities, doubtless. But does that manner reveal the whole of Miss Burton? I think not. If you wish to be left to your quiet existence, you must curse the fate that gave your face that trick it has of transforming itself when you forget your ladylike dignity. And those eyes of yours, my dear. They tell me that you are a woman of deep feeling and passion. They excite me. There, have I succeeded in paralyzing you with shock?"

"If your purpose is to seduce me," she said, her voice low, her eyes firmly fixed on the ground ahead of her, "I must tell you that you waste your time, my lord. You are a type of man I despise."

"A type?" he said. "You could scarce have wounded me more. Do I have no individuality, ma'am?"

"No," she said, "I think not. There is a certain type of man who has good looks, charm, and wealth, and believes that the world is here to cater to his every whim and that every female must be falling over her own feet to attract him. You are such a man, I believe. But I am not such a woman."

"Indeed," he said, and the teasing note in his voice had been replaced by a somewhat biting edge. "You almost tempt me, ma'am, to go to work to proving you wrong. But, alas, it has never been my practice to seduce either married ladies or virtuous unmarried ones. That principle has left me a very obvious choice, has it not? No, my dear, my intentions toward you—if intentions I have—are entirely honorable. I do not, by the way, call a kiss a seduction, do you? I fully intend to kiss you before the winter is out. I have a notion that it will be an interesting experience."

"If you enjoy having your face slapped, then I must agree with you, sir," Vera said.

He laughed and patted her hand again, his good humor restored. Georgiana turned at that moment to make some observation, and both couples started back in the direction of the gates. The conversation became general.

Ralph had accepted a dinner engagement for himself and his wife that evening at the home of Lord Standen, whose acquaintance he had made during the past weeks in the House of Lords. Lord Standen shared his concern for social reform and had several interesting ideas that had drawn Ralph's attention.

Ralph arrived home before Georgiana in the afternoon and waited for her in the drawing room. Gloria was bright with the news that David Boscome was coming to London for a few days as soon as he could leave his parish, in order to see her and discuss their wedding plans. His mother, Ralph noticed, made no comment but continued with her embroidery.

"Mama," he said, "will you wish to go to Chartleigh early in December? You know so much more about organizing big events than anyone else in the family. I am sure your presence will be invaluable."

She looked up. " Well, as to that," she said, "I have indeed had much experience. Chartleigh expected me to oversee all our entertainments, you know, even though we always had servants enough to see to things themselves. And if Gloria is really set on this marriage, I suppose I had better make sure that everything is done as it should be."

Ralph smiled. "It will be the grandest wedding the countryside can remember, I am sure," he said. "Whatever would we do without you, Mama?"

"Well," she said, clearly gratified, "I have always known my duty, Ralph, and I have always tried to teach you and Gloria and Stanley yours."

He crossed the room to kiss her on the cheek. "I think I am going to tell you of a Christmas present I have been planning for you," he said. "I would like to keep it a secret, but I think the gift would be so much the better if you helped plan it. How would you like to have the dower house, Mama, and a free hand to decorate it and furnish it as you choose?"

She looked up at him sharply. "The dower house?" she said, frowning.

"You always liked to entertain when Papa was alive," Ralph said, "and I know that you were greatly respected as a hostess. It has struck me that perhaps you feel inhibited somewhat now that I have a wife. Perhaps you feel you are no longer free to treat the house as your own and to plan your own entertainments. I would not wish you to feel that way, Mama. I would like you to be mistress of your own establishment—provided you will promise me that I shall always be welcome there.''

He was leaning over his mother's chair, smiling gently down at her. She patted his hand after a moment's hesitation.

''You have always had a generous heart, Ralph,'' she said. ''I will grant you that. If only you had some of your dear papa's firmness of manner, you would promise very well. I will not be cheap, you know. The dower house will need a great many changes before it will be a suitable establishment for me.''

''I told you, Mama,'' he said, straightening up and laying one hand on her shoulder, ''you may have a free hand. It will be a Christmas present that will come to you with all my love.''

Gloria had been listening quietly from across the room. ''Mama,'' she said now, ''I believe that if you look very closely, you will find that Ralph's gentleness of manner hides a remarkably firm character. I am exceedingly proud of my brother.''

Georgiana saved Ralph from the embarrassment of having to reply. Though as to that, he thought as his eyes alighted on his wife, this was a moment he had been dreading all day. He had not seen her since before his visit to Kensington the night before. He had not known quite how he would face her without his guilt and shame showing for all to see.

Georgiana beamed on everyone, her eyes sliding away from Ralph so that he was saved from the ordeal of having to meet her gaze. She was flushed from walking and was unusually animated. She started talking immediately, telling them about visiting her mother and sister and finding Roger there, going walking with him and Vera and having the good fortune of running into her old friend Dennis Vaughan, who had been obliging enough to walk with them for fifteen minutes and tell

them all about his summer at Brighton, where he had
actually seen the Regent's pavilion, which he judged to
be a monstrosity and an uncomfortable building to be
inside because Prince George kept it so hot that ladies
were always fainting all over the place, but Prinny never
would admit that it was less healthy to exclude all fresh
air than it would have been to risk some drafts now and
then.

The dowager cut off this breathless monologue by
telling her to sit down and pour herself some tea from
the pot, which was still hot. Ralph had been watching
her with growing wonder. What had wrought this
change? Had Roger or this Vaughan had something to
do with it? He knew a sudden stab of guilt over the fact
that she had to seek companionship from men other
than himself. He had given up taking her out in the
daytime when it became clear that they could not be
alone.

"Do you have enough energy left to go out for dinner
tonight, Georgiana?" he asked.

She turned her attention to him, and the flush on her
cheeks seemed to deepen. "Oh, where?" she asked.

"Lord Standen has invited us together with some
other guests, I believe," he said. "I said we would
come."

"That would be lovely," she said, her voice sounding
breathless to his ears. She smiled.

"You really should do less walking, my dear," the
dowager said to her. "You will ruin your complexion. If
you are going out tonight, I would suggest a rest for an
hour. You do not want shadows under your eyes. There
is nothing more calculated to make a person look
hagged."

Georgiana turned the smile on her mother-in-law.
"That is a good idea, Mother," she said. "If you will
excuse me, I think I shall take your advice. Will my blue
satin and lace gown be suitable, Ralph? And my
pearls?"

"Perfect," he said, rising to open the door for her. "And your complexion looks very far from ruined to me, dear."

He followed her upstairs a few minutes later. It was far too early to get ready for dinner, but he too felt that a rest might do him good. He was having a hard time keeping his eyes open.

He was soon in a pleasantly drowsy state, lying on top of the covers on his bed, his hands linked behind his head. There was a fire crackling in the grate, giving off a cozy warmth. He was glad that he and Georgiana were going out to dinner. Just the two of them. She had seemed quite delighted when he mentioned the engagement to her. He had expected some opposition. Lord Standen's parties were not renowned for the gaiety of the entertainment they offered. Rather, they were usually gathering grounds for intellectual conversation and the interchange of political ideas. Perhaps Georgiana did not know that.

She had seemed so happy and glowing when she returned from her walk. He had seen her like that only at Chartleigh, when she was planning her dinner party. He wished she could always be thus. He wished he could bring her to life like that. She had been walking with her sister and with Roger and the unknown Dennis Vaughan. It must have been this old friend of hers who had made her so happy.

Ralph sighed. He knew so little about her. He had never thought to ask her to tell him about herself. She had been in London since early in the spring. She had taken part in all the whirl of the Season. She had been presented at St. James's. And she was young, attractive. Was it not likely that she had many friends of whom he knew nothing? She had probably had several admirers. Was there anyone in particular whom she had had to renounce in order to marry him? he wondered. Perhaps this Vaughn was someone she had loved? But no, he did not think so. Surely she would have looked tragic this afternoon if she had met him under such circumstances. She had seemed genuinely delighted by the meeting.

But she had smiled at him. She had readily agreed to accompany him to Lord Standen's. She had consulted him about the gown she should wear. And she seemed to have chosen something with which she could wear his pearls. He must not miss the opportunity with which she was presenting him. If there was a chance that a warmer relationship between them could develop this evening, even if only a friendship, he must not lose it.

He wanted Georgiana very badly. Not just her body, though he ached for that. He wanted her companionship, her respect, her love. And that need had only intensified since the night before. Ralph closed his eyes and relived his encounter with Sally Shaw. He no longer wished to think of her by name. He did not wish to picture her as she had appeared at the opera. He wanted only to remember how she had felt in his arms.

She was small and very shapely, her skin soft and incredibly smooth. He had not expected her to be naked. But he gloried now in the memory of his hands moving over her, learning some of the mysteries of a beautiful woman's body. And she was beautiful. It was a tragedy that she sullied that beauty with paint. He supposed that there was something extremely sordid about what had happened. He had coupled with a woman he did not know, a woman whom he had not even seen close. But it had not seemed sordid. She had offered herself sweetly and undemandingly. He had felt no fear of clumsiness or failure as he discovered inside her body the delights that he had dreamed of for several years.

She must be very skilled in her art. She had shown no signs of distaste or boredom, and no impatience to be rid of his weight or his person when it was all over. He found himself all impatience for the two days to pass until he could be with her again.

Did he feel guilty? He rather feared that he did not. He had been unfaithful to the wife he claimed to love, and he planned to repeat the infidelity, probably many times. He should despise himself. He had only to think of Georgiana to know that it was she he wanted. And could one want two women at the same time? He very much suspected that one could. Georgiana was beyond his reach at present. He was not quite sure why this was so. There was no nameable barrier between them, but there was a very real one nevertheless.

He had begun their marriage all wrong, giving in to timidity just at the time when he had most needed to be decisive. He was sure that if he had consummated their marriage on their wedding night, they could have made the adjustment to married life and begun to build an affectionate relationship, even if the process had taken time. He might have been clumsy. He might have hurt her. It might have been a very unsatisfactory wedding night. But it could have been lived down. The fact that he had left her had paralyzed all future action. Not only for him. There had been that one occasion when he had been close again to making love to her. But she had lost her courage.

It was a ridiculous situation they found themselves in. Ralph was sure that most people of his acquaintance would hold him in the utmost contempt if they knew. Here he was, with the courage to hire himself a whore and take his pleasure with her, yet terrified into inaction by the mere thought of going to his wife, who slept nightly in a room adjoining his own. He really did not wish to dwell on the thought. It shook to the roots his newfound sense of manhood.

Georgiana. His love. His biggest failure in life.

13

THE EVENING at Lord Standen's townhouse was indeed quite different from anything Georgiana had expected. Most of the guests were male, and most were considerably older than either she or Ralph. Normally she felt quite unselfconscious in a crowd and could converse with the greatest of ease with whoever happened to be near her. On this occasion, she felt out of her depth. This was no frivolous social occasion.

Yet Ralph, she noticed with some interest, seemed immediately to be in his element. After some introductions had been made on their entry into the drawing room, he drew her into a group that was talking animatedly about something to do with taxes and land reform. She did try at first to follow what was being said, but her attention quickly wandered.

It was caught by a young lady on the other side of the room, almost the only person in the room, in fact, noticeably below the age of thirty, with the exception of her and Ralph, and the man on whose arm the girl's hand rested. He was a slightly built young man with a thin, ascetic face and a shock of unruly black curls, a marked contrast to the blond beauty of his companion. Georgiana had been introduced to both a mere few minutes before, but she could not remember their names.

She caught the eye of the young lady, who smiled and beckoned her. Georgiana removed her hand from Ralph's arm and crossed the room.

"Do join us, Lady Chartleigh," the girl said. Her

beauty was quite flawless, Georgiana saw. "I daresay you are rather dismayed to find yourself in company with so many dry old sticks. I must not say that very loudly, of course, but Standen's parties are not strong on excitement."

"Oh," Georgiana said. "I had not realized I was looking so bored."

The girl dimpled. "I used to be terrified of him," she said, "Until Nigel told me that my own opinions are quite as valuable as anyone else's. I must say I still stand in some awe of all this superior intellect. These people all make me feel the merest peagoose. But sometimes the most intelligent people are not the most practical people. Is that not true, Nigel?"

The dark young man looked gravely at her. "Quite so, my love," he said. "But they are also the most powerful people and ultimately will be able to do far more than you or I to set right the inequalities of our social system."

"Lady Chartleigh," the girl said, "I can see that you look quite bewildered. And how foolish of me to forget that when one is introduced to twenty new faces in fewer minutes, one is unlikely to remember a single one of them afterward. This is my husband, Nigel Broome. He is Standen's brother, you know, though you would never guess from looking at them, would you? I am Sylvia Broome. Like you, we have been married only a few months."

Georgiana relaxed. Here was someone as ordinary as herself, a girl of her own age, surely. In fact, now that she looked more closely, she seemed to remember having seen Sylvia Broome before, probably at some of the social events of the spring. She smiled and began to talk.

It was a strange evening. No cards. No dancing. No music. No charades. Just conversation, and lots of it. But Georgiana had made friends with Sylvia and Nigel Broome by the end of it. They were a fascinating couple, she found. They were deeply devoted to each other although physically they seemed such a mismatch. Sylvia had a habit of prefacing much of what she said with "Nigel says . . ." And he never failed to listen with the whole of his attention to everything she said, no matter how seemingly frivolous.

What made them most fascinating to her, though, was the fact that they did not spend their days in fashionable idleness. Not for them the constant fight against boredom that she knew from her own life and which had often led her into all sorts of troublesome scrapes. Nigel ran a school for destitute boys in their own home. They had twenty enrolled, though actual numbers fluctuated quite alarmingly, they confided. It was their sole ambition to give the boys enough of an education to enable them to get positions as servants or perhaps even clerks.

"When you see the reality of the situation, you quickly lose your larger ambitions," Nigel Broome explained. "We have no dream of reforming the world. If we can be of small help to a mere handful of boys so that they have some future instead of none at all, we will feel that our venture has been a success. As Sylvia once said, the ocean is made up of little drops of water. Each little drop is as important as any other."

"But in your own home!" Georgiana said, turning to Sylvia. "How can you bear it?"

"The adjustment has certainly not been easy," the girl said, laughing. "I lived a retired and very pampered life in the country until my guardian brought me to London this year, you know. But Nigel says that being able to adapt to change is part of maturing, and Nigel is always there to calm me down when I am ready to say I can take no more. It is a challenging life, Lady Chartleigh. Looking back, I can hardly recognize the girl I was a mere few months ago—a timid, frivolous ninnyhammer of a girl."

"You were never that, my love," her husband said gravely.

Ralph joined them partway through their conversation. He sat beside Georgiana and smiled at her. She felt a rush of warmth. How good it was to sit thus with one's husband, conversing with another equally young but very interesting couple. There was something very domesticated about the scene. And how horrified by the very notion she would have been only a couple of months before. Sylvia Broome was right. One did change very quickly after marriage—even after a very incomplete and unsatisfactory marriage.

"How does your brother react to your project?" Ralph asked Nigel Broome. "He seems very set on bringing about sweeping social changes in the country."

Nigel smiled. "I am afraid we do not always see eye to eye," he said. "It might seem surprising since we have very similar ideas. But my charge is always that my brother's head is in the clouds. Airy notions do not bring about the changes that are so desperately needed, or if they do, those changes come about so slowly that whole generations suffer in the meanwhile. He charges that my solution helps so few people that it is quite worthless. We keep the peace by agreeing to disagree."

Later, in the carriage on the way home, Ralph took Georgiana's hand, something he had not done for a while. "Are you very tired, my dear?" he asked.

Georgiana yawned. "Mmm," she said. She was resisting the urge to rest her head on his shoulder. As it was, she had allowed the motion of the carriage to tilt her sideways so that her shoulder was propped against his arm.

"I am glad the Broomes were there," he said. "I had not met them before, though Standen has spoken of his brother. He was betrothed to Sylvia Broome, you know."

"Who?" she asked.

"Standen," he said. "But something happened and she was forced to marry his brother."

"How strange," she said. "I would say she has made the wiser choice, though, even though Lord Standen is vastly more handsome than her husband."

He turned his head and smiled down at her. His cheek brushed against her hair for a moment. "Did you like them?" he asked. "I was afraid for a while that you would be dreadfully bored, Georgiana."

"I would not have minded," she said gallantly. "You like that sort of gathering, do you not, Ralph? I think you must be very intelligent and have a very superior education. I must seem very dull to you. I have not read very much and I have never thought very deeply about any really important topic."

"Georgiana!" he said, turning toward her in the darkness of the carriage and squeezing her hand. "Do not belittle yourself. You have not had occasion, perhaps, to think a great deal on serious matters. But you have qualities of character that I find most enviable. You have the courage and the warmth to show to advantage in almost any situation."

"Oh," she said. "Ralph, when I talk to someone like Sylvia Broome, I think of how very useless my life has been. And I do admire her tremendously. But I do not believe I could live her kind of life. To have one's home invaded by boys from the street! I think I should become cross beyond all belief and be screeching at them like a barn owl before a day was out."

He laughed and drew her arm through his so that her shoulder rested comfortably against his arm again. "Then I must be careful never to suggest opening a school for boys in Middleton House," he said. He added quietly, "But I must find something to do, dear. I am not quite sure what. Will you mind?"

She shook her head and gave in to the temptation to rest her cheek against his shoulder. They rode home in companionable silence and climbed the stairs together to their rooms. Ralph stopped outside her door and looked down at her.

"I hope it has not been a dreadfully dull evening for you," he said.

How could she convey to him the fact that any activity this evening would have been a delight provided only she could see him and be in the same room as he?

"I have enjoyed it," she said. "I think I have learned something about your life, Ralph."

He smiled and brushed the fingers of one hand against her cheek. "You are a very sweet person, Georgiana," he said.

She felt herself become breathless. What stopped her from reaching out and putting her hands against his chest or around his neck? Or from taking his hand and opening the door of her bedchamber as she had the night before in a different house? And what prevented him from taking her in his arms? Or leaning across her and opening the door himself? What was it that was between them when there was no apparent reason for any barrier at all?

They looked into each other's eyes only long enough to know that there was no breaching that invisible wall yet. He bent his head and kissed her very softly on the lips.

"Good night, dear," he said.

"Good night, Ralph."

The formality of their words rang in Georgiana's ears as she stood on the other side of the door a few moments later, leaning back against it, the tears wet on her cheeks.

For the next two days Georgiana was very restless. It seemed to her that the time would never come when Roger would again take her to Kensington and she would again don her disguise for her meeting with Ralph. She was all impatience. In the meantime she tried to interest herself in what was going on around her. She went shopping with Gloria for more bride clothes, visited Lady Beauchamp with her mother-in-law, visited her own parents on the occasion of her father's birthday, and wandered around Middleton House, examining each room with a critical eye and imagining how it would look with some changes.

She was only just beginning to digest the fact that this

house was now hers, that she was its mistress. It was a magnificent house, but the furnishings were heavy and old-fashioned. Georgiana hated furniture loaded down with ornate carvings and gilt trimmings. She much preferred simple elegance. And reds predominated far too much in the house, she felt. She would like softer tones to make the rooms lighter and more airy. She would like to see all the family portraits arranged in the upper gallery, where there was light and space enough to show them to advantage. If she had her way, they would all be removed from the living rooms and replaced with landscapes.

She wondered what Ralph would say if she told him of her ideas. She certainly foresaw battles with his mother, who could not seem to accept the presence of Georgiana in what she still considered as her own home.

And Georgiana had a visitor. Dennis Vaughan called on the first afternoon and stayed for a whole hour. She heard someone else at the door while he was with her and was disappointed to discover that it was not Ralph. She would have liked her old friend to meet him. They would have nothing in common, of course. Dennis would appear quite trivial-minded beside Ralph. She even admitted to herself with a little twinge of surprise that she wanted Dennis to see that she had married someone above the ordinary touch. She recalled feeling just before her marriage that she would be ashamed for her friends to see the sort of man she had been forced into accepting.

It was Stanley who had come in. He came and talked with Dennis for a while before leaving the room again. Georgiana was starting to feel rather uneasy around Ralph's brother. He was always civil, but she had a feeling that he disliked her and disapproved of her. He could not possibly be more unlike Ralph. She put him from her mind.

She spent a pleasant evening with Ralph the day after the Standen party. The rest of the family had been invited out after dinner, and Georgiana followed her husband to the library.

"Do you mind if I sit in here to do my embroidery?" she asked. "I shall not disturb you."

"Of course not, Georgiana," he said. "I merely came to choose a book. I intended to join you in the drawing room."

"Would you not prefer to stay here?" she asked. "It is a much cozier room."

And they sat, one on each side of the fire, for an hour or more, she sewing, he reading, with scarcely a word passing between them. Just like an old married couple, Georgiana thought with deep content. So life should be at times. One could not forever be going out, searching for any activity that might alleviate boredom for a few hours.

She looked up under her eyebrows at him a few times. He was quite engrossed in his reading. She might have felt some resentment against his books, which could take him so completely away from her. But he looked very endearing, slouched down somewhat in his chair, one elbow propped on the armrest, his hand pushing at his hair, which was looking more disheveled than usual. His face held a slight frown of concentration.

Men must be very different from women, she concluded. He seemed utterly absorbed in his book, just as if he had never visited a certain house in Kensington two nights before and just as if he had made no plans to go there again the following night. Had it really meant so little to him? Was it perhaps just a light flirtation for him, something he would have indulged in even if their marriage was a normal one? She did not care to investigate that thought further. Or did the meetings mean something to him, but he had the ability to put them out of his mind? Could men compartmentalize their lives, love and all its associated emotions being but one compartment? That thought too was not an attractive one.

She could not think of anything else but their liaison. Two nights ago she had given herself to her husband for the first time. It was not an event to be forgotten in a moment or shrugged off as a thing of little importance.

It had been such a very physical act, so much so that she could not be in the same room as Ralph now without feeling an ache of awareness of him. She could feel him now, his long leanness pressing down on her, his manhood a hard and welcome pain inside her. Just a glance at him now could set her heart to thumping and her womb to throbbing.

How could he sit there reading, oblivious of her very presence, when she could not wait for tomorrow night, when it would all happen again? Tomorrow she would not be frightened or unsure of herself. She would be able to enjoy every moment. And she hoped it would last longer. So much waiting for a mere few minutes of delight! Of course, she thought suddenly, Ralph did not know that it was she with whom he had lain. But how could he not know? How could he not feel now that it must be she?

Ralph, she thought, stitching away sedately at her embroidery, when I married you I hoped that I would be able to tolerate you. After a few days of marriage I thought that perhaps I might be able to develop an affection for you. Now I think I might be in a fair way of falling in love with you. She glanced up at him again, startled by her own thoughts. He was looking at her.

"I am very dull company, am I not, dear?" he said. "Would you like to come to the music room and play for me?"

She smiled across at him and shook her head. "No, carry on reading," she said. "I know that is what you like to do, Ralph. I think perhaps I will choose a book too. The only trouble is that I am not a reader and do not know where to start. What would you recommend?"

He put down his own book and got to his feet. He held out a hand to take one of hers. "Let us see," he said. "Poetry? Perhaps you would enjoy Thomson's *Seasons*." He took a slim leather-bound volume from a shelf and handed it to her. "Or a novel? Richardson's *Pamela* is quite readable, though you might find that the sentiment is somewhat objectionable. It is a very long book, too."

"Oh, dear," Georgiana said when he set three volumes in her hands. "This is all one book? Let me try the poetry, Ralph. Is it easy to understand?"

"Shall we read it together?" he suggested. "Perhaps if we put our heads together, we can interpet any lines that are a little difficult."

"You are very tactful," she said. "What you really mean is that you will be able to explain the meaning to me."

"You belittle yourself, Georgiana," he said gently, and he pulled up a chair alongside hers while she folded up her work and put it away in its basket.

When she was in her own room later, Georgiana marveled at the fact that she too had forgotten all about Kensington in the hour they had spent together with the book. Ralph was a born teacher. They had both talked about the poetry, but she knew that her own insights had been drawn from her with skilled questions. She had never dreamed that reading could be such an absorbing activity. And she had not thought in the last few days that her intense awareness of her husband could be anything but sexual. For an hour she had been totally captivated by his intelligent and active mind. She had been borne upward by it, beyond herself.

She had been actively disappointed when Ralph's mother and sister arrived home and came into the library to share some tidbits of gossip they had heard during the evening visit. The spell was broken. She was again herself. He was again Ralph, the husband from whom she was estranged, if that was the right word. She supposed that two people must at one time have been close if they could be estranged. They were again the couple whose marriage had never made a proper start. Still the couple who said good night at a respectable hour and retired to their very separate chambers.

She started to long for the following night again.

* * *

Ralph handed his caped greatcoat and beaver hat to
the porter when he reached the house in Kensington. He
resolutely put from his mind thoughts of Georgiana and
the very happy turn their relationship had taken in the
past two days. They were in a fair way to becoming
friends, he felt. But they were far from being lovers still.
He would not think of her for the next hour. He had
waited with impatience for three days for this moment.
He was going to enjoy it.

She was waiting in the dimly lit sitting room as she
had been before. She rose to her feet when he entered as
she had then. It was almost like going back in time. He
crossed the room to take her gloved hand. It was quite
impossible to see her face beneath the heavy black veil.
But he did not wish to do so. He would be repelled to see
the hennaed hair and the features of a stranger. He
raised her hand to his lips.

"I do not like to think of you alone on the streets
coming here and leaving," he said. "Will you change
your mind about taking up residence here for a while,
Miss Shaw? It can be easily arranged, you know."

She shook her head. "No," she said in that whisper
she had used on the other occasion.

It must be that she had other lovers, he thought, and
pushed the thought from his mind. He was not sure yet
if he wished to set her up as his mistress, under his sole
protection. But he thought not. For him this was to be a
very temporary interlude.

"Shall we go into the other room?" he asked.

This time he found his way to the bed with rather
more ease than he had the last time. He did not think he
had ever been in a room from which even the faintest
glimmer of light had been so ruthlessly excluded. He
undressed and climbed into the bed.

She was already there, naked as before, but warm this
time. Excitingly warm. He propped himself on one
elbow and clasped her shoulder, pushing against it until
she turned over onto her back. And he began to explore

her body, unafraid tonight, savoring every move, post-poning the moment when he would mount her body and give himself up to the demands of his physical need.

Her shoulders and arms were very delicate and slender. Her full, firm breasts were a surprise in contrast. So very feminine. He touched them lightly at first and then with greater boldness, molding them in his hands, touching the tips with wonder as he felt them harden against his thumbs. He lowered his head hesitantly and kissed one hardened nipple. He took it into his mouth and sucked gently. The girl pushed up against him and made a low sound in her throat.

His hands slid lower as his mouth moved to the other breast, spanning her tiny waist, pushing down on her flaring hips, tracing the outside of her legs and then her inner thighs. Her flesh was even warmer than his hand. She was burning him. His hand nudged at her thighs with some urgency and she opened for him. He buried his face between her breasts and felt her with his hand. His fingers explored her, caressed her, gloried in the heat of her.

And then her fingers were tight in his hair, the upper part of her body arched toward him, and he was rising to meet her, toppling her to the bed again, bringing himself down on top of her nakedness and pushing up urgently into the soft heat beyond where his fingers had reached.

His arms went around her slight little body and he buried his face against her soft curls as he thrust and thrust into her, heedless of gentleness, heedless of the moans that escaped her, heedless of everything except the elemental need to reach that moment of glory when all the tensions of his desire would be released into the woman's body that he possessed.

She was shaking slightly beneath him when he came to his senses again. He did not know how long he had been lying thus. Had he been sleeping? He rolled off her, but kept his arms around her and brought her with

him. He held her close against him and pulled the
blankets up around her shoulders. She was still
trembling.

"Did I hurt you?" he asked. "I am sorry. I forgot to
be gentle."

"No," she whispered, "you did not hurt me."

And what an absurd thing to have said, he thought.
This girl had doubtless been subjected to indignities that
he could not even dream of. It was not in her power to
object to the treatment she received in a man's bed. She
was paid to be compliant.

Ralph felt a twinge of distaste for what he was doing.
This was a person he held in his arms, a woman doubtless with dreams and hopes and feelings. He tried to
put a face to the physical presence he could feel. But he
could not. He could not associate the pretty and rather
vulgar little dancer of the opera house with the soft and
still slightly trembling body that cuddled against him.

She was Georgiana's size. Just thus Georgiana would
feel, if she could ever overcome her fear of him
sufficiently to cling to him so trustingly. He closed his
eyes and laid his cheek against the soft curls of the
dancer and imagined that they were dark, glossy curls
instead of garish red ones. It would be so easy to
fantasize, to imagine that it was his wife with whom he
had just made love.

The girl had stopped trembling. She had relaxed
against him. Her breathing had become deep and even.
She was sleeping, Ralph realized in surprise. Somehow
he had not expected a paid whore to sleep after such an
encounter. He would have expected her to be eager to be
gone, her work done for another night. Perhaps she was
really tired? What must it be like to be forced to work
on after a night of dancing in order to earn enough
money to make a living?

He was glad she was sleeping. He did not feel like
leaving yet. He did not want to lose contact with her and
know that several more days must pass before he could
hold her again. He remembered the way she had offered
herself to him with something like urgency just before

he entered her. He remembered the sounds she had made as he moved in her. Did she feel she must be an actress in bed as well as on the stage? She surely could not have been feeling the eagerness her actions had suggested.

He was so inexperienced, Ralph thought ruefully. Not that he was really sorry. He did not think he would crave contact with the muslin company once this particular liaison was at an end. If only his marriage to Georgiana could be set right, he would be perfectly content to explore the world of sexual delights with her and to learn further pleasures with her.

The girl woke suddenly with a start and Ralph hugged her to him, knowing that however disappointed she might be, and however unfair to her he was being, he must have her again before he left. He rolled with her on the bed and was relieved to find that she accepted this new duty without objection or hesitation.

He took her quickly and deeply, his eyes tightly closed, seeing and feeling his wife beneath him. And she lay submissively beneath him, this girl, perhaps living out her own fantasies.

14

SEVEN WEEKS PASSED with amazing rapidity. Georgiana lived them almost in a dream. She knew that her life was not a satisfactory one, that there would have to be many changes before she could feel that there was stability and true contentment in her home. But this knowledge was of the head. With her heart she was happy, almost deliriously so. Perhaps the present state of affairs could not continue indefinitely, but she would not think of that. She would enjoy the present for what it was worth.

She was in love with Ralph, deeply, headlong, passionately, head over heels in love. And she felt that the fact must show on her face. She could not feel as she did and show no outer sign, surely. She tried not to look or behave differently from usual. She went about her day-to-day activities as if nothing had changed in her life. But she was convinced that one day Ralph must look at her and know the truth.

The wonderful thing was that she had fallen in love with him in his two persons. She was in love with the lover who came to her and bedded her twice each week. She was equally in love with the husband who showed no physical sign of attachment, but whose behavior toward her suggested a growing affection.

She had not expected that physical love could become a craving for her. She had looked forward to marriage as a means of being independent of her parents and becoming someone of consequence in society. She had thought of the physical side of it with some misgiving, as something she must get used to, since men appeared to need it and it was necessary anyway for the begetting of children. She had been prepared to endure.

But Ralph could rouse her body to unimagined delights. She did not know how he did it. He had no more experience than she. Less, in fact. He had never even kissed before his marriage. His skill must be instinctive, a part of his natural gentleness of manner probably. He could do things to her with his hands and his mouth that reduced her to raw sensation. And his driving presence inside her body could lift her beyond feeling, over the edge into blissful nothingness. And he was always there afterward with warm arms and body to cradle her back into this world and back into her body.

It was not always like that with him. Sometimes he took her without first using his hands to excite her. But she found that she enjoyed these encounters equally. Perhaps even more. When she was aroused she forgot everything except her body's need. She forgot Ralph and even herself. On the other occasions she could remain fully aware of what was happening and could enjoy thoroughly the knowledge that it was her husband embracing her, occupying her body, moving in her, making those low sounds of pleasure that he always made against her hair as he climaxed. One did not need an earth-shattering experience to enjoy the marriage act, she found.

She almost lived for those nights. And she willed time to slowness when they were together. With the exception of the first time he had come to her, he always took her twice. And she found herself loving more than anything the time between, when she could cuddle against his body, warm and relaxed, knowing that soon, but not too soon, he would turn her onto her back again or lift her astride his body and they would be one again. She always smiled into the darkness when he apologized for needing her more than once. If he just knew! Just for the luxury of spending a whole night with him she would have let him take her ten times!

It had been an agony to her to have to tell him one

night that she would be unable to keep their next regular appointment. A whole week had passed with no more than a chance touch of his hand at home. But she might have avoided the frustration. Nothing had happened in its regular monthly pattern, and nothing had happened in the more than three weeks since.

Her newness to sexual activity must have upset her system, Georgiana decided. She could not be with child. It could not happen that quickly or that easily, surely. Besides, would she not know if she were pregnant? Surely one could not have one's husband's child on one's womb without feeling it there. And did not women vomit and have the vapors all over the place when they were in such a delicate situation? No, she was not with child.

She hoped she was not! As it was, she was beginning to realize that she had trapped herself into one of her hopeless tangles, except that this one was worse than any of the others had ever been. Life was wonderful at the moment. But sooner or later she was going to have to reveal the truth to Ralph. And how would he feel about it? He would feel a fool, probably, to discover that he had been sneaking away at night to make love to the wife who slept nightly a few feet away from him. And she could not afford to make Ralph feel foolish. He had very little self-confidence as it was.

Soon now she was going to have to find a tactful way to tell him. She certainly did not need to be pressured by the presence of a baby pushing her out of shape. How quickly did one develop a bulge, anyway?

But it would be wonderful to have a baby with Ralph, she thought despite herself. As soon as he knew the truth and their marriage had become a normal one, she would ask him if she might have one. Though she supposed that she need not ask. Once he was making love to her nightly in her own bed, it would happen in its own good time, she rather suspected. Oh dear, she was so inexperienced, so woefully ignorant. She, who had thought just a few short months ago that she knew everything there was to know!

But her love for Ralph was developing not only through their clandestine meetings. She was getting to know him in an everyday setting and growing to love the person he was. She could not imagine why she felt as she did. He was not at all the sort of man she had always admired and associated with. She had always liked men who were strong and confident and physically very active. She had liked daring men, ones who were willing to take a risk and accept a wager for the sheer fun of doing something out of the ordinary. Warren Haines had once wagered a great deal of money on his ability to outdrink a notorious heavy drinker. He had won the bet and spent three days in bed violently ill. And Georgiana had admired him tremendously.

She had not liked Ralph at first because he was not a "manly" man. Whatever that description meant. Whatever was manly about being able to outdrink a fellow fool and half-killing oneself into the bargain?

Ralph was incredibly gentle. Somehow he managed to keep the peace at home, even though the atmosphere between her and her mother-in-law was frequently tense. She had noticed that he somehow succeeded in making both women feel as if they had his support. And she could not be offended at his not turning against his mother. She could see that he genuinely loved the dowager, whom she found it extremely difficult even to tolerate. She had heard about his plans to give his mother the dower house at Chartleigh for a Christmas present. And she marveled at the way he had made his mother enthusiastic for a move that should have upset her dreadfully.

They had been driving to the lending library one afternoon when Ralph drew the phaeton to a sharp halt and handed her the ribbons. He vaulted down into a crowded street and reappeared with a scruffy little dog in his arms. She had half-noticed the dog being beaten with a stick as they approached but had thought very little of it. Such sights were quite common. Ralph deposited the mutt in her lap before climbing to his seat again, and she gave a little shriek as she noticed the grime of its fur and the blood on one side that immediately stained her pelisse.

Ralph apologized and moved to take the dog into his own arms again. But first he took a linen handkerchief from his pocket and laid it gently against the creature's injured side. And she felt ashamed of her concern for her own appearance and tender toward the man who had noticed the suffering even of a small animal in the crowded streets of London. The mutt, now clean and healed of its wound, spent its days in the kitchen, where the cook constantly threatened to do away with it for being always under her feet and just as constantly fed it the choicest scraps of food from her store.

And Ralph was educating her, though she thought he would be surprised if he realized that she put the matter that way to herself. She was learning to enjoy reading when he was in the same room. One of the greatest pleasures of her days came when they sat together and shared a book, discussing some poem. She talked and gave her views, but she loved to listen to him interpret a passage that had seemed to her to have a very obvious meaning. He could see depths of thought that had completely passed over her head. And yet there was no intellectual conceit in him. She doubted that he even realized that his ideas were of such greater value than her own. He always listened to her attentively.

He took her to art galleries and museums, places she had always shunned as dry gatherers of dust and worthless junk. She would still not have enjoyed the visits greatly, she admitted, if Ralph were not there to explain things to her and bring to life an object that was just that to her and no more. She started for the first time to believe that it would be a pleasurable experience to travel to Florence and Milan and Rome and all those other places that many travelers visited out of a sense of duty only.

With Ralph she was learning that one did not need to be constantly out and doing in order to bring meaning and enjoyment to life. Not that they shunned the brighter entertainments. Now that more and more members of the *ton* were returning to the capital for the winter, there were frequent invitations. And they refused only those they genuinely could not keep. They attended parties, musical evenings, theater parties, even one ball.

Ralph did not shine at such entertainments. He was not naturally sociable. But he did not shun contact with others. He could be relied upon to seek out someone—usually a female—who was isolated from the company for one reason or another. And he would sit quietly conversing with these people—aging spinsters, young girls without either looks or fortune, even chaperones, who were usually beneath the notice of the *ton*. If some of his friends from the House of Lords were present, of course, he would be engrossed in serious conversation.

Georgiana loved to keep an eye on him while she danced or chatted with gayer companions. She was inordinately proud of him and came very close to quarreling loudly with Dennis Vaughan one evening when he joked that Ralph blended in quite well with the row of chaperones amongst whom he sat for one particular set.

One afternoon Ralph took her to visit the Broomes. They did not live in the most fashionable part of London. Georgiana felt apprehensive. The school would be in progress. Were they to expect noise and chaos and dirt?

She was pleasantly surprised when a maid ushered them into a tiled hallway and took their coats. The only sound was a distant, unidentifiable murmur. And the hallway, though rather small, was neat and spotlessly clean. Sylvia Broome came hurrying down the staircase before they could be shown into any room, her hands extended.

"How wonderful!" she said. "I am so happy you have come. We do not have very many visitors during the daytime. Some people, I believe, think that they will be coming into a den of thieves if they set foot in here."

She laughed lightly and instructed the maid to take Lord Chartleigh to her husband.

"That is, if you wish to meet our boys?" she said, eyebrows lifted in inquiry.

"I had hoped to do so," Ralph said. "Will your husband mind?"

Georgiana was taken to a cozy sitting room by her hostess, who immediately rang for tea. And she found again that she liked this girl, who was the same age as herself yet who seemed very mature.

"I am so happy to see you, Georgiana," Sylvia said. "I lived a quiet life in the country until last spring, you know, but I always had my cousin with me to talk to. She is on a wedding trip in Italy and like to be away for almost a year if Edward has his way. And I do miss her. Do you mind my calling you by your given name?"

"My friends call me Georgie," Georgiana said.

Sylvia laughed. "I like it," she said. "It suits you. You used to be quite a madcap, didn't you? I remember hearing of your racing in the park during the fashionable hour, when it is considered quite unacceptable to move faster than a slow crawl."

"Oh dear," Georgiana said. "That does seem to be a long time ago. Is it your cousin who married the Earl of Raymore? I heard of his wedding a few months ago."

Sylvia nodded. "We were both most fortunate," she said. "We both made love matches. Is it not wonderful to love one's husband? I can tell that you and Lord Chartleigh are very attached to each other too. He is a lovely person. I had not met him before Standen's party."

"He has been at university," Georgiana explained. "He is only one-and-twenty, you know. Three years older than I. I had not met him myself before . . . Well, he offered for me at our second meeting, you see. It was an arranged marriage."

"How dreadful for you!" Sylvia exclaimed. "But how wonderful to discover that your parents had allied you to the very man you would have chosen for yourself if given the chance."

"Yes," Georgiana agreed. "Except that I do not believe I would have had the good sense to choose him. I have grown to love him since our wedding."

Sylvia laughed again. "I was foolish enough to let Nigel talk me into betrothing myself to his brother," she said. "It was only afterward that we realized that it was each other we wanted. I had to think of a desperate scheme to set things right. I still feel almost guilty when I think of it. Almost! But when I look at Standen, I know that we would have been very unhappy. As a brother-in-law I can admire him and even feel affection for him. As a husband I would have feared him and come to hate him."

The hour that passed until Ralph and Nigel Broome joined them in the sitting room seemed no longer than five minutes. Georgiana found a very easy friendship developing between Sylvia and her. The other couple had promised to dine with them before they left for home.

Ralph was impressed with Nigel Broome's school. He talked to her on the journey home about his own dream of doing something worthwhile with his time and fortune and position of influence. Chartleigh was a large estate. Could he set up some sort of project that would occupy the people from the village workhouse? he wondered. Charity was not the answer. He could give all the inmates of the institution enough money on which to live in comfort and still not beggar himself. But that would not restore their self-respect or satisfy their human need to feel in control of their own lives and destinies. It was jobs they needed. What did Georgiana think?

Georgiana had never done any thinking along those lines. She was in the habit of agreeing with the general feeling of her class that the poor were poor because they were idle and lazy. But she had learned respect for Ralph's mind. If he said these people needed jobs and faith in themselves, then it must be so. She felt a warm glow of happiness that he would discuss his thoughts with her and ask her opinion. Just as if she were a real person who mattered, instead of a feather-brained female who needed to be bullied to stay out of scrapes.

"I don't know, Ralph," she said. "But I am sure you will think of a solution. And I know it will be the right one. And if it means spending a great deal of money, you are not to mind me. I shall be quite content to stay at Chartleigh if we cannot afford to keep up the town house. And I have quite enough clothes and faradiddles to last me until I am quite middle-aged."

And what was more, she thought in some surprise as he laughed in amusement and assured her that he did not think they would be reduced to utter destitution, she meant it. She could live naked on a desert island for the rest of her life, provided Ralph was there with her, she thought with all the intense unrealism of one newly and deeply in love.

They were a happy seven weeks.

They were not quite so happy for Ralph. He was happy when he was with Georgiana and when he was with Sally. But he could find no peace of mind when he was alone.

He was delighted with the way his relationship with his wife was developing. She appeared to have lost her fear of him and a fragile friendship was growing. He was making an effort to spend more time with her, to get to know her, and to share something of himself with her. The last was not easy to do. Ralph had always been a very private person. He was accustomed to being alone, to feeling somewhat despised by most of the people with whom he was forced to associate. He had accepted his essential loneliness.

It was not easy for him to open his mind to his wife and risk indifference or ridicule. He took her to look at paintings and other works of art that meant a great deal to him. It would have hurt to find her impatient or openly contemptuous. And he shared some of his favorite works of literature with her, mostly poetry over which he had pondered for years. He knew that she was not a reader, that she had no use for the education that had been offered to her as a girl. She had told him as much.

He found true delight in discovering that she was receptive to the important things of his world. She had no confidence in her own opinions. She constantly belittled the power of her own mind. But she had an intelligence that seemed to have been untapped in her eighteen years of life. Her ideas were fresh, untainted by the opinions of books and scholars. More than once she gave him a fresh insight into some work he had long been familiar with.

And she showed no reluctance to use her mind. It seemed as if she genuinely wished to enter his world, to be a companion to him. One evening she had been invited to join a theater party with her own family. Knowing that he would be at home alone if she went, she had chosen rather to remain with him. They had spent the evening in the library, quietly involved in their own pursuits until she took a volume of Pope's poetry from a shelf and drew a chair close to his. She had smiled eagerly and handed him the book when he closed his own and put it down.

But it was not his wish to change her. He delighted in her gaiety, which he had so little suspected when they first married. She loved company and shone when other people were around her. She seemed made to dance, to converse, and to laugh. It became his practice to accept invitations that his own inclination would have led him to refuse. He did not particularly enjoy these parties, but he delighted in watching her, her face animated and flushed, her small, shapely figure always at the center of activity.

She was very popular with men; he guessed it was because she always looked directly at them and talked quite candidly. She never put on feminine airs, and she never flirted. Perhaps it was because of that fact that it never occurred to him to be jealous. And she did not ignore him. She always appeared to know where he was in a room and frequently looked across at him and smiled. He was very proud of her. How other men must envy him his wife!

He thought several times of trying to begin a physical relationship with her. There seemed to be no reason why he should not. She appeared to like him. She certainly made no attempts to avoid his company. But he was afraid. Things were going perhaps too well between them. He did not have the courage to risk losing all by forcing himself on her before she was ready. He would wait a little longer. He loved her too dearly to risk losing her.

His relationship with Sally Shaw had become much more serious than he had ever intended. He had certainly not planned for it to last so long. He had merely wanted to gain some experience and some confidence. He now had both and there was no reason to continue seeing her. But he found that he could not face the thought of losing her.

When he was with her, he was happy, utterly so. She had a perfect body. He had never failed to be totally satisfied with their couplings. He knew a feeling of well-being when he was with her that stayed with him for the days in between. Had that been the whole of it, though, he felt that he would have been willing to put an end to their affair.

But that was not the whole of it. There was something more than the physical between them. Why was it that one of his favorite times during their hour together was the spell between their lovemaking when they would merely lie together, their arms wrapped around each other? Why was he always so reluctant to leave her even when his body was thoroughly satiated?

He knew the reason. He was in love with her. No, not exactly. Not in love with her. In love with Georgiana. He was still repelled when he forced himself to recall with whom he was so frequently intimate. Once he even went to the opera, alone, just to remind himself of how she looked. He was appalled. His box was quite close to the stage. He was even more aware than on the previous occasion of the heaviness of the paint on her face and the artificiality of her hair color. He had gazed at her, quite unable to associate the unseen yet very familiar body of his mistress with this vulgar-looking creature on the stage.

She caught his eye at one point and smiled at him. No. Leered. There was a coquetry in her look that repelled him. He left the theater almost immediately and never went back again.

He found that he did not put her face to the body of his mistress. It became his fantasy that it was Georgiana he held. It was her with whom he made love. Sometimes he deliberately slowed down his own impulses so that he might give her pleasure. He would play with her with his hands and his mouth until he knew she was ready for his entry. And then he would move in her, denying his own climax until he knew by some instinct that she was ready for hers. And he would release into her at the very moment when he knew she would shudder against him and give that smothered cry he was becoming used to.

Why would he do so for a woman who was merely earning her living thus? It was in her interests to have the business over with as quickly as possible. He did it for Georgiana, dreaming that it was she to whom he was giving a pleasure that he knew was often denied women. He refused to puzzle over the surprising fact that he was obviously giving pleasure to a practiced courtesan.

He could have been happy if, like many men of his class, he had seen no wrong with having a wife and keeping a mistress both at the same time. But when he was alone, away from the pull that both women exerted on his heart, he did see wrong in what he was doing. What he had done had never been right, but at least at first it had been a purely business arrangement with a very definite motive on his part.

Now it was a lot more than that. The girl still rendered him a service. He still paid her well on each occasion. But there was a relationship between them for all that they did not exchange a dozen words during their encounters. In a strange way that defied words, he loved her. And the longer he had her, the more he grew familiar with her body, the more they slipped into happy routine, the harder it became to give her up.

Yet he loved his wife more deeply with each passing day. Quite passionately. He wanted her desperately. And he despised himself for making love to her through the body of another woman. Ralph's self-esteem was not growing any greater despite the vast improvements in almost all other areas of his life.

On the whole, he was not a happy man at the end of the seven weeks, when everything changed.

15

LEAVING MIDDLETON HOUSE for a few hours late at night in order to go to Kensington and back again had become a matter of some routine for Georgiana. Her maid helped her don the heavy black dress and a dark cloak. The veils, she had not put on until she arrived at her destination. The same maid then checked to see that the back stairs were deserted and let her out through a side entrance. The door was left unbolted so that she could return again without disturbing anyone.

Roger's plain carriage always waited around a nearby corner to take her to Kensington and to return her at a prearranged hour. Roger had accompanied her on the first two occasions, but he no longer did so. As he had explained, he could think of rather more entertaining ways to spend his evenings than in conveying his cousin's wife to clandestine meetings with her husband.

"And quite frankly, my dear Georgie," he had added, "the sight of your flushed face when you return reminds me painfully of all that I am missing on my own account."

Georgiana had never come even close to being caught. Eventually she abandoned some of the caution that had always set her heart to thumping at first. She did not even have her head covered by the hood of her cloak the night she saw Stanley. She was hurrying along the pavement on her way to the carriage. He was walking toward her on the other side of the street.

She immediately felt panic. She hastily raised her hood, lowered her head, and hurried on. She did not think he had seen her. Certainly he did not hail her or cross the street. She breathed a sigh of relief when the postilion handed her into the carriage and she was on her way. But she remembered the near-disaster. The next time she was far more cautious, though on that occasion the street seemed deserted. She thought no more about the matter.

Two evenings later there was a ball at Viscount Roth's mansion on Charles Street. It was an occasion Georgiana much looked forward to. Entertainments on a grand scale were still fairly rare. She dressed with particular care in a pale green velvet gown that had just been delivered from the modiste's. Its design was very simple, but she thought that it showed her figure to advantage. She wore Ralph's pearls with it.

The ballroom was surprisingly crowded. It seemed that everyone who was anyone had been invited. Georgiana's card began to fill with flattering rapidity. Ralph claimed the first set and the supper dance. Roger, Dennis, Stanley, other acquaintances: all signed her card. She was rather surprised at Stanley. She felt he did not like her. And besides, he rarely danced. He felt it to be a rather juvenile activity, she guessed, and cultivated a mature image by playing cards and playing rather deep, she had heard.

She thoroughly enjoyed the first part of the evening. The set with Ralph was too soon over, but she had the supper dance to look forward to. And she could see from her card that it was a waltz. Dennis Vaughan amused her with the story of his latest escapade, in which he and a friend had put frogs into the carriage of Lady Sharp, who had boasted at a dinner party that she was a strong-minded female and never had the hysterics or the vapors.

"We watched from the bushes at the end of the evening," he said, "and she had both. It was vastly entertaining."

"I wish I could have seen it," Georgiana said. "I know the lady and she certainly lacks sympathy for other people's weaknesses. 'Hard-minded female' would have been a more apt description, I believe.''

Lord Beauchamp was in high good humor and soon had her dimpling and protesting against his teasing. What could have been happening to his dear Lady Chartleigh, he wondered, that she was looking so satisfied with herself and so starry-eyed these days? If he were her husband, he would consider the matter worth investigating.

Stanley had written his name next to a waltz. He knew the steps, Georgiana discovered, though he danced without flair. She resigned herself to a dull half-hour, wishing that she were dancing with some of the more accomplished partners around them.

"I am onto your game, you know, Georgiana," Stanley said quietly, close to her ear.

"What?" she said.

"I am onto your game," he repeated. "I know what you are up to."

She drew her head back and looked into his face, startled.

"Did you think I had not recognized you?" he asked. "That was a fond hope. The street was deserted except for the two of us. Of course I saw you."

"When?" she asked, looking mystified. She knew immediately that it was a stupid reaction.

His eyes were cold as he looked back at her. "The night you were on your way to an assignation with my cousin," he said very distinctly.

"With your cousin!" she said. "You mean Roger? How absurd, Stanley. Of course I was doing no such thing."

"You cannot bluff your way out of this," he said. "Do you think I am quite stupid? I was not certain beyond any doubt that it was you. And when I followed you, I was not quite certain that the carriage was Roger's. I waited for three more nights before I saw you again. And that time—it was just two nights ago—I was ready to follow your carriage. I know Roger has a house in Kensington where he takes his ladybirds. Of whom you are one, Georgiana."

"Oh, no," she said urgently. "You are mistaken, Stanley."

"You are a liar," he said, "among other things. I will never understand why Mama chose you for Ralph. From all I have heard of you, you have been a trouble-maker and a man-chaser since you have been in London. And you have not changed. Poor Ralph. He may be older than I, but he knows a great deal less about life. He probably has no notion that he is being cuckolded."

"No," she said. "You misunderstand the situation entirely." Could they be having this mad encounter and still be performing the steps of the waltz? she wondered.

"And by Roger," he continued as if she had not spoken. "Roger has always run after every skirt within sight, but I did not think that even he would stoop this low."

"There is nothing whatsoever between me and Roger, Stanley," Georgiana said firmly, trying to take charge of the situation. "You should be sure of your facts before making such accusations. I hope you have said nothing of this to anyone else."

"You would like that, would you not?" he said. "And the worst of it is, Georgiana, that you may get your wish. Ralph and I are very different, but he is my brother, and I do love him. I do not believe he would be able to cope with the knowledge of what you are."

"I love Ralph too," she said haughtily. "And you are not to interfere between me and him, Stanley."

"God, how I loathe you," he said. "You are a slut and a whore."

Georgiana pushed blindly against his shoulder and dodged her way through the dancers in the direction of the doorway. She had only one thought: to reach the ladies' withdrawing room before she disgraced herself by vomiting all over the floor in public. She succeeded, but only just in time. She felt as if her whole stomach were going to come up, as well as its contents. She was dabbing at her clammy face with a lace handkerchief when her mother came rushing into the room.

"Georgie!" she exclaimed. "Whatever happened, child? Your papa was furious when he saw you leave the dance floor in that scandalous haste. He was convinced you had quarreled with your brother-in-law and were airing your differences for all the world to see. But I knew it might be that you were unwell. Poor baby. Is it something you ate?"

"I think it must be," Georgiana said shakily as her mother fussed around her, bringing a wet cloth from the pitchers of water that stood on a stand against the wall.

Ralph was pacing outside the room when they left it a few minutes later, and rushed to assist her to an anteroom attached to the ballroom. He was sitting beside her holding one of her hands while her mother was soaking a handkerchief in eau de cologne when the dowager Lady Chartleigh came bustling in, followed by Gloria.

"Roth keeps the house far too warm," she said. "I have been telling Gloria this half-hour past that I feel quite faint. I am not at all surprised that you do not feel quite the thing, Georgiana dear. You have not stopped dancing. Yes, that will be just the thing, Lady Lansbury. Do you need my vinaigrette, dear?"

"Georgie is not faint," her mother explained. "She has an upset stomach. Something she ate at dinner, doubtless."

The dowager's manner changed instantly. She seated herself in a vacant chair and smirked at her son and daughter-in-law. "Then why is it that all of us are not ill?" she asked archly. "We all ate the same dishes. I would wager there is some other cause."

Georgiana, who was responding to the comfort of Ralph's hand and shoulder pressed against her own and beginning to feel the blood return to her head, looked up sharply.

"I do believe, Lady Lansbury," her mother-in-law

continued, smiling broadly, "that it may not be a great
length of time before you and I will be changing our
status to that of grandmama. Gracious, how old that
does make me feel. Shall we hope for a boy the first
time."

Ralph's hand closed rather tightly around
Georgiana's. He looked acutely embarrassed, she saw in
one fleeting peep up at him. She did not know quite
where to look or what to say. She said nothing. Neither
did Ralph.

"For sure, I suppose it is possible," Lady Lansbury
said. "I did not even think of it. Is it true, Georgie? But
there, we must not press the matter. You will let us
know as soon as you are sure, which you may not be at
the moment, I daresay."

"Shall I summon the carriage, dear?" Ralph asked
her. "Or would you prefer to sit quietly here for a
while? Perhaps you would like a drink."

"Yes, I should like that, please," she said, smiling
up at him in gratitude. "Will you sit here with me for a
while, Ralph? I am so sorry to have been silly. I do not
know what came over me."

The older ladies stayed with her until Ralph returned
with a glass of cold water and then left them alone. She
felt very depressed as he settled himself beside her again
and took the hand that was not holding the glass. It was
all over, then, this happy part of her life. She would not
be able to keep up the Kensington visits with Stanley
spying on her. She would have to tell Ralph the truth
and risk his anger or his humiliation or whatever other
emotion he would feel when he knew of the terrible trick
she had been playing on him for more than a month. If
she did not tell him soon, Stanley might well do so.

She should tell him now. It was the obvious course to
take. There was nothing to be gained by delay. Besides,
she was becoming more convinced that her mother-in-
law was probably right. She could never remember
vomiting in her life. Ralph was silent beside her,
perhaps feeling that she needed quietness. She should

just open her mouth and let the words come out. But it was so good sitting here beside him, feeling his concern for her health. She felt tired, too tired to cope with the emotions that would be unleashed by her words. She leaned her head sideways against his shoulder and felt comforted. She closed her eyes.

Vera Burton was unaware that her sister had been taken ill. So was Lord Beauchamp. They had withdrawn from the dance before she made her very public exit.

They had started to waltz, but Vera had twice accused her partner of drawing her indecently close during the turns.

"If I did not do so, ma'am," he replied, "you might spin off in a direction quite different from mine. Imagine how very conspicuous you would feel if that happened."

"A waltz does not have to be danced as if it were a flat-out gallop along an open green, my lord," the usually docile Vera said tartly. "I believe you quite deliberately turn fast just so that you may have the excuse to draw me close. I find the experience quite repugnant."

"Do you?" he said. "I can hardly blame you. I do believe the tips of your breasts actually brushed against my coat for the smallest fraction of a second. Scandalous goings-on indeed, ma'am. Enough to give a maiden of the strongest constitution the vapors. Would you like to swoon quite away and give me the pleasure of carrying you off the floor?"

"I do not know why I even consented to dance with you," Vera said. "You never do anything but insult me, sir."

"I?" he asked with raised eyebrows. "Insult you? You malign me. Did I say that I shrank from contact with your breasts? On the contrary, my dear. I felt a distinct thrill of desire."

"You are insufferable!" she said, her cheeks aflame. "Return me to my mother immediately, sir."

He stopped dancing, made her a mock bow, and

offered his arm. But he led her to an alcove across which
curtains almost met.

"If I returned you to your mama in your present
agitated state," he said, "she would do me the injustice
of agreeing with you. Besides, this seems to me to be an
excellent opportunity to discover just what those lips
really do taste like."

"Don't you dare touch me," Vera said, backing away
from him into the alcove. "You . . . you rake!"

He threw back his head and laughed. "Tell me," he
said, "why are your cheeks flaming quite so red and
why is your bosom heaving as if you had just run several
miles? Is it all outrage, or is it partly excitement? If you
are totally honest with yourself, do you find that
perhaps you want to be kissed? I find it hard to believe
that what I am feeling can be entirely one-sided."

He had been moving toward her so that he now stood
directly in front of her. She stood flat against the wall,
her hands splayed against its surface on either side of
her. She stared up at him, her eyes wide, and said
nothing.

He laughed more softly. "You are incurably honest,
are you not, Vera?" he said. "You cannot deny your
own feelings of desire, yet you would not for the world
admit them. So you stand mute."

"I will not be trifled with," she said. "I will not be
used for your amusement so that you can boast of your
conquest of an aging, plain spinster. I will not." Her
voice was trembling.

"Vera!" he said. "Are you talking about yourself?
Aging? How old are you? Two-and-twenty? Three?
Four? My next birthday takes me into the next decade,
you know. And plain? I might have agreed with you
after our first meeting, though your eyes have always set
your appearance above the ordinary. But it is some time
since I have even had any reservations about calling you
beautiful. Your fashionable new hairstyle has greatly
changed your appearance. You cultivate a prim
expression that tends to make one assume you are plain.

But any sort of emotion transforms you into a quite remarkable beauty. And I do frequently arouse emotion in you, even if only indignation, do I not, my dear?''

"Don't," she said. "Don't make mock of me."

He shook his head slowly. "I don't," he said. "And I do not trifle with you. I want to kiss you. May I?''

"Will it make any difference if I say no?" she asked, some bitterness in her voice. "You will do as you please anyway."

"I will tease you and shock you to my heart's content," he said, "because I suspect that doing so brings me closer to the real Vera. But I will not interfere with your person against your will. Had you not realized that about me?''

She shook her head. "I am not used to light flirtation," she said, "and I make no apology for my lack of experience."

He smiled. "You are procrastinating, ma'am," he said. "Will you be kissed?''

"Yes," she said almost defiantly. "Yes, I want you to kiss me."

She came into his arms and held up her face to his. He gazed into her eyes, which were looking full into his.

"Ah, you feel right," he said. "Slender and yielding. Now, how do they taste, Vera?''

He lowered his head and opened his mouth over hers. She jerked back in some shock, but when he waited for her without moving, she lifted her arms up around his neck and put her lips against his again. And she gave herself up to his embrace, allowing him to bite at her lips, to part them with his tongue, and to take possession of her mouth. Instinctively, without thought, she arched her body to his. She lost touch with her surroundings.

Roger did not. He broke the embrace slowly after a couple of minutes. "Mmm," he murmured, his mouth against her ear. "Every bit as tasty as I suspected. God, how I want you."

"If I might interrupt!" a clipped voice said from the opening in the curtain.

Vera pushed in panic against Roger's chest. Lord Beauchamp himself turned lazily.

"Ah, Stanley," he said. "You have damnable timing, my lad. Can you not see that I am occupied with important business at the moment?"

"You are all too frequently involved in important business, Roger," Stanley said coldly. "When one wants to talk to you, one just has to interrupt. You are usually occupied with the sister, though, are you not?"

Roger's eyes narrowed on his cousin. "Your meaning, my boy?" he asked.

"You are pawing one sister almost in full view of a roomful of people," Stanley said, "and bedding the other in secret."

"I think," Roger said languidly, turning and taking Vera lightly by the elbow, "that we should not bore Miss Burton with this strange conversation, Stanley. Perhaps we can talk later? Or tomorrow? Come, ma'am, I shall help you find your mama."

"What do you mean?" Vera was very white. Her eyes were fixed on Stanley.

"He is an impudent pup, ma'am, who has not been taught how to behave in society," Roger said, grasping her elbow more firmly and trying to steer her past his cousin.

"What do you mean, sir?" Vera asked, trying to shake her arm free of Roger's grasp.

"I mean that Lord Beauchamp"—Stanley spat out the name—"keeps my sister-in-law and your sister as his mistress. That is what I mean, ma'am."

"Do try not to make a complete idiot of yourself, my dear lad," Roger said pleasantly. "Obviously you are under some misapprehension. We will discuss this alone. It is very bad *ton,* you know, to have alluded to such a matter in the presence of a lady. I see you need a lesson in manners."

"How can you make such an allegation against my

sister?'' Vera asked. She was even whiter than before, if that were possible. "What is your evidence?"

"I have seen her with my own eyes," Stanley said, "leaving home at eleven o'clock and being driven away in Roger's carriage. And I have followed her and seen her enter a house in Kensington that Roger owns and uses for his dealings with women. It does not take a great deal of intelligence to draw a conclusion."

"And you would be wrong, Stanley," Roger said wearily. "Damnably wrong, my boy."

"Is it true?" Vera turned to him with wide eyes and trembling lips. "Has Georgie been going to your house?"

He closed his eyes briefly. "Yes," he said, "it is true. And now there is no point in my saying any more, is there? You will already have drawn the same conclusion as this young hothead. And I cannot say I blame you. I can only suggest that you confront your sister with your knowledge."

Vera gazed at him a moment longer. Then her hand flashed out in a stinging slap across one cheek. "You are despicable," she said. "Despicable! You are even lower than I thought. 'Rake' is too good a word to describe you."

She gathered her skirts in her hands and rushed from the alcove. Lord Beauchamp made no move to follow her. He folded his arms across his chest and stared at his cousin. He ignored the stinging welt across his cheek.

"You young fool!" he said contemptuously. "If you have such a filthy suspicion, damn you, can you not wait until you can confront me with it without involving an innocent female? Even for one so young, I find your behavior quite unforgivable. One does not discuss such matters before ladies, Stanley. I have a mind to take a whip to your hide."

Stanley flushed painfully. His hands were clenched into tight fists at his sides. He nodded his head. "Oh yes," he said, "it is a nice try, Roger. You think you can throw my youth in my face. You think you can make my talking openly before Miss Burton the main issue here. Quite frankly, I don't care a damn that she knows. She has a right to know just so that she may avoid being next on your list. But the main point here is your affair with my brother's wife. It has to end.''

"Stop behaving like a prize ass, Stanley," Lord Beauchamp said. "As it happens, I have never had so much as a carnal thought about Georgie. But even if I had, even if I were in the middle of a hot affair with her, do you think I would put an end to it merely because I was ordered to do so by a headstrong young puppy? Go back to the dancing, my boy, and leave your brother and his wife to run their own affairs. And me to take care of mine.''

He smiled and shrugged his shoulders and made to walk past Stanley. But his cousin stepped across to stand in his way, determination in his face.

"No," he said. "I came here to deal with this matter. I have no wish for my brother to know the truth, and I am not sure he would do anything decisive about it even if he did. I must deal with you myself.''

Roger looked bored. "Oh no, youngster," he said. "You are not about to throw a glove in my face, are you? But I notice with relief that you do not have one.''

"You will meet me nevertheless," Stanley said. "Name your weapons and your seconds, Beauchamp. Or own yourself a coward to the world.''

"Oh, really, Stan, my lad," Roger said, "You would leave immediately if you just knew what a very amusing spectacle you make at the moment.''

"You are a scoundrel and a rake and a damned wife stealer," Stanley said. "And this time you have chosen a suitable partner. My sister-in-law, the Countess of Chartleigh, as I have just finished telling her, is a liar and a slut and a whore.''

Roger passed a weary hand over his face. "You are a tenacious young puppy, aren't you?" he said. "You must know I cannot allow you to get away with that description of someone I know as a lady. Very well,

Stanley. Pistols it will be. Tell me who your second is to be and I shall make sure that someone calls on him tomorrow morning to make all the proper arrangements. Damn you to hell, my stupid lad. Perhaps you would like to check your facts more closely before exposing your brains to be blown out."

"Jeremy Allistair," Stanley said curtly. "I have already asked him. I shall write down his direction for you."

Lord Beauchamp waved a dismissive hand. "I know him," he said. "Now that you have had your way, my boy, take yourself beyond the range of the toe of my shoe, will you?"

Stanley made what he deemed a dignified exit.

16

RALPH WAS IN his library the following afternoon, poring over a report from his bailiff at Chartleigh on the progress being made on the laborers' cottages and on his findings with regard to the dower house. Everything appeared to be progressing satisfactorily. In little more than a month's time they would all be going into the country to prepare for Gloria's wedding. Then he would be able to superintend the building himself, and his mother would be better able to decide on the changes she wanted in her new home.

He looked forward to the move. Sometimes, he felt, one's life fell into a routine that was difficult to break. His own life was at such a stage. Definite changes needed to be made. He must end his affair with Sally Shaw, and he must consummate his marriage to Georgiana. He was quite clear in his mind that both moves must be made. If he continued to see the dancer much longer, he might never be able to give her up. And give her up he must. Somehow, although he loved Georgiana with every fiber of his being, he knew that he would not be able to make love to her if he were still conducting his affair with the other girl.

And he must consummate his marriage. There was no reason in the world why he should not do so. He knew now that he would be able to make love to Georgiana without causing her undue pain. And he believed that he would also be able to give her pleasure once she had got over her initial fright. Most important of all, he felt that a deep enough friendship had grown between them to diminish her terror. She seemed to feel some affection for him, even.

But it is one thing to know what one should do, even what one wishes to do, and quite another to do it, Ralph felt. Somehow he needed a change of circumstances to force him into organizing his life along more satisfactory lines. A move to Chartleigh would force him to give up his mistress. It would also bring him into closer daily contact with his wife.

He was a little worried about Georgiana. He had never known her to be ill. Yet last night she had looked quite ghastly for a while. She had sat with her head on his shoulder and her eyes closed for fully half an hour before rallying a little and announcing that she would go into the supper room with him. But she had hardly touched the food he put on a plate for her.

And this morning she had vomited again, rushing from the breakfast room when Stanley had set a plate of kidneys down on the table across from her. He had not wanted her to go out this afternoon, but she had insisted that she was quite recovered and that she had promised her mama to go shopping with her. He supposed that her mother was quite capable of looking after her if she should become ill again. He would certainly call a physician if she had a recurrence of the strange sickness.

He turned hot and then cold as he recalled his mother's guesses of the night before. How embarrassed he had been. And how mortified poor Georgiana must have felt. He had not dared look at her. He tried to return his attention to the letter from his bailiff.

Ten minutes later the butler interrupted his thoughts by announcing the arrival of Miss Burton. Ralph jumped to his feet. He had almost forgotten that his reason for being at home at this unusual hour was the note he had received from Vera that morning asking to see him. His curiosity on receiving that letter returned to him now.

He held out a hand to his visitor and smiled at her. "Hello, Vera," he said. "How are you? Do come in and have a seat. There is a warm fire. It is cold outside today, is it not?''

"Thank you,.'' she said, and he noticed immediately that her normally calm manner had deserted her. "I knew that Georgie was to go out with Mama this afternoon. That is why I asked to see you at this hour.''

"Indeed?'' he prompted, hiding by his kindliness of manner his surprise.

"What do you make of it, Ralph?'' she asked. "You seem very calm, which suggests that you do not believe a word of it. And you may say it is none of my business. You would be right too, of course. But Georgie is my sister and we are very close. I did not have one wink of sleep last night.''

Ralph was frowning down at her. "What are you talking about?'' he asked. "Has something happened?''

She stared at him for several moments and then her eyes grew round with horror and one hand crept up to cover her mouth. "Oh,'' she said, "is it possible you do not know? Did no one talk to you about it?''

"About what?'' Ralph asked, laughing briefly at the expression on her face.

Color rushed into her cheeks. "Oh no,'' she said. "It did not occur to me that you would not . . . It is nothing. I merely heard that . . . I thought perhaps . . . I heard that Georgie was ill last night. I wondered what the truth of the matter was.''

Ralph seated himself in the chair opposite Vera's. "Now,'' he said, "what is this all about, Vera? And do not tell me you have come to inquire about Georgiana's health. If that were so, it would have been sensible to come when she was at home. Besides, you could have found out the truth about her sickness from your mother, who was right there. What is it that no one thought to tell me?''

"I cannot,'' she said. "Oh, I cannot say anything if no one else has. Oh, curse me for walking into this. I shall never forgive myself.''

"I think I might find it hard to forgive you too if you

do not satisfy my curiosity soon," Ralph said. "Tell me, please, Vera. Whatever it is, it must be something I should know if you took for granted that I did know. And if it concerns Georgiana I must be told. Please? She is my wife."

Vera was now as pale as she had been flushed a few moments before. "It was your brother, Stanley," she said. "I daresay it is as Lord Beauchamp said. He is just a hotheaded boy who does not quite know what he is talking about. I am sure there can be no truth in what he said."

"And what did he say, Vera?"

"He said . . ." Vera looked at the ceiling and drew a deep breath. "He said that Lord Beauchamp is keeping Georgie as his mistress. Oh, it cannot be right, Ralph. I do not know why I even listened to such nonsense."

Ralph was very still. "On what grounds did he make his accusation?" he asked. "Surely you must have asked him that?"

"Yes," Vera admitted. "He said that he had seen her leave this house late at night and be driven away in Lord Beauchamp's carriage. But it could have been anyone, Ralph. One of the maids, perhaps. And it could have been anyone's carriage. And even if it was Georgie, there is probably a perfectly reasonable explanation."

"And he said no more?" Ralph asked.

"N-no," Vera said. "That is all."

"I see," Ralph said. "And my cousin was also present when my brother said all this, Vera?"

"Yes," she said.

"And how did he respond?"

"He said it was all nonsense," Vera said, "and I am sure it is. He made sure I left quickly. He was furious with Lord Stanley for saying as much in front of me."

Ralph stared at her, his face blank.

"What are you going to do?" Vera asked miserably. "I do wish I had not assumed that your brother would also have spoken to you. I feel quite terrible. I am sure there was no need for you to know. It is all a ghastly mistake, and he probably knows it by now and has apologized to your cousin."

"Yes," Ralph said. "You are doubtless right, Vera. I shall speak to all concerned and find out the truth of the matter. Then we can all have a good laugh about it. Though I might be tempted to break Stanley's head. Roger was quite right. He had no business talking on such a topic before a lady."

Vera got to her feet. "I shall go, Ralph," she said, "now that I have done such terrible damage. I am so sorry. Please do not let yourself doubt Georgie. She is impulsive and occasionally a little wild, but I know she could not do something so terrible. Please believe me."

"She is my wife," Ralph said gently, "and I love her, Vera. I do not need someone else to plead her case to me."

"Of course," she said. "Yes. Forgive me, please, Ralph."

She left the room without further ado, leaving Ralph standing before his chair looking at the door she had closed quietly behind her. His mind refused to function at first. Vera's words revolved in his brain, making no sense whatsoever.

Then he felt anger at his brother. White fury. Had Stanley been in the house at that moment, he would have found himself confronting a brother he had never seen before. Ralph, normally gentle and pacific, to whom reason was of infinitely more value than passion, would have gladly killed him. To accuse Georgiana of infidelity! And to voice those suspicions to at least two other people. He would choke the life out of him!

Ralph was pacing furiously back and forth in the library, slamming one fist into the other palm and trying to guess where he might find his brother at this hour of the afternoon, when he heard sounds of the front door being opened and closed again. He yanked open the door of the library and strode out into the hallway.

"Oh, Ralph, dear," Lady Lansbury called, sounding vastly relieved, "you are at home. Do come and help me support Georgie. She has been quite ill again, the poor baby."

But her words were quite unnecessary. Ralph had seen at a glance that his wife was not well. She was leaning heavily on her mother's arm. The butler was hovering at her other side. Her face, beneath the poke of her bonnet, was ghastly pale. He rushed toward her and scooped her up in his arms and headed for the stairs.

"Send for the doctor immediately," he called over his shoulder to the butler, "and see that he is sent up to my wife's room as soon as he arrives."

"Oh, Ralph," Georgiana said faintly, lifting her arm up to cling to his neck, "how foolish I am. I am sure there is no need of a doctor. I merely need to rest. You will be thinking me a very poor creature."

"Hush, love," he said. "We will have you all tucked up in your bed in a moment and you shall rest until the doctor comes. He will give you something to settle your stomach."

He carried her into her room and set her down on top of her bedcovers. Lady Lansbury followed him into the room.

"I have sent for your maid, Georgie," she said. "What a fright you gave me, my girl. I should have known better than to take you away from home today."

She began to pull off Georgiana's half-boots. Ralph untied the strings of her bonnet and eased it from her head. He left the room when the maid came running in.

An hour passed before the doctor arrived. By that time the dowager and Gloria had returned from their afternoon outing. Ralph was in the drawing room, restlessly wandering about, then aimlessly picking out a tune on the pianoforte.

"Do stop worrying, Ralph, dear," his mother said. "It will be as I said last night, mark my words. Goodness me, men always seem to be taken by surprise by such events, just as if they were not mainly responsible. Georgiana is a strong girl. She will do very

nicely once she has passed this early stage of nausea.
Some women succeed in escaping it altogether. With me
it always lasted for the first three months, but then I
always did have a rather delicate constitution. Chartleigh was never willing for me to leave my bed during
those months.''

Ralph said nothing. Gloria looked embarrassed and
made an excuse to go to her room.

The doctor was shown into the room a few minutes
later. He was smiling and nodding obsequiously. ''Her
ladyship will be as right as rain after some rest, my
lord,'' he said to Ralph. ''Her mother is with her now.''

''Is it anything serious?'' Ralph asked. ''Does she
need medicines? Treatment?''

''Now, do tell us, doctor,'' the dowager said. ''Is my
daughter-in-law increasing?''

The doctor smiled conspiratorially. ''Her ladyship
was most insistent that I say absolutely nothing, my
lady,'' he said.

''Quite understandable,'' she replied, smiling condes-
cendingly at him. ''Shall we put it this way, doctor? If I
were to assume that her ladyshp is with child, you would
not entirely deny that I am right?'' She smirked at
Ralph.

''I certainly could not do that, your ladyship,'' the
doctor replied with a confidential smile. He was rubbing
his hands together. ''But neither could I confirm it. It is
too early to be absolutely certain. But remember, your
ladyship, that I have kept my word to the countess. I
have said nothing.'' He smiled broadly at his two
listeners.

''Absolutely not,'' the dowager agreed, and she
nodded graciously as the man made his bows and his
exit.

''Well,'' she said, turning to Ralph, her hands clasped
across her ample bosom, ''my darling boy! I am very
proud of you. You have wasted no time in doing your
duty. Oh, I do hope it is a boy, Ralph. An heir. Dear
Georgiana! I must go to her immediately.''

"Mama!" Ralph said sharply. "Remember that the doctor said that he cannot know for certain yet. And he promised Georgiana that he would say nothing. It was wrong of him to drop hints the way he did. Besides, she is unwell. She does not need any excitement today. Her mother is the best person to look after her at present, I believe."

"That is my boy," his mother said approvingly. "You learn to protect her, my darling. It is most fitting while she is increasing with your heir. I shall wait until tomorrow. Surely she will have told you by then, Ralph. And remember, you must act as if you have been taken completely by surprise."

"Yes," Ralph said. "Excuse me, Mama. There is something I must do."

He succeeded in reaching the library and closing the door before his legs buckled under him and set him down with a thud in the nearest chair.

Georgiana was lying on her bed staring up at the canopy above, her hands clasped behind her head. She should summon her maid to take away her empty cup and saucer and snuff the candles for the night. But she did not feel like settling to sleep yet.

What a predicament she had got herself into. She was with child. She had not needed the doctor to tell her so. Indeed, the doctor had been very cautious about agreeing beyond all doubt that it was true. But she knew very well that it was. And one part of her was delighted, elated. It seemed like heaven on earth to be carrying Ralph's child. It was going to be a boy, she had decided, and he was going to look exactly like his father, even to the good-humored mouth and laughing eyes. She would see that he was happy enough.

At least, she thought, it might have seemed like heaven if she could just have sent Mama downstairs after the doctor had left, to send Ralph to her. She could have held out her arms to him as he came into the room and waited until he sat beside her. And then she would have told him and he would have hugged her and kissed her and they would have proceeded to live happily ever after.

The trouble was that she could not do any of those things. And through her own stupidity, as usual. At least she had had the presence of mind to make the doctor promise to say nothing about her condition as he left the house. And of course, Mama had promised too. It would be unimaginably awful if Ralph found out that part of the truth first, before he found out the other. Her stomach felt quite unsteady again at the mere thought of his discovering that she was increasing when he believed her to be still virgin.

But even though she had ensured that he would not find out, she still felt under pressure. She must let him know about the identity of his "mistress" without delay. And for several reasons. She could not keep her condition a secret from him for more than a few days at the most. It would be unfair. And there was always the danger that that imbecile Stanley would take it into his head to blurt out his suspicions to Ralph after all. That would pose a major embarrassment.

It was perfectly clear to her now, of course, that she should have told Ralph the truth a long time ago. After their second or third encounter at Kensington would have been the ideal time. By now she felt paralyzed by inaction just to think of broaching the topic with him.

"By the way, Ralph, you know that girl you visit in Kensington twice a week?"

No, much too casual an approach.

"Ralph, I have something to tell you that will make you dreadfully angry, but I hope you will forgive me when you have had time to think about it."

No, far too bland, meek, and mild.

"Oh, Ralph, dear, I have a shocking confession to make, but I know you will laugh with me once I have done so."

Worse and worse. Perhaps she should just burst into

tears. Or get dressed in her black outfit and have her maid send Ralph up. Or . . .

Georgiana pulled a pillow from behind her head and hurled it over the foot of the bed. The other pillow followed it two seconds later. She felt better for a moment, until she realized that the display of temper had brought her no nearer a solution to her problem.

Well, she decided, climbing out of the bed in order to retrieve her pillows, she would set herself a limit of two days. Tomorrow, if she was as brave as she thought she was, or the day after, if she was the coward she feared she was, she would go to Ralph and make a clean breast of the whole thing. She would not let it go beyond two days.

And once she had cleared up everything with Ralph, she would go after that Stanley. A slut and a whore, indeed! It was a great blessing that her stomach had forced her to run the night before. Otherwise, she would probably have brought permanent disgrace on Ralph's family and her father's by punching him in the face. Impudent, silly boy! He deserves no better. And the disgrace might almost have been worthwhile. At least she would have succeeded in making an idiot of him.

Georgiana rang for her maid and lay down again on the bed. She clasped her hands loosely across her abdomen and gave the canopy a self-satisfied smile. When she was putting herself through the agony of telling Ralph about her recent exploits, she must fortify her courage by remembering how glorious it was going to be to tell him about his child. He would be so surprised and so happy. Ralph would make a wonderful father. She just knew he would.

He had seemed touchingly concerned about her earlier in the evening when he came to see her for a few minutes. He had refused to sit down and had been pale and ill-at-ease. Poor Ralph! He probably imagined that she was dying at the very least. He had been on his way out. She smiled. At least she knew he was not going to

keep an assignation with another woman. The next
Kensington night was tomorrow. The thought sobered
her. She would not be able to go, of course. But the fact
that she was supposed to do so must make it all the more
important for her to talk to Ralph tomorrow.

She smiled at her maid and directed the girl to snuff
the candles. She would try to sleep and dream up some
magically tactful way to break the awful truth to her
husband.

Ralph in the meanwhile was being shown into Lord
Beauchamp's dressing room, where his lordship's butler
was helping him into a particularly well-fitting
evening coat.

"Ah, Ralph, my lad," he said cheerfully, "looking
for company, are you? I am on my way to a card party.
Do you care to join me?"

"No," Ralph said. "But I would like to have a word
with you before you leave."

"Well, fire away, my boy," Roger said, smoothing
the fine lace of his cuffs over the backs of his hands
while his valet pulled the coat into place across his
shoulders. "Oh. You may leave, Perkins. I believe you
have done a good enough job that your reputation will
not suffer when I appear in public."

The valet gave a doubtful glance at his master's
neckcloth, which still lay in its starched perfection on
the dresser. But he turned and left the room, closing the
door quietly behind him.

"Well," Roger said heartily when they were alone, "I
can see from your face, my boy, that you know. So I
might as well save us both from the tedium of pretending ignorance and surprise. It is a dreadful coil, Ralph.
He took me completely by surprise, you know, and I
had said pistols before having a chance to think. Quite a
disastrous choice! I shall delope, of course, but that will
leave me dreadfully exposed to the young lunatic's
bullet. Is he a good shot, by any chance?"

"My God," Ralph said. "What are you talking about?"

Roger looked back at him and then closed his eyes for a few moments. "I should have put us both through the tedium," he said. "You did not know after all, did you?"

"No," Ralph said. "You are talking about Stanley, are you not? A duel? Has the world gone mad?"

"I seriously fear young Stan might have," Roger said, turning and picking up the unfolded neckcloth. He proceeded to arrange it himself, with the aid of the mirror in front of him. "You should seriously consider packing him off to Oxford, Ralph. He could work off his energies there in acceptably unruly undergraduate activities. He maneuvered me very handily into accepting his challenge and then I blurted out pistols without a thought to the consequences. Someone is likely to get killed, and I very much fear it might be me."

"Is it true?" Ralph asked quietly.

Roger swiveled sharply on his chair. His brows were drawn together. "Is what true?" he asked.

"Is Georgiana your mistress?" Ralph asked. "I swear if it is true, Roger, I shall kill you myself before you even leave this room."

Roger pulled the half-tied neckcloth off his neck again and slammed it down on the dresser. He got to his feet. "Damn you, Ralph," he said. "I never thought to hear you ask me such a question."

"I want to know if it is true," Ralph persisted.

"No, it is not true, dammit!" Roger replied.

"Is it true that she had been leaving the house and driving away in your carriage late at night?" Ralph asked.

Roger sat down again. "Look, Ralph, my lad," he said, "I think you should have a good talk with Georgie. I can't say any more."

"Can't or won't?" Ralph asked.

"Won't," Roger said firmly. "But there has never been anything remotely improper in my relations with your wife, my boy. If you will just look at me and remember who I am, I think you will know that I am speaking the truth."

"If that is so," Ralph said, "why did you accept Stanley's challenge?"

"There were reasons," Roger said reluctantly. "I am fond of Georgie, you know, and she is married to my favorite cousin."

"What did he say about her?" Ralph asked.

"You would not want to know, my boy," Roger assured him.

Ralph moved for the first time since he had entered the room. He began to pace the floor. "You cannot fight this duel, Roger," he said. "When is it supposed to be, anyway?"

"Tomorrow morning," Roger said. "At dawn, of course. Everything has to be dramatic with young Stan."

"It must not take place," Ralph said. "You must just send him word that you have changed your mind."

"Spoken like a true man of the world, my lad," his cousin said, grinning despite the seriousness of the topic. "And where would I find a hole deep enough to hide my head in for the rest of my life, may I ask?"

"You cannot fight!" Ralph said vehemently, coming to a halt in front of his cousin. "Do you realize how appallingly public the whole affair will be if you do so? I will not have that happen to Georgiana."

"I must confess the thought has bothered me somewhat," Roger admitted. "But I am afraid this thing has gone rather too far, Ralph. I don't know quite why it is, my boy, but people like me take affairs of honor rather seriously, you know."

"I shall put a stop to it!" Ralph said firmly. "I shall look for Stanley until I find him tonight. And I shall make sure that he does not keep his appointment tomorrow. He will come to apologize to you, Roger.

And if there is any fighting to be done, I shall do it. Georgiana is my wife, for heaven's sake, and my brother and my cousin are about to fight to the death over her! She is not your concern or my brother's.''

He turned and stalked from the room. Lord Beauchamp turned back toward his dresser with a shrug and a half-smile and regarded the ruined neckcloth ruefully. He rang for his valet.

17

AT HALF-PAST FOUR the following morning, Ralph was sitting in his brother's darkened bedroom. He had not bothered to light any candles. He was feeling worried and had to force himself to sit still. Pacing up and down the room would bring Stanley home no sooner. Indeed, his worry stemmed not so much from the lateness of the boy's return as from his fear that he would not return at all before his dawn appointment with Roger.

Ralph had searched for him. The trouble was that he did not know which places Stanley was in the habit of frequenting and could find no one who knew of his plans for the evening. Finally, at well after midnight, he had been forced to give up the search. There was always the possibility, anyway, that while he was wandering the streets, Stanley would be at home in his bed.

He had been in this room for two hours, interminable hours during which every sound outside the house drew him to the window. He had had no idea that a street in London could be so noisy at night.

Ralph tried to force his mind to stay on the main issue. He must see his brother in time to stop the duel. Duels were rare enough in these days to become immediate items of news. By noon of tomorrow—no, today—half the population of London would know the location of the fight, the outcome, the identities of the duelists, and the cause of the quarrel. The thought did not bear contemplation. Georgiana would be the talk of the town.

Besides, it was an unjust quarrel. Roger was not

keeping Georgiana as his mistress. Stanley, probably in a burst of youthful idealism, had decided that challenging his cousin was the only way to preserve the family honor. As it was, he was about to make a fool of himself. An expensive fool. He might end up dead, though Ralph recalled suddenly Roger's decision to delope, to shoot his pistol into the air rather than risk injuring his opponent. But Stanley could well end up killing Roger, and he would have to live with the guilt for the rest of his life. Indeed, he would be in a great deal of trouble with the law if any such thing occurred.

That madcap Stanley! Ralph felt a return of the intense anger he had felt when he left Roger's house. If there were a quarrel, if there were reason to challenge anyone, it was not Stanley's place to do any such thing. Georgiana was Ralph's concern, not his brother's. Yet Stanley had not even come to him with his suspicions. Why not? Did he wish to spare him pain? Or did he consider his older brother too weak to set his own house in order?

And was he too weak? Ralph could no longer keep his mind away from the thoughts he had been blocking all night. What was the truth concerning Georgiana? She was with child. The doctor had said he could not be certain yet, but he must have been quite well satisfied of the fact to drop the hints he had the previous afternoon. And his mother seemed confident that Georgiana's symptoms fit such a condition. He knew it was true. There was a dull certainty inside him that it was true.

She was not Roger's mistress. He did not know quite why he should trust the word of his cousin, but he did. Roger was not her lover, but someone was. And Roger knew who. His mind passed wearily among all the male acquaintances who danced with her and talked to her and occasionally even walked out with her or took her driving. There were several, notably Dennis Vaughan, whom she had known quite well before their marriage. But there was no point in trying to fix the blame. He had no way of knowing.

Ralph closed his eyes and rested his forehead on the palm of his hand. He would never have thought it. He would have wagered his life on her honor even against some of the most damning evidence. But one could not argue against a pregnancy. She had a lover. She, whom he had been afraid to touch in the last two months lest he give her an everlasting terror of physical love, had taken someone else for her lover. She had threatened at one time to do so, and he had not believed her. He had thought her merely overwrought.

And their relationship had seemed to be improving so well. He had thought that she was growing to like him, even to feel affection for him. Yet she had a lover. He wondered if she had made love with this unknown man just once or if they had a regular relationship. He could not bear to think of either possibility. He felt terribly depressed. Pictures of an unutterably dreary future came to his mind unbidden. No longer could he hope for a close marriage relationship. Perhaps she would leave him entirely now that she was to bear this other man's child. And if she stayed, what? Would he be willing to forgive her? Would he be willing to accept her child as his own? He would have no choice but to do so unless he chose publicly to denounce her.

He could never do that. She was Georgiana, his wife. His love.

He tried to feel anger. He tried to work himself into a fury. His wife of little more than three months had been unfaithful to him. She had taken herself a lover. She had let him think her a shrinking virgin and all the time she had been sneaking off to make love with another man. And Roger, by the sound of it, had aided and abetted her. He should hate her. He had every right to turn her off.

But he could not do it. He could not whip himself into a rage. And did that denote weakness? Would he not be burning with righteous fury if he were any sort of a man?

The truth was, he could not find it in himself to condemn his wife for a sin of which he was equally guilty. He had taken a lover too, had he not? For the past two months almost he had been conducting an affair with an opera dancer, and enjoying it too. He had been finding the experience so thoroughly satisfactory that he had been unable to force himself to give it up. And he had begun and continued the affair despite the fact that he had a wife whom he loved and with whom he was trying to build a good marriage. The affection he had shown to Georgiana in the past weeks was not hypocritical merely because at the same time he had been making love to another woman.

Of course, it was different for a man. A man's freedom to taste pleasures other than those offered in his wife's bed was generally recognized. Most men would not even think of feeling guilty about keeping mistresses. Most wives probably knew of their existence. Many perhaps did not care. They would be called upon less frequently to perform the tedious duties of the marriage bed. And a man could do no great harm by his extramarital affairs. He did not run the danger of bearing bastard children.

The trouble was, Ralph thought, getting up restlessly from his chair and wandering to the window yet again, he could not convince himself of the truth of this argument. The truth was that both he and Georgiana had pledged themselves to fidelity at their wedding. They had sworn before God. Could his breaking of that pledge be less serious than her doing so? The answer could only be no. He could not possibly stand in judgment of her when he was at least equally guilty.

At least equally! He was probably more guilty than Georgiana. Had he shown more force of character after his wedding and in the months since, it was probable that she would not have been tempted or driven to err. He had not been a husband to her at all. In the last few weeks, perhaps, he had been a friend. But a woman needed more than friendship from her husband.

Tomorrow—later today—he was going to have to confront Georgiana. He must let her know that he was aware of her condition and he must get her to tell him the identity of the father of her child. He must confess his own infidelity. And together they must talk long and seriously about their future. He was really not sure if anything of value could be salvaged for that future. Could they begin again to build their relationship? Could they recapture the affection that had been growing? Could they learn to trust each other again? Would he ever be able to win her love?

They must try. He must persuade her to try. It would not be easy. Even without her pregnancy it would be difficult. But it must be done. Somehow he must bring himself to accept what could not be changed. He must accept the child as his own, even if it was a boy and must be named as his heir. Even if a son of his own, if there ever were one, would have to take second place. He loved Georgiana. And she was his wife. And no one had ever said that marriage was easy.

Ralph looked up startled as the door was opened abruptly and his brother stepped inside. After dozens of visits to the window over the last two hours and more, he had after all missed Stanley's arrival.

Vera was preparing to walk to Middleton House to visit her sister the following afternoon. Her mother, of course, had whispered the news of Georgiana's probable condition. Unlike her mother, though, Vera could not feel any elation. She had a dreadful fear that perhaps her brother-in-law was not the father of the child. Perhaps responsibility lay with that unspeakable rake Lord Beauchamp.

She was more than ever sorry that she had been to talk to Ralph the day before. It had been an incredible *faux pas* on her part to assume that he would know about his brother's suspicions. She had merely wished to discover the truth and to ask if there were anything she could do. All she had probably done was to alert Ralph to the possibility that Georgie's child might not be his.

She felt that she must go to see her sister and somehow offer her support. Besides, she needed some outing to cheer herself up. She had been thoroughly depressed since two evenings before when she had committed the great folly of allowing Lord Beauchamp to kiss her. She could not imagine why she had done so. She had never liked the man, had never for a moment been deceived into thinking him worthy of her regard. Yet she could not even feel the satisfaction of knowing that he had forced his attentions on her. She had actually given him permission to kiss her!

Vera was pulling on her gloves as a footman opened the doors into the drawing room so that she might bid her mother farewell. She felt a lurching of the stomach and almost lost her poise when she saw Beauchamp himself standing there talking to her mother. He looked as cool and as elegant as if he had never entertained a sinful thought in his life.

Vera inclined her head stiffly in his direction. "I shall be on my way, Mama," she said. "I shall see you later."

"You are on your way to see Georgie," Lord Beauchamp stated. "I have your mama's kind permission to escort you. Do I have yours, Miss Burton?" He made her an elegant bow.

"It is merely a sisterly call that I make," she said stiffly. "I would not put you to any trouble, my lord."

"No trouble in the world, I assure you, ma'am," he said cheerfully. "It would be my pleasure."

With her mother sitting there smiling affably, Vera had no choice but to accept the offered company. She turned and preceded him from the room.

"If you held your spine any straighter," Lord Beauchamp said conversationally when they had reached the pavement outside, "it would shatter from the tension." He took Vera's hand and tucked it beneath his arm.

"Kindly release my arm, sir," she said staring straight ahead. "I am perfectly capable of walking without any support."

"But consider my reputation," he said, "if I should be seen to be walking along beside you without offering you the use of my arm. I should never live down the ignominy, Vera."

"And I have not given you leave to use my given name," she said.

"Ah," he said with a sigh, "can this be the same young lady who melted into my arms but two nights ago and enslaved me with the passion of her kiss?"

"I would have thought the least said about that evening the better," Vera said tartly.

"Why?" he asked, looking down at her with raised eyebrows. "Do you find words inadequate to express how you felt? You are quite right. Perhaps we should drop the topic of kisses until we are in surroundings conducive to a repetition of the action."

"You have deliberately misunderstood my meaning," she said. "And why are we turning at this corner, sir? My sister's house is straight on."

"So it is," he said. "But the park is in this direction."

"I am not going to the park, my lord," Vera said quite firmly. "Certainly not with you. If you will kindly release my arm, you can continue to the park and I shall continue on my way to my sister's."

"Now, why should I wish to walk to the park alone?" Lord Beauchamp asked. "Sometimes I wonder about your intelligence, Vera."

She stopped walking, resolutely drawing him to a halt. "Enough!" she snapped. "I am tired of this verbal sparring that we always seem to become involved in. I have no wish to walk with you, sir, and no wish to speak further with you. I wish you will leave me alone. And Georgie too."

"Ah, Georgie," he said, turning to her and covering her hand with his. "She is at the root of all this, is she? Come, Vera. You will walk to the park with me—"

"No, I will not."

"Don't interrupt," he said. "It is ill-mannered to do so. You will walk to the park with me and we shall talk about this quarrel that you seem to think we have. And if you still believe you have a grievance at the end of it, I shall conduct you to my cousin's house and say good-bye to you. I shall not bother you ever again. Is that fair enough?"

"Fair enough!" she agreed abruptly after a moment's consideration.

"Good girl," he said, patting her hand and resuming their walk. He chatted about inconsequential matters while they picked their way through the more crowded streets around the entrance to the park, and steered her through the gates. Inside, the paths and the grass were nearly deserted.

"Now," he said at last, "you may let fly at me, my dear."

Vera said nothing for a while. "Tell me if it is true," she said finally, looking away from him toward a clump of trees.

"No," he said, not even pretending to misunderstand, "of course it is not true. I am wounded to think that you have even had any doubts."

"How could I not have doubts?" she cried passionately, turning a flushed face to him. "There is your reputation, your very forward behavior to me, your familiarity with Georgie, your admission that she has been leaving home late at night in your carriage, her pregnancy. How could I avoid being suspicious?"

He was grinning suddenly. "Is Georgie in a delicate way?" he asked. "That is new to me. And that will certainly put her into a nasty predicament."

"Then there *is* something going on," she said, "and you know about it. How can you stand there and smile?"

"Merely because your sister has got herself into an unbelievable scrape," he said. He held up a hand as she opened her mouth to speak. "And it has nothing whatsoever to do with immorality, Vera. I can tell you with some certainty that the child is Ralph's, that there is no possibility of its being anyone else's. And I believe I can assure you with equal certainty that those two are almost indecently in love with each other. There are merely a few tricky misunderstandings to clear up. I am not at all sure which of them is in the worse tangle. But to be quite honest with you, at the moment I do not feel like affording them another thought."

Vera looked doubtful. "And has Lord Stanley

accepted the fact that he made a mistake?'' she asked.

"I have no idea,'' he told her. "He made a very formal and abject apology this morning. But I could not tell if it was spontaneous or not. It struck me at the time that he might have been under pressure from whoever gave him the black eye and swollen lip.''

"Ralph?'' Vera asked, saucer-eyed.

"I think you must be right,'' he said, "though Ralph always seems the veriest lamb. But there was once a similar occasion when he became quite unreasonably violent on behalf of a female. It was only that memory that made me give up my conviction that Georgie was the architect of Stanley's morning face. I cannot think how Ralph found out, but he knew by last night, when he appeared in my dressing room breathing fire and brimstone. Only now does it strike me that I was probably most fortunate not to share young Stan's fate.''

"I told Ralph,'' Vera admitted. "I assumed that he knew already, you see.''

"Then you are probably my savior,'' Lord Beauchamp said, raising her hand to his lips and making her a bow. "My brains might be splattered on a barren field by now had it not been for you.''

"A duel?'' she said, her eyes wide with shock. "Lord Stanley challenged you?''

"Vera,'' he said, "I do wish you would not do that with your eyes in such an exposed part of the park. It is most unfair. Knowing how your lips taste is far more tantalizing than merely imagining, I find. Yet the two occupants of that barouche and those two pedestrians on the horizon would doubtless have forty fits apiece if I did what I badly want to do.''

"I wish you would not talk so,'' Vera said, turning abruptly and beginning to walk again.

"We are very different from each other, are we not?'' he said, falling into step beside her, and taking her arm again. "Do we have anything in common at all, Vera?''

"No,'' she said, "I think not. Unless it is a tendency to speak our minds.''

"Is that why we have all these deliciously exhilarating arguments?" he asked.

"I fear so, my lord," she agreed.

"Would we be very unwise to marry?" he asked.

Vera looked at him, startled. "To marry?" she said faintly. "Surely there is no question of such a thing."

"What did you expect?" he said. "An offer of *carte blanche?* I would not dare, you know. It must have taken a full hour a few nights ago for my face to recover from the sting of your slap. And that was only from a supposed dishonoring of your sister!"

"I have not expected anything," Vera said. "I am an old maid, my lord, past the age of marriage."

"Ah, yes," he said. "I had forgotten. Do you wish to lean more heavily on my arm, ma'am? You need not fear that I shall totter under your weight, though I am far more advanced in years than you."

"Don't make fun of me," she said. "I think you should take me back now, or I shall be too late to visit Georgie."

"To hell with Georgie," he said cheerfully. "I really want to know if a marriage between you and me would have a chance of success. I believe I must be quite mad to consider such a possibility, of course. You have been prim and disapproving since I met you, if one disregards those minutes when you were kissing me. Why do I feel that there is a deeper, more passionate nature to love if I can but penetrate your defenses?"

"Perhaps there is nothing," she said in some agitation. "Perhaps I am as dull and as much of a killjoy as I appear to be."

"Perhaps," he said. "And perhaps I am no more than the shallow rake you take me for. Do you believe there is more to my nature, Vera? Do you think there is anything of value to make it worth your while to become better acquainted with me?"

She hesitated. "I sometimes like to believe so," she said. "I do not know."

"Or is love alone enough?" he asked.

"Love?"

"Well," he said, "I certainly am quite in love with you, and I am almost certain that your own feelings are engaged a great deal more than you will admit even to yourself. Could you bring yourself to marry me, Vera? I have not lived an utterly worthless existence, you know. I manage my estates myself and have made them solvent again since my father's death. Much of what you seem to have heard is true, I will admit. There have been many women in my life. But I have never ruined an innocent girl or cheated with any man's wife. And I believe I can safely promise that you will be the only woman in my life from this moment forward."

"Oh, please," Vera said. "Please, I am so confused. I do not know what to say."

He drew her to a halt again. "I think I will not make you a formal offer now," he said. "I have not spoken with your father, though I thought of doing so earlier. You are going down to Chartleigh for Gloria's wedding and for Christmas, are you not? I shall be there too. Shall we agree to an unofficial understanding until after Christmas? In the meantime we can get to know each other without the barrier of this apparent hostility that has been between us from the start. And we can discover if there is anything to bring us together in addition to love. Shall we, Vera? And plan a spring wedding if we still feel after Christmas that we cannot live without each other?"

"I have not said that I feel that way at all," Vera protested feebly.

"Then say it now," he said urgently. "Don't fight with me any longer. Tell me."

She looked up at him and smiled ruefully. "Very well," she said. "I do love you, Roger, though I cannot think of a single reason for doing so. There, are you satisfied, sir? All this is quite against my better judgment, you know."

"Quite," he said. "I think in consideration of your very advanced age and my fast approach to my thirtieth birthday that we should perhaps make that wedding very early in the spring, don't you?"

"But there is no official betrothal, is there?" she asked.

"Absolutely not," he agreed. "Shall we say unofficially early in the spring? You know, love, if we veer to our right just a fraction, we shall be on a collision course with those trees. A mere twenty paces if we sharpen the angle slightly thus. And this particular tree trunk in front of us looks to me like a very suitable shield from prying eyes. Come and kiss me."

"But, Roger," she protested, "is it not dreadfully vulgar to embrace almost in public?"

"Oh, dreadfully, love," he agreed amiably. "But I shall not tell if you will not. I take it your answer is yes, since I have not had to drag you back here. And you see how slender you are in comparison with the tree trunk? No one who is not a determined prowler will even know we are here. Kiss me, Vera."

"I really ought not," she said, putting her arms up around his neck and lifting her face to him. "Roger, you cannot really love me, can you?"

"No, not at all," he said, feathering his lips across hers in a manner that set her to tightening her grip on his neck. "I could think of no other way of maneuvering you behind this tree than to say I did. And I fear that I shall have to marry you just in order to get you into bed. How you do blush, darling. You will probably force me to extinguish the candles on our wedding night, will you not?"

"Roger," Vera said from between her teeth, " will you stop this very improper talk and kiss me!"

He drew his head back and grinned down at her. "My apologies, ma'am," he said. "I had not realized you were quite so desperate."

He lowered his mouth to hers and leaned his weight against her so that she was pressed against the tree, only his arms wrapped around her protecting her from its rough surface. But it is doubtful that Vera would have noticed anyway. She had melted into his embrace, her body molded against his in a manner that would have severely shocked her in a more rational mood.

18

GEORGIANA WAS SITTING in the library sewing. It was an activity she did not particular enjoy, but she certainly did not feel like reading this afternoon, and she was very reluctant to sit doing nothing. She had made an excuse to leave the drawing room, where the dowager and Gloria were entertaining Lady Beauchamp. She did not know how long Ralph would be. She had not seen him at all that day. She hoped he would come in before dinner, before her resolve gave way. She blocked thought from her mind and concentrated on her sewing.

She heard him come into the house and looked up from her work, wondering if he would come here immediately or if she would have to send upstairs for him. The door opened quietly even as she was straining her ears for sounds of his movements, and she could feel her cheeks flush and her heart begin to thump as she met her husband's eyes across the room.

"Ah, Ralph," she said, "I thought I heard you come in." Too hearty, she thought in dismay, listening to her own voice.

He smiled at her. "Hello, Georgiana," he said. "I was hoping I would find you at home. How are you feeling today?"

"Oh, far better, thank you," she said. "I wanted to go shopping this morning, but your mama would not hear of it. So I have stayed at home like a good girl. I am even sewing. See?"

"I am glad you are feeling more the thing," Ralph said.

They could go on like this for several hours, until it would be too late to say anything before dinner, Georgiana thought. She threaded her needle through the cloth on her knee and put her work aside. "Ralph," she said, "I wish to talk to you."

His hand rose quickly. "I have something to say to you, too," he said. "May I go first?"

She should say no, Georgiana thought. She was not about to lose her nerve. "Please do," she said meekly.

Ralph sat in the chair opposite hers and looked at her quietly for a moment. "I would like us to decide together, Georgiana," he said, "whether it is possible for us to start again. We have not had a real marriage thus far. I want it to become real. Now. Today. Tonight. Is it too late?"

Georgiana stared across at him, at his mouth, slightly upturned at the corners, at his kindly, vulnerable eyes, his unruly hair. She shook her head slowly, not taking her eyes from him.

"The fault has been entirely my own," he said. He flushed somewhat. "I hurt you on our wedding night and frightened you. I know you were afraid for me to touch you after that. And knowing that, I became afraid too. I had no experience at all, Georgiana. I really did not know how to go on. I did not know how not to give you pain."

"I should not have told you that," Georgiana said breathlessly. "My tongue always runs away with my sense."

Ralph leaned foward. "I love you, Georgiana," he said. "I fell in love with you the second time I saw you, and my love has deepened with every day since. You are so very beautiful and so full of life. And you have a mind that is willing to develop and grow. I want more than anything to have you as my closest friend and my lover."

Georgiana opened her mouth to speak, but he did not stop.

"And now that I have said that," he continued,

"what I have to say next will seem all the more inexplicable and reprehensible to you. Probably it will hurt you. But I must tell you. I have committed a terrible sin against you. For the past two months I have had a mistress."

He paused, looking across at his wife in the deepest apprehension. Georgiana leaned back in her chair and said nothing.

"You are shocked," he said, "and you have every right to be. I have no excuse. I knew what I was doing, and I quite rationally chosen to begin this affair. My reason sounds very silly. I thought that if I could gain some experience with another woman, I would be better able to soothe your fears and give you some pleasure without pain." He flushed again.

"And have you gained what you wanted?" Georgiana asked.

"I suppose so," he said slowly. "But I have learned a great deal more. I have learned that infidelity arouses terrible guilt feelings. I suppose I wanted to feel more of a man. But I have broken a vow I made to both you and God, and in so doing I have made myself less of a man."

"What is she like?" Georgiana asked. "Is she beautiful? Do you love her?"

"I love you," he said, looking earnestly into her eyes. "And yet . . ."

"And yet?" she prompted sharply.

"I don't know if you will understand," Ralph said. "I probably should not even talk of such matters to you. Such women are generally seen as creatures to be used and despised. Almost as if they are non-persons. I never spoke to her, Georgiana. Indeed, I never even really saw her. But she was real. She is real, a real person. She has thoughts and dreams and problems. She was probably driven to becoming what she is. She is as precious to herself as I am to myself or you to yourself. She cannot be dismissed as a creature of no account merely because she can be labeled a whore. And I have

contributed to her degradation. In this way too I have
sinned.''

"I am sure she would not see it that way," Georgiana
said.

"It is nevertheless true," he said. "And I feel I must
do something about it. I must see her once more,
Georgian, and offer her the means to live independently
if she so wishes. I am sure you will find this hard to
believe, but this too I must do."

Georgiana shook her head.

"It pains me," he said, leaning even farther forward
in his chair and looking quite agitated, "that any
woman can be driven to that way of life. How desperate
must be the circumstances, Georgiana, for a woman to
be forced to sell her body. And what about men of their
class? What alternative do they have but to become
thieves and footpads or to lose themselves in gin? We
must set our minds to beginning some sort of industry at
Chartleigh soon. Weaving or spinning, perhaps? At
least maybe we can offer the poor of our own part of the
world an alternative to going into the cities in search of
employment that simply is not there."

Georgiana smiled warmly at him. "I shall help you all
I can," she said. "And you will do well, Ralph. You
have a gift for relating to the poor and winning their
affection."

The eagerness died from his face as he looked back at
her. He eased himself back in his chair a little and
flushed. "I am sorry," he said. "I have gone completely
off the point, have I not? I am almost afraid to ask the
question again, Georgiana, now that you know what
sort of husband you have married. Is it possible for us
to begin again, to pretend perhaps that our wedding has
taken place today?"

The smile had been gradually fading from
Georgiana's face. She still had her story to tell. And it
was becoming more and more difficult to tell it.

"Ralph," she said impulsively, "will you kiss me?

You have not done so for such a long time. Please will you hold me?''

He stared at her for a moment before jumping to his feet, his smile crinkling his eyes at the corners. He reached out both hands for hers and, when she placed her own in them, pulled her up and into his arms. She held her face up eagerly. He had never kissed her at Kensington.

He kissed her eyes, her temples, her cheeks, her throat. Georgiana closed her eyes and abandoned herself to his will. She did not try to participate or to guide him to her mouth, where she wanted him to be. She placed her hands on his shoulders and surrendered.

And finally his mouth was on hers, warm, gentle, seeking. He parted his lips and played with hers until she did likewise. And she shuddered and pressed closer when the tip of his tongue outlined her lips, exploring the warm, moist flesh behind them and penetrated beyond the barrier of her teeth.

Georgiana moaned and his hand came behind her head to steady it and the kiss became deeper and more urgent. She began to feel that familiar throbbing low in her abdomen. She felt heat rising like a wave toward her head. She wanted him. She wanted her husband.

"Oh God," he said, lifting his head and clasping her to him, his cheek against her hair. "Oh God, Georgiana, is it possible that you can feel as I do? Then what have I driven you to, love? What have I done to you?"

She pushed at his shoulders until she could look into his troubled face. "What do you mean?" she asked, wide-eyed.

"I know about the child," he said. His face was tormented. "I know that you too have had a lover."

Her eyes grew round with horror. "You know?" she said. "How?"

"The doctor was indiscreet," he said. "He did not break his promise to you, but his hints said as much as words. I told you about myself, love, so that you would know that my own actions have been worse than yours.

I don't know how you feel about the . . . the father. I don't even want to know who he is. But please give our marriage a chance. The baby will be ours. I shall never again allude to the fact that biologically it is someone else's. Come back to me, Georgiana."

"You would do this for me?" she asked. She lifted one hand from his shoulder and put back a stray lock of fair hair from his forehead. "I love the child's father. Very, very dearly."

He closed his eyes and bent his head forward. He drew a deep breath. "It would never work," he said. "If I were to release you so that you would be free to go to him, you would be ostracized from society. And I don't believe you would be happy under those circumstances. I wish you could be happy. I would give almost anything to see you happy."

"I can be happy with you, Ralph," she said quietly.

"Can you?" he asked a little sadly. "We should not have married, should we, Georgiana? We are both too young, perhaps. I should have allowed you to wait for love."

"I want to be married to you," she said.

He smiled. "I shall try to make you forget the greater happiness," he said. "I swear it, love. You wanted to talk to me. Were you going to tell me about the child? It must have taken a lot of courage to work yourself up to telling me that."

"I wish it were only that," Georgiana said, looking him straight in the eye.

"There is more?" he asked.

"Yes, I am afraid so," she said, "and you are not going to like me very well when you have heard it, Ralph."

"Am I not?" he said, releasing his hold on her. "Perhaps we should sit down again."

Georgiana was disappointed. She felt it would be far easier to tell him when she was close enough to hide her face against his shoulder if need be. But she was reassured when he clasped her hand, sat down in the chair that she had recently vacated, and drew her down onto his lap. He settled her head on his shoulder and wrapped his arms around her.

"Now, tell me," he said. "What is this dreadful confession?"

"Well," she said, "I have in my workbag a large bundle of money that I was going to begin by giving you. Shall I get it? It is just beside the chair."

"No need," he said. "What is its purpose? Did you steal it?"

"No," she said. There was a pause. "I earned it, actually."

"Indeed?" he said. "And what have you been working at to earn money? Do I not provide you with enough?"

Georgiana ignored the last question. "I have been earning it by allowing a gentleman to make love to me," she said distinctly. Her mind was telling her with equal distinctness that she was approaching this whole confession in quite the wrong way.

Ralph's body jerked quite convulsively. She put an arm up about his neck, thinking that at any moment she was going to be hurled to the floor.

"You have been doing what?" he asked hoarsely.

She said nothing. She merely tightened her grip on his neck and burrowed her head under his chin until her face was safely hidden in the hollow between his shoulder and neck.

They sat thus for a long time, absolutely still.

"My God," he said at last. "Oh my God. Georgie!"

"Are you very angry?" she asked, her voice muffled against his neck. "Please say you will not kill me. I shall never have the courage to move my head, you know."

She suddenly missed the comfort of his chin against the top of her head and realized that he had put his head back against the chair. There was a long silence again. This one lasted for several minutes. Georgiana found every second an excruciating agony, but she had no more power to lift her head than she had to stop breathing.

His next words took her completely by surprise.

"Why, you little rascal!" he said. "I suppose Roger put you up to it?"

"Oh no!" She lifted her head without thinking and presented a flaming face to his view. "I had to use all the wiles at my disposal to persuade him to help me. He thought it a quite scandalous idea."

"I should think so too," he said.

"I thought you were afraid of me," she said in a rush. "I thought that with me perhaps you felt yourself incapable . . . That is, I thought perhaps you could not . . . Ohhh!" She burrowed her face back into its safe hiding place again.

One of his hands came up to fondle the back of her head. "You were partly right, you know," he admitted. "But, you rogue, Georgie. You utter scamp! When I think! Why did you not tell me the truth when I had proved to you and to myself that I was not incapable, as you so delicately put it?"

"I was afraid you would think I had made a fool of you," she said, "and turn from me in disgust. I could not bear to give you up, Ralph. I loved so much the . . . That is, I enjoyed . . . Oh, I never thought I could be such a stuttering miss." She withdrew her face from safety and looked him severely in the eye. "I derive enormous pleasure from being in bed with you," she said defiantly.

Ralph began to laugh. "I wish you had completed the other sentences too," he said. "I always thought you were a lady, Georgie. Ladies are not supposed to have such feelings, you know. And they are certainly not supposed to talk about them."

"Are you very angry?" she asked anxiously.

"No," he said, serious again, "I think not. But the memories are crowding at me. My God, that was you! So beautiful, Georgiana. So very . . . giving. It is no wonder that I have been confused by the fact that I loved two women."

"Did you love me there?" she asked wistfully. "I was not merely a . . . a body to you?"

He shook his head. "No," he said. "There was more

than that. You must have felt it. I did not merely use
you. Did you not know that? I made love to you each
time except perhaps the first. I wanted more than just
my own pleasure. I wanted to make you happy too. And
I succeeded?''

"I love you," she said, linking her hands together
behind his head and leaning back from him to the full
extent of her arms. "I love everything about you. Not
just the things that happened there. I admire your
intellect and your learning. I love your kindness and
concern for everyone you know and even for people you
do not know. I love your gentleness. You are so very
truly a gentleman, Ralph. And my very dear love. I am
so proud that you are my husband."

"Oh my God," he said suddenly, closing his eyes and
putting his head against the back of the chair again,
pressing back against her hands. "I have just thought of
something else."

"What?" she asked sharply.

He opened his eyes and looked at her so that she had
that familiar feeling of being about to drown in the gray
depths. "Your child," he said. "It is mine."

"Of course it is," she said, and watched in wonder
the tears spring to his eyes. "Oh, my dear love, of
course it is your child. It is going to be a boy, you know,
and he is going to be just like you so that when you are
old and gray, I shall be able to look at him and
remember just how handsome you used to be. Though
as for that, you will always be handsome to me. And I
shall always insist that he mind his father so that he will
learn all the valuable things of life from you.
He could learn nothing from me except how to get into
stupid scrapes, and I don't want him to be wild. Maybe
our second son can be a madcap, or even one of our
daughters. But not our first son. Not your heir. I will
not stand for it."

"Georgie," he said, tightening his arms around her
and bringing her against him again. "My love, I cannot
adjust my mind to reality at the moment. My child.
Inside you now. Here, is it?" He laid a hand lightly

against her abdomen. "Our child. I cannot believe it."

He laid a cheek against the top of her head and they sat silent for a while. His hand still rested against her womb.

"Am I keeping you imprisoned here?" he asked. "Perhaps you have other things to do, Georgiana. We must have been here an hour or more."

"Well," Georgiana said. She was playing with a button on his waistcoat, twisting it dangerously in one direction. "I thought that perhaps . . . I mean, it is only just past teatime, is it not? I thought . . . But perhaps you would rather not. I mean . . . Oh, here I go again. Just listen to me." She released the button, which spun back crazily to its original position, and sat up.

She fixed her husband with that severe eye again. "Would you care to convey me to my bedchamber and make love to me?" she asked.

"Now, Georgie?"

"And tonight too, if you wish," she said, her expression not faltering.

"Now, what do you mean by 'convey?' " he asked. "It suggests being carried. I can just picture the butler's face if I were to carry you out of here and up two flights of stairs, can't you? And Mama's, if she happened to come out of the drawing room just as we reached the first landing."

"I shall walk," Georgiana said with great dignity. "Are you coming?"

"I invite you to try to stop me," Ralph said. "I hope you realize that there is still some daylight outside, Georgie."

She looked her inquiry.

"I want you just as you have presented yourself to me at Kensington," he said.

"Oh," she said, and blushed. "I shall be very embarrassed."

"Good," he said. "You deserve a strong dose of embarrassment, my girl, after having the effrontery to invite your husband to bed in the middle of the day."

"Are you shocked?" she asked.

"No," replied Ralph, taking his wife's hand and linking it through his arm before turning toward the door, "merely chagrined that you made the suggestion before I had a chance to, my love."

"I shall leave it to you in future," she said meekly, "provided you promise that it will be quite frequently, Ralph."

"Georgie!" he scolded, opening the library door wide enough that they could pass through to the hallway together. "Whatever made me think in the long-ago days of my youth that that nickname was inappropriate for you? You almost do not deserve the longer form, you know."

Georgiana smiled in thorough self-satisfaction and wriggled her arm farther beneath her husband's until her shoulder touched his in a quite scandalously public promise of intimacies to come.

About the Author

Raised and educated in Wales, Mary Balogh now lives in Kipling, Saskatchewan, Canada, with her husband, Robert, and her children, Jacqueline, Christopher, and Sian. She is a high school English teacher.